THE
DEPTHS

Also by
NICOLE LESPERANCE

The Wide Starlight
The Nightmare Thief
The Dream Spies

NICOLE LESPERANCE

THE DEPTHS

RAZORBILL

RAZORBILL

An imprint of Penguin Random House LLC, New York

First published in the United States of America by Razorbill,
an imprint of Penguin Random House LLC, 2022

Copyright © 2022 by Nicole Lesperance

Razorbill & colophon are registered trademarks of Penguin Random House LLC.

Visit us online at penguinrandomhouse.com.

LIBRARY OF CONGRESS CATALOGING-IN-PUBLICATION DATA IS AVAILABLE.

ISBN 9780593465363

Printed in the United States of America

1st Printing

LSCH

Design by Tony Sahara
Text set in Walbaum MT Std

For Ciaran.

THE
DEPTHS

Chapter

1

THERE'S A VIDEO OF me dying on the internet, and I can't stop watching it. My mother says it's morbid and I need to stop. I know she's right, but every night before I sleep, I pull the blankets over my head, turn my phone's volume whisper-low, and curl my body around the tiny screen. I only need to type the first letter of my name; it fills in the rest.

Adeline Spencer freediving accident

A boat crowded full of people sits rocking beside a square of ocean, cordoned off by white PVC pipe. It's a perfect tropical day, the sun glinting off the flat aquamarine. I'm just about to complete an underwater dive of sixty-three meters, as deep as a nineteen-story building is high. No weights, no fins, nothing but my own body to propel me.

Everyone is screaming.

Not cheering. *Screaming*.

Droplets of water fleck the camera lens. Three divers—my safety divers—break the surface, cradling me among them. My eyes are open and flat; my mouth is slack.

Breathe, Addie, breathe, they're shouting.

But in the salt-spattered video of water and panic, I don't

breathe. The camera pans closer, zooms in on the pink foam slipping down the side of my jaw. The trickle becomes a burst, pink turns crimson, and everybody on the boat falls silent. In her flowered sundress, my mother leaps into the water and thrashes toward me. Her wide-brimmed hat floats away into the open sea.

One of the safety divers wipes away my bloody foam and presses his mouth to mine, blows a sharp exhale through my teeth.

Breathe, yells everyone on the boat. *Addie, come on. Breathe!*

I hear them now, but I didn't then. That's the part I can't wrap my head around. That's why I keep watching this. I see myself—I see my body, but I don't think I'm in there. I don't understand what it means, where I went if the inside part of me left my body. All because of a silly mistake I made, pushing through pain instead of turning around like I should have.

The video ends as they're pulling me onto the boat. For eight and a half minutes, they say, I was dead. But I don't remember bright lights or long tunnels or warmth or unconditional love, like people say is supposed to happen. There wasn't any heaven or hell or anything in between. Five hundred and ten seconds of my existence are just gone. I keep pressing the replay button, cycling through the video over and over, but I never get any closer to understanding. It haunts me, this question I'll never be able to answer.

Where did I go?

Chapter

2

EULALIE ISLAND IS crescent shaped, its inner edge a powdered sugar beach lined with swaying palm trees. Beyond the palms lies a forest so lush and vibrant that the word *green* doesn't feel adequate to describe it. The scent of dead seaweed and tropical flowers floods my nostrils and lungs, filling them with an itchy need to cough.

Beside me, the seaplane bobs, tethered to the dock. It was a long journey from Saint Thomas, soaring over islands and islands that grew smaller and flatter until they were just sandbars, then gone. For a long time, we floated through a cloudless sky over an endless ocean, and there was nothing but blue. It took every ounce of my strength to not yank the plane door open and dive into that blue.

But I didn't. And now we're here. At the private island that's going to be my private prison for the next two weeks. I'm the third wheel on my mother's honeymoon with a man who wears pressed khaki shorts and belts with little whales on them. She was too afraid to leave me alone with my injuries after the accident, and I'd never admit this out loud, but I'm glad she didn't.

"Come on, sweetie!" She waves from the beach, her other arm wrapped around David's waist. It doesn't feel right that one twenty-minute ceremony can make you someone's daughter, step- or not. But she's been planning this honeymoon for almost a year, and I am not going to ruin the trip for her. I pull an elastic off my wrist and twist my sweaty, light brown hair into a knot on top of my head.

"Go ahead, Addie." Ken Carpenter, the island's bearded caretaker, leaps onto the seaplane to help the pilot with our suitcases. "Melinda will get you folks settled in at the house, and we'll bring your bags up."

"You're going to love it." His wife, a woman in a billowing caftan with silver-streaked hair, gives me a sympathetic smile. Everyone here seems to already know about my accident, which is both embarrassing and a relief because I won't have to explain why I unexpectedly cough up blood sometimes. Leaving the seaplane—and that gorgeous turquoise water I'm not allowed to dive in—we head for the beach. A stone jetty stretches out even farther than the dock, with a white lighthouse at its end.

The scent of flowers is so strong I can taste it, sweet and cloying and tinged with something almost rotten. It thickens as we approach the forest, and I swallow hard, then take a shallow breath.

Don't cough.

"Isn't this spectacular?" says my mom as we join them on the beach. I plaster a smile onto my mouth and nod.

"Just wait until you see the rest," says David, though he's never been here before either.

Melinda leads us onto a packed-dirt path that cuts through

4

the woods, and as we pass under the leafy canopy, it takes a few seconds for our eyes to adjust to the dimness. My mother grabs my wrist.

"Oh, Addie, look!"

White flowers bloom absolutely everywhere: hibiscus and lilies and amaryllis and so many more that I don't know the names of. Crowding the bushes, peeking out of the shrubs underfoot, climbing the trees in slender vines. Not a single blossom or bud that isn't white. I take a slow, soupy breath, willing myself not to wheeze. I am *not* going to ruin this trip. Not after I almost made her miss her wedding.

"So pretty," I say.

Melinda swats a bug from her face. "It gets humid down here, but don't worry. There's always a breeze up at the house."

Sunlight sifts through the giant ferns overhead as I stop to catch my breath. A thousand birds are shrieking, though I can't see any of them. I wonder if they're all white like the flowers. As beautiful as this is, I can't wait to find the house and the breeze so I can get this floral stench out of my lungs.

Ahead, Melinda, David, and my mom are climbing a set of stone steps, but I don't think I can make it up just yet. My face is hot and cold at the same time, and black specks flit in my vision. Bending low, I brace my hands on my knees. If I can train myself not to breathe for seven minutes, I can train myself not to cough. And I can train myself to heal. It's just a question of control. Mind over matter. Slowly, the need to clear my lungs eases, and I lean back against the trunk of a huge old tree.

Shutting my eyes, I breathe, gently breathe, and let it all settle. I try to find my center, my inner silence, but lately whenever things get quiet, my brain circles back to the accident. The same nagging thoughts circle like flies, constant reminders that everything is different now. That *I'm* different now, even though I still have no understanding of what happened to me when I died.

Something pulls me out of my thoughts, bringing me back to the flower-filled woods. It's too silent, I realize. The birds have stopped screeching. The insects are no longer buzzing. Then something rustles behind me, and a child's laugh plinks like a music box.

"Hello?" I call.

The back of my neck tingles like someone's watching me, but if they are, they could be anywhere in this chaotic jumble of plants and trees. They could be hiding an arm's length away and I'd never know.

"Hello?" I repeat. "Is somebody there?"

Again, that laugh, high-pitched and the slightest bit broken, and it sounds nothing like a bird. That sound is human.

Leaves rustle suddenly, and I jolt as a black cat slinks out of a white-flowered bush. It swishes against my shin, and as it dashes away up the steps, I have to bend over again to catch my breath and let my rocketing heartbeat calm.

"Kylo, you naughty thing! How did you get out again?" Melinda's voice floats down through the eerily still trees. Slowly, my panic fades, but the crawling sensation on my skin does not. That laughter definitely wasn't a cat. I'm sure it was a child.

"Is someone there?" I call.

The forest is silent.

Chapter

3

THE HOUSE—IF you can call the cluster of round, thatched-roof bungalows connected by covered walkways a house—sprawls on a cliff overlooking the ocean at the island's southern point. On the forest side is a pool surrounded by lounge chairs and potted plants that are even more exotic than the ones in the woods. All white flowers too.

David owns a chain of luxury hotels, and instead of spending their honeymoon at one of his properties, he and my mom decided to skip all things hotel-related so he wouldn't think about work. I'm not sure how they even found this island—apparently it's one of those places where you need to know somebody who knows somebody to rent it.

It's strange having this much money all of a sudden. I'm still getting used to the massive, eco-unfriendly house we now live in, David's collection of gas-guzzling vintage cars, the way he just pays for anything without ever asking how much it costs. And somehow, this tropical retreat—or island oasis, or whatever people call these things—hits me fresh. David's not my dad, and I don't want to get too comfortable in this unreal, wasteful lifestyle. I'm only borrowing it until next year when I turn eighteen and make my own life. Whatever that's going to be now that everything's turned upside down.

My fingers find the silver medallion hanging around my neck, tracing the raised shape of Saint Brendan. I'm not religious, but he's the patron saint of sailors and divers. It used to be my lucky charm. Now it's just a reminder of what I can't do. My doctors say I'm not allowed to dive until my lungs are fully healed, and that could take months, maybe a year. Maybe never.

"Addie!" Melinda beckons from the open doorway of one of the bungalows. Inside, a pillowy white barge of a bed floats on a sea of blue tile. French doors framed with gauzy curtains open onto a cliffside patio and the endless ocean.

"Your mom told me blue is your favorite color." She adjusts a vase of white lilies the size of my head. "We thought you'd like this bungalow best, but let me know if you'd prefer a different one and we'll bring your things there."

"It's perfect." I slip off my flip-flops and let the cool of the tiles soak into my feet. "Do you have a house on the island too?"

Melinda beams. "We live in the lighthouse."

"Wow, that sounds amazing." It never occurred to me as an option, but suddenly all I want in the world is to live in a lighthouse, surrounded by water and sky.

"We love it," she says. "Come over anytime, and we'll show you the view from the top."

A gust of wind sends the curtains billowing. Beyond the bungalow's open back door, bushes rustle and leaves crunch. A sudden pain shoots through my chest. Both hands fly over my mouth to stop the cough from barking out, but it's too late.

Flecks of scarlet land on the blue tile. Melinda is busy arranging the flowers, and I step on the blood to hide it.

"Do you have . . . any kids?" I wheeze, thinking of the laughing child in the woods.

"Two boys." Melinda plucks a browning petal from one of the flowers and sighs. "Billy's fifteen, and he should be here with your bags any minute. As for his older brother, Sean, well, I hope he'll put in an appearance at some point, but it's impossible to drag him away from his video games. You know how it is."

I don't have time to play video games or watch much TV— correction: I didn't use to have time—but I nod anyway. "And there's nobody else on the island?"

"No one," says Melinda. "This is your own private paradise while you're here."

I cringe at the word. Paradise is one of those places I might have gone after dying, but didn't. And as gorgeous as this island is, it's not my idea of paradise if I can't dive. Not to mention, no paradise would have that inexplicable, creepy laughter I heard in the woods. It must have been a bird— there are probably lots of strange species on an island this remote—but I still don't love the idea of that laugh following me around for two weeks.

A skinny, blond-haired boy appears in the doorway with my suitcase. He's a couple of inches shorter than me, and he seems unsure of where to stand, his bare feet shuffling left and right.

"There he is!" says Melinda. "Addie, this is Billy."

"Nice to meet you," I say.

His tanned, freckled cheeks flush. "You too. Where should I put this?"

"On the bed is fine, thanks." I'm not used to people waiting on me, and I don't know if I'm supposed to give him a tip, but that seems somehow wrong.

Billy strains to lift the suitcase, then dumps it onto the bed with a thump that squeaks the springs. He swabs his forehead dramatically. "What did you fill this thing with, rocks?"

"Billy!" says his mother, but I let out what feels like my first genuine laugh since my accident.

Don't cough.

"Actually, that's my blacksmithing equipment," I say with a grin. "You have anvils here, right?"

Billy laughs. "Of course we do! They're down by the squash courts."

"We don't have squash courts or anvils, Addie." Melinda rolls her eyes. "I hope that's not going to be a problem?"

"Definitely not." I couldn't make it through two minutes of squash without coughing up pieces of my lungs. "And as for the suitcase, it's just some projects I brought to keep me busy since there's no internet here."

My therapist says I should think of this trip as an opportunity to find out who I really am—the me who isn't a freediver. I'm not sure there *is* a me outside of diving, but I brought along some activities I've never had much time for. A journal and multicolored gel pens. A half-finished embroidery project that makes me feel like a character from a Jane Austen book. Introductory French, Dutch, and Mandarin workbooks. An origami kit. A book about gardening. The problem is, I'm not very good at any of these things, and whenever I try to do them, my anxiety ratchets up instead of settling like it's supposed to. My mom says I just need to be patient, but then I feel terrible about not being good at being patient.

"We have the world's slowest internet at the lighthouse if you ever need to use it," says Billy. Even though he's technically standing in one spot, his bare feet never stop moving, scuffing, shuffling.

"That's great, thanks," I say, and his cheeks go pink again. Something beeps in his pocket, and he pulls out a walkie-talkie.

"Yeah, I'm here," he says.

There's a squawk, then an unintelligible burst of static and words.

"Be right there." Billy shrugs and pockets the walkie-talkie.

"Just give us a shout if there's anything else you need," says Melinda. "Oh, and a postcard came for you earlier this week. It's on your bedside table."

I glace at the card on the table, and my stomach sinks. "Thanks again."

"See you around," calls Billy.

Once they're gone, I wipe the blood off the floor. Then I pick up the postcard and lie on the bed. It's a photo of sandy yellow mountains sprawling into a turquoise sea. In the center of the ocean lies a deep blue hole.

Dahab, it says in flowing script at the bottom.

My two best friends, Evie and Mia, are training in Egypt

right now, diving in the Red Sea with our coach for the whole month of July. I was supposed to be there too. Instead I died, and now I'm in hell. Stomach clenching, I flip the postcard over.

It's gorgeous here, but all we do is eat, sleep, and train. Hopefully Grant will give us a break this weekend so we can explore. But it's not the same without you. We miss you so much!

$E + M$

I'd give anything to be in Dahab with no free time to sightsee or enjoy the beach. Evie and Mia are my closest friends, but they're also two of my biggest competitors, and the gap between them and me is widening by the day. I'm stuck here with all the free time in the world, and they're getting stronger, faster, and more efficient. Grant says one of us is going to break a world record someday, and it was supposed to be me. I'll never catch up with the others at this rate.

With a sigh, I toss the postcard across the room and it skids under the dresser. Shutting my eyes and pretending I'm on an Egyptian beach, I cycle through my breathing exercises, which are supposed to help my lungs heal but mostly just serve as an excruciating reminder of how broken I am.

___

Dinner is cold roast chicken and potato salad that Melinda left in our well-stocked fridge, along with two frosty bottles of white wine. David and my mother are halfway through the first bottle, and we're sitting at a glass-topped table by the cliff's edge. A wooden staircase runs down the cliff to a strip of beach that's not visible unless you're looking right over the side. The floral stench has mostly dissolved in the ocean breeze, but the air's still thick and I still want to cough.

"You were right about this place, Carrie." David tops off my mom's glass and his, then leans back in his chair. "I feel ten years younger already."

"You look it too." The flirty grin she gives him sours my stomach. This trip isn't about me, and I'm trying to be as selfless as I can, but there are some things you shouldn't have to picture about your own mother. She tips her glass to her lips. "We'll see how you feel after a couple of days with no internet."

David gives me a meaningful look. "It'll be good for all of us to disconnect."

He's clearly implying it'll be good for me not to watch that video of myself all the time, but I bet he'd be obsessed with death too if he could watch himself doing it. David thinks freediving is too dangerous and my mom should force me to stop competing, but she and I made a decision that we'd wait and see how I recovered. Of course I'm going to recover, and we do not need a third opinion.

Don't snipe at David. Don't ruin their first night here. Don't cough.

He pushes an empty wineglass in my direction and tips the bottle over it, a peace offering.

"David!" says my mom, but he waves her off.

"Relax. It's not like she's driving anywhere." He winks at me, and he's got flecks of mayonnaise on his chin, and I still don't understand how this is my actual family now. Before my mom can snatch the glass away, I take a long gulp. The wine is tart and just barely fizzy, and it chills my scorched throat. Minutes later, the glass is empty and everything's softer and I don't need to cough, but I would like to sleep for three days straight. Maybe until it's time to go home again.

David clears the plates and returns with the other bottle of wine. This time, he just refills my mother's glass and his. She stretches her legs out under the table, resting her bare feet on his knees, and I have to look away, but there's only that wide, beautiful sea that I can't dive in.

"I think I'll go to bed," I say.

"Are you feeling all right?" Her forehead creases with worry.

"Yep, just tired. Enjoy your evening, okay?"

Just not so much that I can hear it. My jaw goes tight at the thought. Their bungalow is several structures away from mine, and I mentally thank Melinda for that.

"Don't sleep too late," says David. "Ken's giving us a tour of the island in the morning."

"In seventeen years, Addie has never slept past seven a.m." My mom laughs. "Not once. Love you, sweetie."

"Love you too." I blow her a kiss, give David an awkward wave, and head for my bungalow that's bigger than most people's apartments. As I flick on the light switch, the ceiling fan whirs to life, scattering lily petals all over the floor. Ignoring the mess, I brush my teeth in the blue-tiled bathroom and change into my pajamas, a pair of soft gray shorts with a matching tank top. Even with all this travel and fatigue, I don't know how I'll fall asleep without watching that video. I check my phone one more time. No signal, and the battery is almost dead.

There's a stack of blank postcards on the table beside the lilies, but I can't bring myself to write back to Evie and Mia yet. I'm worn out from pretending this is all okay so other people won't feel bad.

At the foot of my bed lies a little nosegay of white flowers bound with a blade of grass. I don't remember seeing it earlier. As I pick it up, something black falls out. A centipede the size of my index finger. With a shriek, I drop the bouquet and swipe the insect off the bed. It hits the floor with a small, wet slap, and tears sprout in my eyes as it scuttles into the shadows. What a stupid thing to cry about. It's just a bug. Swiping the tears away, I climb into bed and pull the cool sheets over myself.

I want to go home. I want my old life. I want to go back in time and change everything about the day I died, take back all those mistakes. As I cycle through my breathing exercises, I call up the memory, the perfect weather and sparkling sea. The searing pain in my left sinus that I kept ignoring as I hit negative buoyancy and let gravity pull me toward the bottom of the ocean.

The pain building, getting worse and worse no matter how many times I equalized the pressure in my ears. A hazy turn at the end of the line marking sixty-three meters, a foggy and agonizing ascent feeling like my eye was about to pop out of its socket. I tried equalizing one last time, this time with a different technique I knew wasn't a good idea, allowing seawater to flood into my sinuses. A method my coach told us never to use. A series of terrible mistakes I should never have made. And then everything went away.

The memory switches to the internet video, playing on the screen of my mind instead of my phone. My slack mouth and dead-fish eyes. The water lapping around my face, dancing over my chin. The pink foam. The screaming.

The Addie I'm watching doesn't hear them.

I don't hear them.

I don't hear.

I don't.

Later, the mattress dips as my mother sits on the edge of my bed. She runs her fingers through my sweaty hair, smoothing the bumps and tangles as she hums a strange song I've never heard before.

"Can you pass me my water bottle?" I mumble.

She doesn't answer, and I rub my eyes, squinting in the darkness.

It's not my mother sitting on my bed. It's a young woman with wild black curls framing a face that's so sunken and pale it looks like a skull. With a gasp, I sit up.

She's gone.

Chapter

4

I SWITCH ON the bedside light. The room is empty, aside from me and that centipede that's probably still lurking somewhere. The french doors and the back door are shut. With a shudder, I turn the lamp off again. It was only a dream, just like all the other frantic, lurid nightmares I've been having since the accident. My therapist says they're normal after such a traumatic event, but all I can think is that my brain is just one more part of my body that I can't control anymore.

It's not as late as I thought, just after midnight. The room is stifling, even with the fan on, and my skin is crawling so badly I contemplate taking a shower, as if I could somehow wash this feeling off. The lilies gleam ghostly in the darkness, their stench unbearable. Outside, the ocean whispers, whispers. Untangling myself from the sweaty sheets, I climb out of bed and unlatch the doors.

A glittering swath of stars streams from one horizon to the other. Everywhere smells of salt and damp and flowers. Before I realize where I'm going, my toes find the edge of the first step leading down to the beach, and it's all so beautiful and surreal that I might still be dreaming. I used to sleepwalk as a child, used to wake up and find myself in all sorts of strange places, but it's been years since the last time. As I float down the steps, the bungalows' outside lights fade, replaced by moon and starlight.

Come, whisper the waves.

Down I drift until my feet sink into sand, and I don't stop until bath-warm water is lapping around my thighs. Maybe I am still dreaming. If this were a dream, I wouldn't have to stop. I'd wade out into the heart of the ocean and nothing would matter.

The waves hush around me, whispering me deeper, and I follow, my feet sinking into silt. Water seeps over the hem of my shorts, laps around my waist, eases the ache in my chest, and takes my weight. I'm home again. As I roll onto my back, my hair floats out like a halo. The galaxy overhead is endless and soaring, more white than black.

There's a gentle sideways current, and I let it take me. The beach drifts slowly past, moon-shadows of palm trees casting long lines of black. The syrupy flower scent is still there, but I can almost ignore it with the salt on my lips.

I'm dreaming, I'm dreaming, and nothing is bad, nothing hurts.

Time slows and stretches as I float, and then there's a different shape on the beach among the palm tree shadows. It's a person, a boy sitting with his knees pulled up and his face buried in his arms. My feet graze the sand to stop my drifting.

"Billy?" I say.

He gives no indication of having heard me.

I swim closer, keeping my chin level with the surface. He's bigger than Billy, sturdier, and he's wearing only a pair of black shorts. His hair is the color of ashes, and his shoulders hitch in a haphazard rhythm. I should be afraid of this boy in the night in the middle of nowhere, but he's crying. I drift closer.

"Sean?"

His head snaps up. He's nineteen or twenty, with wide-set eyes like Billy's but less roundness in his face. The tears on his cheeks glint silver in the moonlight, and he's beautiful in a way that makes my chest ache even more than usual.

"Hello?" he says uncertainly.

It should feel strange, crawling out of the ocean in the middle of the night like some mythical creature, but maybe I'm still dreaming and it isn't strange at all.

"Are you Sean?" I say, rising slowly to stand at the tideline.

The boy gapes at me, at my dripping pajamas. "Yeah. Are you . . . real?"

Of course I am, is what I mean to say, but what comes out is "Sometimes I wish I weren't."

It's not that I wish I didn't exist. I wish I didn't exist in this ugly parallel life I've stumbled into where I'm not a freediver anymore. And now that I've watched myself die, I'm not sure I know what existing even means anymore.

Sean's silent for a minute, his expression unreadable. "Me too," he says.

The ocean's still whispering promises and secrets, but I don't want to drift away again, not yet. Crossing the sand, I sit beside him.

"I'm Addie," I say, though he hasn't asked.

"You remind me of a seal, Addie," he says.

I laugh, surprised. "I do?"

He nods. "The way you move when you're swimming. Like it's more natural than being on land."

"It is." I grind my clenched fists into the sand.

"I wasn't expecting somebody like you," he says, and my heart jitters at the many things that could mean. "Wasn't there supposed to be an older couple on their honeymoon?"

"There is," I say. "It's my mom's honeymoon. But I had an . . . accident, and even though the doctors say I'm not in danger anymore and I just need to rest and heal, she didn't want to leave me alone for two weeks. She was going to cancel the trip, but it was so important to her and I begged her not to. She said the only way she'd go was if I came too, so . . ." I swallow the itchy tickle in my throat, not wanting to cough in front of him. "Here I am. Total disaster."

"Maybe not total." He gives me a small, sliding smile, and warmth pools in my stomach.

"Addie!" A man's voice rings out, making us both jump. It's David. My new dad. I want to go back to my dream; I want to crawl back into the sea.

"Sweetie? Are you out here?" My mother's voice breaks with fear, and it looks like I'm already ruining her honeymoon. Down the beach, a flashlight beam searches the ocean's surface. I stand, brushing the sand from my sticky legs.

"I'd better go. I'm not supposed to be out here."

"Me neither." Sean stands too. He's taller than I thought, his shoulders lean and broad, and I wonder if he's a swimmer.

His eyes search my face like he's trying to figure out if I'm actually real, despite what I said. "Do you mind not telling anybody you saw me out here?" he asks.

"Sure. I mean, no, I don't mind." It's not uncomfortable, him staring at me like this, but it jumbles my words.

"Adeline Avery Spencer!" calls my mom's frantic voice.

"I'm coming!" I turn back to Sean, cheeks burning. "I'll . . . see you around, I guess?"

"I hope so." He gives me that sliding smile again as he makes his way to the water's edge.

"And I'm sorry," I say.

Knee-deep in the black water, he pauses. "For what?"

"For whatever made you cry."

He laughs quietly. "It was nothing."

"Addie!" wails my mother. "Adeline!"

"I'm here!" The flashlight beam swings in my direction. I turn back to say goodbye to Billy's brother, but he's already far out in the water, his head slipping into the depths.

Chapter
5

WHEN I WAKE, the lilies in the vase are pale pink. At first I wonder if Melinda snuck in when I was sleeping and changed them, but the petals that the ceiling fan scattered on the floor are pink too. So is the little nosegay that held the centipede. My thumb traces the underside of my Saint Brendan medallion. This place is equal parts beautiful and unsettling.

It almost feels like last night on the beach was a dream, like it only could have existed in my imagination, but my skin is salty and my damp pajamas are hanging in the bathroom. After a quick shower, I pull a postcard from the top of the stack and find a pen.

> *Hey Evie and Mia,*
>
> *Eulalie Island is beautiful. I thought this trip would be torture, but maybe it's not so bad after all. Say hi to Grant for me. Miss you!*
>
> *Addie*

I slip outside to the terrace. No one else is up. The clouds on the horizon are edged with orange and gold, and the air is light with the perfect freshness of dawn. In the forest behind the bungalows, the flowers are pink now too. I wonder if they'll turn white again as the day goes on. It's hard to believe those are the same woods that felt so sinister yesterday. Today, it's a perfect island paradise, as Melinda would say.

I wonder if Sean will make an exception and come out of his room now that he knows I'm here. His presence makes this trip slightly more interesting, though I'd still rather be in Dahab. It's probably not a great idea to get involved with some boy I'll never see again, but I'm not planning to get involved. I'm just . . . intrigued.

And I've got more important things to think about. I unroll my yoga mat by the pool and unclasp my medallion, coiling it up on the ground beside the mat. If I'm going to recover, I need to be strong. A dragonfly lands on the corner of my mat. Its narrow body is pearlescent white, and the veins in its wings are tinged with the same pale pink as the flowers.

After a few centering breaths of flower-flavored air, I start moving through the Ashtanga primary series. My arms sweep up like wings, gathering the whole blue sky, and then I dive forward like I'm plunging into the sea. As my body bends and my muscles stretch, the ruckus of birdsong fades along with the chatter of my mind. The jittery stress of the past few days begins to drain out of me. Nothing will ever clear my mind as fully as diving, but this is closer to that peace. The nagging thoughts of death are still present, still circling, but I'm letting them go, one by one.

Another dragonfly, this one with a pink body and white-veined wings, lands on the opposite corner of my mat.

"Good morning, sweetie!"

I wobble in my triangle pose. The dragonflies flit away.

"How are you feeling?" My mother stretches out in a lounge chair with a cup of coffee, crossing her long, tanned legs.

"Fine." I plant my hand on the mat and twist the other way for revolved triangle.

"Can you believe these color-changing flowers?" she says. "I've never seen anything like it."

It's hard to speak with my body folded in two different directions, so I let out an agreeing grunt.

"Melinda told me the island was special, but I had *no idea*." She laughs, her entire face radiant, and I can't remember the last time she looked this happy. She should have been like this on her wedding day, but she was too busy worrying about me. And I was too busy coughing blood into tissues.

Untwisting my torso, I step out into a long lunge and tip sideways. Something sharp catches in my chest as I swing my arm overhead. If I keep breathing, keep stretching, keep making myself strong, my body will heal. I refuse to fail at healing.

My mom scoots to the end of her lounger. "I just wanted to say thank you."

"For what?" As I switch to the other side, my chest catches in exactly the same place. I need to spend more time on my breathing exercises.

"For humoring me and coming on this trip."

Humoring somebody means letting them choose a restaurant you don't like, not giving up a trip to Egypt that you spent a year saving up for, on top of abandoning your only ambition in life. But that isn't her fault.

"I mean it," she says, crossing the terrace and slipping into a mirror image of my pose so we're facing each other, heads tipping sideways. "This can't be easy for you in so many ways, and you haven't said a word about it. Are you sure you're okay?"

"Yes." I jump my legs wide apart, then bend forward until the top of my head rests on my mat. She moves to the other side of me and bends until she's upside down too, looking at me through her legs. Her wood-bead necklace slides down over her forehead and we both laugh.

"If at any point you become not-okay, you'll tell me, right?" She pulls off the necklace and dips back into the pose. My mom's been practicing yoga since the nineties. It used to be her thing until I learned how helpful it was for diving. She was thrilled when I started going to classes, though these days she prefers a gentler style than I do.

"Right," I say. It feels wrong to lie while doing yoga, like we're supposed to be our best selves while we're practicing. But being my best self means letting my mother enjoy her honeymoon after everything we've been through. I swing up to standing, and the world warps and tips as my blood rushes back to its usual places.

"Good morning, yogis! Or should I say, namaste." David flip-flops out of the house wearing his standard khaki shorts and a T-shirt of some ancient band that might be cool if it didn't also appear to be ironed and starched.

"Hello, my love," trills my mom, and I wonder if she ever spoke to my dad like that. Maybe before I was born, before they started fighting all the time.

My diaphragm pinches as I dip forward again with my hands clasped behind my back.

Don't cough. Work harder on healing.

"Did you take your heart pills?" she asks him.

"Sure did," says David. "Have you seen my binoculars anywhere?"

"I'm sure we packed them." She steps into her sandals, and the two of them leave me alone on the terrace. I try to ease back into the yoga poses, but my focus is gone and the sickly perfume of all those flowers is making my eyes water. A sudden, sharp cough hits me without warning. Droplets of blood patter onto the concrete. The white and pink dragonflies land beside the droplets, and it almost looks like they're touching my blood with their tiny front legs. Testing it. Tasting it. I press one hand over my mouth and swat them away with the other.

"Um. Are you all right?"

I turn to see Billy hovering uncertainly beside a planter stuffed with baby-pink blossoms, and I deeply wish people would stop asking me that.

"It's normal after a lung squeeze," I say, trying not to look at those flecks of my insides that are now on the outside. "You should have seen what I was coughing up a week ago."

He pushes the brim of his orange baseball hat up and squints at me. "That's kind of badass."

The screen door swings open, and Billy snaps his cap back down. "Morning, Mr. Donovan."

"Please, call me David." With an enormous pair of binoculars hanging from his neck, David holds the door open for my mom, who's wearing her wide-brimmed hat. "Is it time for our tour already?"

"My dad's down at the bottom of the stairs with the golf cart," says Billy. "Whenever you're ready."

"Addie, do you need to get anything before we go?" says my mom.

Aa-dee-dee, sings a bird deep in the woods, and then another one joins in. *Aa-dee-dee-dee-dee*.

Goose bumps wash over my skin. The birds weren't singing like that yesterday, or the entire time I've been out here doing yoga. It's almost like—

No. Obviously the birds aren't saying my name. It's just the heat and the humidity and the pain in my chest that's making it hard to think straight.

"Hon?" My mom's cool hand on my sweaty arm makes me jump. "Are you ready?"

I drag myself back to reality and scoop up my medallion from the ground. "Just need to get my sandals."

Chapter

6

"GOOD MORNING, DONOVANS!" calls Ken from a six-seater golf cart surrounded by a riot of pink blossoms.

"I'm not a Donovan," I mutter, trailing everyone down the steps. Sean didn't come, which I guess doesn't surprise me, considering what Melinda said about him and his video games. He said he hoped he'd see me again, but maybe I'm not intriguing enough for him to give up his usual routine.

Aa-dee-dee-dee, a trilling, invisible bird calls. *Dee-dee. Dee-dee.*

Nobody else mentions that it sounds like the birds are calling my name. Shading my eyes, I peer into the trees. I can't see any birds, but I can't shake the feeling that they're all up there watching me, which is absurd. Sometimes I think my brain hasn't fully recovered from all that time when I was dead.

David joins Ken in the front of the cart, my mom and I squeeze into the middle seats, and Billy perches on the rear-facing bench.

"Did all of the flowers on the island really change color overnight?" asks my mom.

Ken shifts the cart into gear, and we lurch forward. "Looks that way, doesn't it?"

"Is that normal?" I say.

Behind me, Billy laughs. "Nothing about Eulalie Island is normal."

The way he says it makes my scalp prickle.

Jerking the wheel to the right, Ken swings us onto a dirt path heading in a different direction from where we came in yesterday. "What Billy means is this place is very unique. We've never seen the flowers turn pink, per se." He makes air quotes around the words, then grabs the steering wheel just in time to keep us on the path. "But sometimes things like this happen. It's all part of the island's charm."

"It certainly is charming." My mother trails her hand through a passing bush, pulls out a blush-colored amaryllis, and tucks it into the band of her hat. I hope there aren't any centipedes in it. Or dragonflies.

"What other kinds of things—" I start to say, but David interrupts.

"So how did this island get its name?"

Ken guns the engine and we skid around a bend. A thick ozone scent fills the air, and the temperature must be eighty-five already. Well over ninety with the humidity. My head feels slow, like it's full of syrup.

"Melinda and I did some research when we first became caretakers of the island," says Ken. "We discovered it's named after a mysterious girl from the eighteenth century."

"How fascinating." My mom leans forward. On her hat, something like sap or nectar is seeping out of the flower. I want to rip it off and throw it back into the bushes.

"Sometime around 1760, an English merchant ship called the *Fortuna* got lost on its way home from Tortola," says Ken. "Nobody could say exactly how it happened. They were following their charts and navigational instruments, but somehow the ship went way off course."

"And ended up here," says Billy.

"And ended up here," repeats Ken. "Which was, at the time, an uncharted, uninhabited island."

"Not totally uninhabited," says Billy.

Ken cranks the wheel and we slide around another turn. "You want to finish telling this story, Bill-ster?"

"Nope."

Ken points to the side of the trail, where an iguana the size of a dog is chewing on a rose-colored gardenia. As lovely as the flowers are, I wish there were more iguanas to eat them so I could breathe a little better and clear this fog from my head.

"By that point, the sailors were almost out of provisions," continues Ken. "So they went ashore to see what they could find."

"And they found her," says Billy.

The path narrows abruptly, and branches slither inside the cart, wiping their leafy moisture all over us. It feels like being licked.

"Hang on, we'll be through in a second," says Ken, shoving a huge banana leaf out of the cart.

"Who did they find?" says my mom once we're clear of the slobbering bushes.

"Eulalie." It's so obvious, I can't help blurting it out. Billy nudges me with his elbow and grins. Apparently he's not the only one who can't stay out of this story.

"According to the ship's log, they found a girl who looked to be sixteen or seventeen living alone on the island," says Ken. "At first, she didn't respond to any of the languages they tried, but she had this uncanny ability to learn. After a day or two, she was communicating in basic English and hand gestures. She told them she'd been on the island since she was ship-wrecked as a small child, and she had no memory of where she was from or even what her own name was."

"Oh, the poor thing!" says my mother, and David nods.

It must have been lonely, living in this livid green jungle all alone. I wonder if the flowers were pink or white when she was here.

"One of the crew members named her Eulalie in honor of his late sister," continues Ken. "After staying on the island for a few weeks and gathering fresh water and provisions, the ship set sail with the girl on board, and this time they navigated back with no trouble. The historical records get spotty after that. Some say Eulalie went to a convent in France; others say she married an English nobleman. But there's no record of her death in either country."

Unlike me, who has a vivid and brutal record of her own death. The first one, anyway.

"Eulalie Island became infamous after that, with people from all over Europe and America trying and failing to find it again," says Ken. "The US government claimed it as part of the Virgin Islands, even though it's pretty far outside the territory. There were all these wild rumors flying around, saying the island's waters had healing properties, that there were magical plants and maybe even hidden treasure in its caves. But it disappeared off the map, with almost all of the ships that tried to find it getting lost."

"Like the island didn't want anyone coming here," says Billy.

A vine slips inside the cart and slithers over my ankle, and a shudder washes over me.

"*We* all made it here just fine," says Ken. "Nobody's had trouble coming to Eulalie Island for years."

Billy reluctantly grunts his assent, and his father continues: "In the early twentieth century, an Italian woman named Lelia Morandi bought the island. She never came here, though—I can only assume the World Wars screwed up her plans—and then the island passed down through her family, though none of them visited, either. But then about five years ago, one of the granddaughters sent a crew to build the lighthouse, the jetty and dock, the infrastructure, and your house. When that was done, she hired me as the caretaker." He shoots a fatherly grin at Billy. "Well, she hired our family, really, and we started bringing people in for vacations."

"I wonder how much she paid for it." David casts an appraising eye at the trees, and I wonder if he could afford an actual island.

"Ouch!" My mom grabs the back of her neck, shiny from the flower's dripping nectar. She tugs off her hat and stares at the saturated brim. "That burns!"

"It's the flower," I say, shuddering and wishing I'd thrown it into the bushes after all. "It's leaking."

"I'm so sorry about that." Ken hands her some napkins from his cup holder. "You must be allergic to the plant. We've got some Benadryl at the lighthouse. Want me to go grab it?"

My mom swabs her neck, then crumples up the napkin and smiles, ebullient as ever. "Don't worry about it. I'm perfectly fine." After shaking the flower out over the side of the golf cart, she sets the hat on the floor between us. I edge my feet away from it.

"Melinda's got a book about the island's history if you want to learn more about it," says Ken. My mother and David make approving noises.

As we climb the hill, the foliage thins and the humidity grows. The patches of sky visible through the trees have turned from blue to ashy gray. At the crest of the hill, we stop. On the other side lies a valley filled with trees and boulders. A thin waterfall trickles into a stream, and nestled on its banks are the remains of an ancient house. The roof is long gone, and the stone walls are covered in thick moss.

Aa-dee-dee-dee, calls a bird through the leafy green.

I sneak a glance at my mom's neck. A faint rash has broken out on her skin.

"Is that Eulalie's house?" she asks as we clamber out of the golf cart. The sky is slowly deepening to charcoal, and the air is practically steam. It's going to rain soon, and my skin prickles with the heat and an odd sense of anticipation.

"No, Eulalie was living in some kind of tree house when

the sailors found her," says Ken. "It's long gone. This is the Wells house." He motions for us to follow him down a winding trail cut into the hill. "In 1843, Abraham Wells, a wealthy Bostonian and an amateur botanist, spent his entire fortune in search of Eulalie Island. Watch your step there, Addie. He hired two ships and a building crew that sailed for eleven months until they finally found it. They left Abraham, his wife, and his two daughters at their brand-new house on the island, with the plan to return with provisions in a year's time."

"Because apparently living in Massachusetts in the eighteen hundreds wasn't boring enough," adds Billy. I rub my nose to hide my smirk.

Ken stops at the edge of the ruins and gestures for my mom and David to step through the gap where a door once stood. "When the ship came back a year and a half later—"

"Because they got lost again," interjects Billy.

"—they found the bodies of Abraham and his wife in their bed. They'd been dead for months. Apparently they got botulism from bad canned food."

The clammy breeze brings a whiff of decay, and I pause in the doorway. "What about their daughters?"

"Two empty graves behind the house are labeled with their names. Lenora and Violet." Ken gestures toward what must have been the yard, which is overrun with brambles and bushes and vines. I can't see the gravestones, but they must be under there somewhere.

"Jeez, that's terrible," says David. "What do you think happened to the girls?"

"My guess is that they drowned," says Ken. "There are strong currents on the east side of the island. They probably got caught in a riptide and pulled out to sea."

"The ocean is a dangerous place." David gives me a meaningful look that I pretend not to notice. I wonder if those girls were conscious when they breathed in the water or if everything disappeared first, like it did for me. I wonder if the nothingness went on forever for them or if they moved past it to somewhere . . . else.

As I step through the ruined doorway, the temperature drops and my skin breaks out in goose bumps. We all crowd into what must have been the kitchen, judging by the blackened fireplace in the corner with half a chimney still attached. In the corner is a small pile of palm leaves with a slight indentation in the middle.

David nudges the pile with his foot. "Looks like an animal nest."

"I'll send Sean out here with a rake and some traps," says Ken. "Before he turns into a sloth."

"Too late for that," mutters Billy.

Sean looked anything but slothlike last night, and I'm irritated on his behalf. Maybe he's just depressed. And with that body, he's clearly getting some exercise. He probably swims every night. Not that I was noticing his body or anything.

Through an open doorway is a smaller space with a broken

metal bedframe that must have been where they found the parents' bodies. I wonder how long Abraham Wells and his wife lay there rotting. If the medical team hadn't managed to save me after my accident, I'd be rotting now too. Or maybe I'd have been cremated, turned into ashes, and stuck in an urn that my mom put on a shelf somewhere in David's house. My eyes start to prickle.

"We think this was the girls' bedroom," says Ken, leading us into a second small space. An ancient harp lies on the floor with a tree growing through its center. Moss and vines cover large sections of the frame, and its ornately carved roses are crusted with dirt. A single string remains stretched across the gap at the top of the scale.

"That belonged to the older girl, Lenora." Billy pokes his face through a hole in the wall where a window once was. "Sometimes at night when the moon is out and wind is blowing in the right direction, you can hear harp music playing all the way up at the lighthouse."

A chill slithers up my spine.

"All right, Bill-ster," says Ken. "Enough with the Halloween nonsense. There's no harp music at night." He turns to my mom and lowers his voice. "Kid's got quite the imagination. He won't even come inside this house."

They all laugh as they wander off to the kitchen, but I can see why Billy feels uncomfortable here. Part of me wants to run out of this crumbling structure and never come back, but another part of me wants to linger. I'd like to sit down with this harp for a while and imagine what it was like for the sisters. I feel a strange kinship to them. We all drowned. We might all have ended up in the same place, except that I got to come back from death and they didn't. I can't help but wonder where their souls went, if they're anywhere at all.

As my parents follow Ken outside, I bend over the harp. Something is drawing me closer, an almost imperceptible hum. I reach down to pluck the remaining string, but it disintegrates the moment my finger touches it.

The buzzing of the insects outside stops. The floral breeze disappears. The trees and plants go photograph-still. The whole island is holding its breath.

Waiting.

Watching.

"I'm sorry," I whisper, easing away from the instrument and scrubbing at the back of my neck, which is crawling like someone's breathing on it.

A fat glob of rain splats onto the harp, then another. It's just a coincidence; the sky's been threatening to rain for ages. Then the heavens open up. Rain hammers down through the trees and pours into the house. The dirt paths turn to muddy rivers, and the waterfall's trickle quickly becomes a gushing roar.

"Everybody back to the cart!" yells Ken.

I back away from the dead girl's harp and run out of her crumbling house.

Chapter
7

BY THE TIME we get back to the house, the sun is peeking out through a ragged hole in the gray, and the deluge has slowed to a patter. Already the air is greenhouse-hot again.

"How about a dip in the pool before lunch?" David pulls off his wet T-shirt to reveal a once-muscular frame now gone saggy. He's got more hair on his chest than his head, and I wonder what my mother sees in him. It's got to be more than just his money, which she's never cared much about. At least he doesn't pick constant fights with her like my dad used to.

She sets her waterlogged hat on a chair to dry, and I hope she's not going to wear it again until it's washed. "What do you say, Addie?"

It feels like my lungs are stuck together on the inside, and the last thing I want to do is cough blood in that pristine pool. Not to mention the fact that it's only five feet deep, which is so unnecessarily shallow. "Maybe later. How's your neck?"

"All better." She tips her head, and the rash is gone.

While the two of them paddle around in the too-shallow pool, giggling and tickling each other, I grab my gardening book and find a hammock by the edge of the forest. Everything is so damp and sticky and oppressive, it's like being inside the mouth of some giant monster. Aimlessly, I start my breathing exercises while flipping through the pages, but the text is so dense and informative, and I honestly couldn't care less about soil quality or drainage.

The morbid thoughts are circling like flies again. Soil reminds me of the two empty graves behind that ruined old house, and I can't stop wondering about my own body if I'd stayed dead. Would I be buried under six feet of soil right now? Or would there be nothing left of me but dust? Sour nausea coats my mouth and throat. I wish I were lying on the bottom of the sea, in water so cold I needed a wet suit, down so deep there was no room for obsessing or worrying—for any feelings at all.

The fern beside me rustles. A child-size hand pokes out, index finger extended, and jabs my ankle. With a jolt, I sit up, sending the hammock swinging. My skin burns cold in the spot where the finger touched it.

"Who's there?" I say, pulse hammering.

The hand flips over, and the finger makes a beckoning gesture.

Aa-dee-dee-dee, calls a bird.

Gulping down the lump in my throat, I glance back at my mom and David, who are kissing in the "deep" end, and shudder. The hand disappears, and a music-box giggle plinks out from the shaking bush. The same laugh I heard in the woods yesterday. There *is* a child here. But why is a strange little kid roaming the island all alone?

I ease my legs over the side of the hammock and stand. "Hello?"

Another giggle. The hand sneaks out of the bush again and slaps my knee. With a yelp, I jump back.

"Hide-and-seek!" calls a little girl's voice. "You're the *it*."

The bushes rustle and shiver.

"Where are your parents?" I don't know where this kid came from, but it seems like a terrible idea for her to be out in a jungle full of centipedes and lizards and creepy old houses.

The bushes go still.

"Dunno," she says in a soft, sad voice that tugs at my heart.

I glance back at the pool, which is now empty. In the minute or so that's passed, David and my mom must have gone inside. The thought of them sneaking off for a quickie turns my stomach, and I try and fail to hold back a cough.

"Gobbless you," says the wiggling bush.

"Can you come out of there?" I crouch to peer into the undergrowth. Two bare feet with filthy gray toenails dance from side to side.

"No, you're the *it*, so you have to find me." The feet spin and dash away.

I try to shove into the bushes where the little girl was, but they're so thick and thorny that I'd need a machete to get through. "Hey!" I call. "Come back!"

Plants rustle farther and farther away, and her tinkling laughter grows faint. I start back toward the house, but my mother's laughing in a muffled kind of way, and so is David. Swearing, I head for the staircase that leads down to the woods. I won't be responsible for letting a little girl get lost. Flip-flops slapping stone, I fly down the steps and almost collide with Billy at the bottom.

"Why are you running?" He looks pale, his eyes watery.

"Are there other people here?" I muffle another cough in the crook of my elbow. "Like, maybe some day-trippers from another island?"

"Uh, no?" Billy sits on the bottom step, pulls an inhaler from his pocket, and puffs it into his lungs.

"Are you okay?" I ask.

He nods, and my eyes dart to the path. She's going to get lost out there, and she'll slice up her feet with no shoes on. "I don't mean to rush you," I say, "but there's this little girl wandering around the woods and I don't know how she got on the island, but she must be lost. I need to help her."

Billy fumbles his inhaler. "What did she look like?"

"I only saw her hands and feet, but they were small. And filthy. She wanted to play hide-and-seek."

Billy lets out a wheezy laugh. "Holy. Shit. Amazing."

I'm getting annoyed. For every second we spend standing here, that little girl is getting even more lost. I don't want to drag Billy along if he's having an asthma attack, but I need to do something. "Why is this funny?" I say. "Who is she?"

"You actually saw her, right?" he says. "Like, definitely *saw* her with your eyes?"

"Billy, I'm going to punch you in about three seconds. I told you I saw her, and then she tagged my leg and said I was it. Well, she said I was *the* it."

Billy bursts into literal giggles and has to suck on his inhaler again. "This is incredible," he says finally. "This is so, so awesome. I'm the one who taught her that game."

"You know, instead of being vague and weird, you could help me look for her," I say. "What if she hides and nobody finds her? Where did she even come from? She doesn't live here, does she?" I gesture at the dripping, pink-flowered plants all around us. Maybe if David finds out this isn't really a private island, he'll be so mad he'll want to leave. He can't really be as easygoing as he acts all the time.

"She doesn't *live* anywhere," says Billy. "Nobody except me—and you, which is so awesome, by the way—can see Violet."

"Wait." I blink hard and swallow another cough. I've heard that name recently. "Violet? As in Violet *Wells*?"

Billy jumps up and shuffle-dances a couple of steps, the asthma attack clearly over. "Oh man, everybody thought I was delusional. They put me on *medication*."

"You're telling me the little girl I saw is Violet Wells, who's been living here since the eighteen hundreds?" I'm having a hard time processing Billy's words.

"Yes. We just established that a second ago." Billy rolls his eyes. "She's just not exactly . . . living anymore."

I get where he's going with this, but it's ridiculous.

"She's a ghost," he says, like it's the most obvious thing in the world.

I snort. "Billy, come on. Who is she really?"

"I'm serious! That's the ghost of Violet Wells."

"Even if ghosts were real, that wouldn't make any sense," I say. "How could she have poked me if she's a ghost? Aren't they transparent or ephemeral or whatever?"

Billy plucks a flower from a nearby branch. "I don't know if you noticed, but stuff doesn't really follow the normal rules here." He shreds the blossom, and as its petals fall to the ground, the pink fades to bone white.

He does have a point, but exotic flowers that change color aren't on the same level as actual ghosts. I'm sure a biologist could explain the flowers, but there's no explanation for a spirit staying behind after death. One explanation does fit, though: Billy's making this up. He's pranking me. Fine, I'll play along.

"So, what, the two dead sisters are just roaming the island?" I set my hands on my hips.

"I've never seen Lenora," says Billy. "I asked Violet about her a bunch of times, but she doesn't seem to know. I also tried asking if she knows she's dead and how she died and what happened to her family, but it's really hard to get a straight answer out of Violet. She must have only been like three when she died. Sometimes I think she sneaks into the lighthouse when nobody is around, because stuff is always going missing."

"You mentioned that harp music at night," I say, zipping my medallion back and forth on its chain and wondering how far he's planning to take this charade. "Is that Lenora?"

"It could be." Billy's eyes dart sideways. "I've heard the harp, but I'm not allowed out of the lighthouse at night."

I narrow my eyes. "Why?"

"My parents don't go out either, unless there's an emergency." Billy shrugs. "My dad says it's so we don't freak out the guests by accidentally running into them in the dark, but sometimes I wonder if there's more to it than that."

Uneasiness worms through my stomach. I can't tell if this is part of the prank. But Sean didn't seem bothered or afraid, and he was out at night. "Does your brother—"

Billy's walkie-talkie chirps, and he pulls it out with a groan.

"I'm almost there, Dad."

"Good," says Ken's crackling voice. "Hurry up."

Billy stuffs the walkie-talkie back into his pocket. "Sorry to cut this short, but I have to get your parents' grocery list for my dad."

I cringe at the fact that David is now one of my parents, but Billy continues, oblivious: "He's taking the boat over to Tortola for supplies and groceries and stuff. And I have a couple of chores to finish up. My dad wants me to set some traps around the island for whatever made that nest in the Wells house. Even though Sean was supposed to do that." Billy grits his jaw. "But if you want, I can take you on the unofficial tour of the island when I'm done."

"Sure," I say. Part of me is still irritated by this ghost prank, but anything is better than staying home with my mom and David.

"Great, yeah, cool." Billy's cheeks are almost as pink as the flowers. "I can tell you more about Violet too. Want to meet back here in like half an hour? We have to walk, though, because my dad doesn't trust me with the golf cart anymore."

I wonder why that is. Clearly this kid causes a lot of trouble. But he's all alone here, and there's not much in the way of entertainment. Plus he's funny, and I have no one else to hang out with.

"Sounds good," I say. "When you get to the house, be sure to, uh, knock first."

He catches the gist of my words and fake gags. "I'll make a lot of noise on my way up there."

"Good idea," I say.

"Okay, so, yeah. I'll . . . I'll see you then." He leaps up the stairs like an awkward baby gazelle, then trips near the top, and I'm not so sure I'd trust him with my golf cart either. Once he's gone, I scan the woods, searching for some trace of the little girl, but she's gone.

Aa-dee-dee-dee, call the birds.

Chapter
8

AFTER BILLY HEADS off with the grocery list, I tell my mom and David through the window that I'm going for a walk, and I wander through the forest, searching for that strange little girl. Even if this is a prank, it makes me uncomfortable. My little cousin, Grace, is four years old, and my aunt would never let her run around the woods alone like that. There are too many places for her to get lost or hurt, and nobody would know until it was too late.

A rosy-peach hibiscus brushes my wrist, giving me an idea. Grace loves when I make her flower crowns, and so do all the kids I babysit. The flowers here are stunning, and as long as I avoid the kind my mother put in her hat, a crown is the perfect thing to lure a little girl out of hiding. Then I can find out who she really is and where her parents are.

Some of the blossoms are soft as velvet, others smooth as a baby's skin, and as I tug them from their branches, they let out little gusts of powdery pollen that tickle my face and make everything feel the tiniest bit crooked. With a lap full of plumeria and jasmine and a lightly spinning head, I sit on the bottom step that leads to our house, and I start weaving them together.

The stems are warm, body temperature, and I can't shake the feeling that they're pulsing like veins. As I braid, sap drips, blood-warm, onto my legs, and I think of all the blood that's come out of my lungs in the past month. It's a shocking amount, although the doctors told me not to panic when I see it coming up, to just focus on getting better.

But maybe, no matter how much I stretch and train, my body will never heal. Maybe I'll have to give up freediving forever. Or maybe David will convince my mom to ban me from diving, and I'll have to wait until I turn eighteen and move out to start training again. By then, Mia or Evie—or maybe both—will have broken the women's national record and left me far behind. I've spent most of my life trying to be the very best at this one thing, and what is the point of wasting all that time if that one thing can be ripped away from me in eight and a half minutes?

"You look like you're about to murder somebody." Billy saunters up the dirt path carrying a blue backpack, his feet still bare. He points to the long machete hooked onto his belt. "Want to borrow this?"

I glance down at the crushed flower in my fist. "No, just sort of having an existential crisis."

"Those are the worst," says Billy.

"Yeah." I drop the broken flower and weave in the ends of the final knot, then hold up the crown to inspect my handiwork. It's even prettier than I expected.

Billy eyes the crown. "That for me?"

"How did you know?" I set it on top of his baseball cap. "But seriously, it's for 'Violet'"—I make air quotes around her name—"so don't break it."

"She'll love it," he says. "But I doubt we'll see her again today. I don't know what she gets up to, but I usually only run into her every couple of days."

"Every couple of days?" There's no way a kid that small would be okay on her own for days at a time. My cousin would be wailing after twenty minutes.

Billy gives me a long look. "Addie, she's fine. She's safe. I promise."

It really must be a prank, then. I can't figure out how he's pulling it off, but maybe the girl belongs to a family who visits the island on their boat, and Ken and Melinda just forgot to mention it. Or they don't know about it.

Aa-dee-dee-dee, calls a bird.

"What's the machete for?" I ask.

"My dad likes me to keep the trails clear. Stuff grows really fast around here." Billy gestures for me to follow him under a dripping banana tree.

"Are there any more ruins like that house?" I ask.

"Nope. Aside from Eulalie, the Wellses are the only people who've ever lived on the island—until we got here. And we haven't had that many guests since then."

We reach a fork in the path. To the right is the way we went in the golf cart this morning, and to the left is a narrow footpath overgrown with trailing weeds and water-beaded cobwebs. Swinging wildly with his machete, Billy charges through, and I give any lingering insects (which I can't see but are probably enormous) a few seconds to scuttle away before following him.

"How come nobody else came here before you?" I say.

"Dunno," says Billy. "The island's been owned by the Morandi family for over a hundred years." He lops the head off a plant with tendrils like octopus arms, and I cringe. "But I've never met any of them."

A gust of wind stirs the plants, and their damp leaves slip over my arms and face as I turn sideways, making myself as narrow as possible to fit through the corridor that Billy has made. "Why not?"

"No idea. You'd think they'd want to hang out in that big fancy house you're staying in." Billy swipes and slashes through more bushes, sending pink petals raining down. "But they don't come here. One of them sends my dad a check every month, and if there's ever a problem, like the generators break or something, we deal with it and they send us more money."

Somehow, the forest grows even thicker as we go, the trees taller and wider and wetter. Enormous orchids with yawning mouths dangle from their branches. As the breeze picks up again, a cloud of pollen drifts out, coating my cheeks and lips. It's faintly sweet. The greenery tips and swirls as the soft thudding of my heartbeat fills my ears. It's so beautiful here. So soft and warm. I'm flooded with the urge to lie back and let the plants cradle me, rock me to sleep.

"Watch out!" A thorny branch catches on Billy's shoulder

and snaps at my face. Just in time, I dodge out of the way, heart pounding. It feels like I've just woken from a dream. Was I seriously just considering lying down in the middle of the forest?

"Sorry about that." Billy pulls the branch aside and wipes sweat from his upper lip. "We're almost there."

"Almost where?" My lungs are starting to stick again, and my knees feel like they're about to give out.

"You'll see." He skirts around a car-sized boulder dotted with lichen and tiny pink flowers. Ahead, Spanish moss dangles from the trees, making a thick curtain. Billy pushes through and holds it open for me.

My breath dies in my chest. The space on the other side of the curtain is wide open, dappled with silvery-blue light and filled with the lapping sound of water. It can't be real. Maybe I really did lie down in those plants and drift off to sleep. Pinching the tender skin on the inside of my forearm, I step farther into the unbelievable space and let my eyes adjust.

A round pool, about a hundred feet across, ripples at our feet. It's bordered on all sides by rough gray stone and flanked by a rocky cliff at the back. The water is clear at the edges, with a ledge of shallow water darkening to a perfect circle of sapphire in the center. A blue hole of deep, deep water, just like the ones in Belize and the Bahamas that I used to dive in. Like the one in Dahab I'm supposed to be diving in. This is too cruel.

Billy sits at the pool's edge and drops his feet in. I crouch beside him, afraid that if I put so much as a toe into that dazzling water, the rest of me will follow whether I mean to or not.

"Is it warm?" I say through teeth chattering with want.

"It's perfect," says Billy.

"What's down there?" I jut my chin at the beautiful blue hole.

"It's a cenote. A freshwater sinkhole." He pulls a granola bar from his backpack, unwraps it, and stuffs half in his mouth. "Want some?"

"No, thanks." I ease my sandal off and touch the tip of my toe to the glassy, cool water. Tiny circles radiate out, slowly traversing the pool. "Anybody ever dive in this?"

"My dad has a couple of times." Billy crams the other half of the granola bar into his mouth, not bothering to swallow before continuing. "But it feeds into a bunch of underwater tunnels and caves at the bottom, and he says it's too dangerous. The tunnels come up in some weird places all around the island, so watch out for random sinkholes if you go wandering."

I brush a chill off my arms. "Well, I don't have a machete, so I probably won't get very far."

"Stick with me, then." Billy grins. "Anyway, you can swim and snorkel here, but no scuba tanks allowed."

"Who needs scuba tanks," I mutter, letting both my legs slide into the water up to my knees. An ecstatic shiver glides from the base of my spine to the top of my head. There's a slight pulse to the water, like a drum is beating somewhere in the depths. Or maybe it's just my own heartbeat, which is still galloping at the absolute perfection of this spot.

Billy grabs a handful of pebbles and tosses them, one by one, into the center of the pool, making circle after circle after circle, their edges crossing over each other. "I heard about what happened to you."

I scoop up a handful of rocks and begin to throw, aiming for the spots where his are landing. "What did you hear?"

"That you're, like, some Olympic-level freediving champion."

A crooked sound slips out of my mouth, and I throw a pebble so far off the mark that it hits the shore on the side of the pool. "There's no Olympic event for freediving, but I was getting close to the US women's national record for constant weight, no fins."

Billy nudges my shoulder with his. "That's pretty awesome."

"Sort of." I lean away. "Did you watch the video?"

"Of what?"

"Of my accident. Of me dying."

He whistles through his teeth. "No, that's messed up. Anyway, you didn't really die."

"Actually, I did." I pull my legs out of the water and rub the chill off them. "No pulse, no breath. I flatlined."

Billy cocks his head, and instead of the sympathy I'm so used to getting from everyone, there's something else in his expression, something questioning. It reminds me of the way his brother looked at me last night. I wonder if I'll sneak out and find Sean again tonight. But then again, he couldn't even be bothered to come on the tour today.

"That happened to me too," Billy says.

I gawk at him. "Really?"

He sticks his skinny legs straight out, splashing his heels in the water. "We used to live in Michigan before here. Not far from a lake." Billy jerks his thumb at the cenote. "Way bigger than this thing. When I was twelve, I went out on the ice by myself and fell in. I was underwater for like two hours before they found me. Dead and blue."

I drop the pebble I was about to throw. "How did they bring you back from that?"

"The cold water saved me." Billy pulls off his hat, along with the flower crown, and runs his hand through choppy blond hair that looks like he cut it himself. "It preserved my brain and my organs and kept them from going to shit."

I nudge his leg with my toe. "Is that the technical term for it?"

"That's exactly how the doctors put it." Billy's eyes crinkle, and I'm amazed that he can joke about this. It still makes me want to throw up.

Billy holds out another granola bar, and I shake my head. He unwraps it, breaks off a chunk, and tosses it straight up, holding his mouth open. The piece bounces off his nose and tumbles into the bushes behind us. With a sheepish grin, he digs it out, wipes it on his shorts, and eats it.

"Do you ever wonder what happened to you in that time?" I say.

"You mean while I was being a human Popsicle?"

"Ew. But yes."

"Do you mean, did I see angels and pearly gates and stuff?" he says.

I should laugh at this obvious joke, but I don't. "Did you?"

He chews, swallows. "Nope. I didn't see anything."

"Just nothing, right?" I say. "That's what happened to me too."

Billy launches another piece of granola bar over his head. This one goes wide, and he grabs it out of the air like he meant to do that all along. "What were you expecting?"

"I wasn't expecting to die, so nothing."

His eyes narrow. "You dive like a mile underwater on a regular basis and it never once crossed your mind that it might kill you?"

"Not a mile." I scoff, but my voice has gone creaky in an embarrassing way. "Anyway, yeah, I'd thought about dying. Of course I did. I just thought there'd be . . . more."

Billy tosses the last piece of his snack and manages to catch it in his mouth. He wiggles with glee as he chomps, open-mouthed. "So you *were* expecting gates and people with wings."

"No, but I thought maybe there'd be a tunnel with a light at the end or, I don't know, I'd wake up being born again as a baby or an eagle or something." I pick up Billy's discarded wrapper and fold it into a neat square. "Just . . . something. Not nothing." My voice starts doing that horrible creaking thing again, and I cover it up with a cough, which is a bad idea because my lungs now think I want them to heave up blood.

"Sorry." I bury my face in the crook of my elbow and try not to be too disgusting.

Billy pretends not to notice the smear of blood I wipe from my arm. "Maybe you didn't have enough time for all that stuff to happen. How long were you gone?"

"Eight and a half minutes."

"Psssh." He waves his hand dismissively. "That hardly even counts. I don't know if I can let you be in my previously dead people club."

My mouth falls open, and then I burst out laughing. "I didn't realize there were eligibility requirements."

Billy rolls his eyes dramatically. "Just wait till you get to the written exam." He tosses another stone into the center of the pool. "But in all seriousness, I think that might be why we can both see Violet and nobody else can."

I scoff. "Any second now, her family is going to show up and you're going to laugh your head off at me."

"Guess we'll see about that," says Billy. "Want to swim before we head back?"

There's nothing I want more in the world. I can't drag my eyes away from that gorgeous blue, its gentle beat still rolling through my legs. I'll never be able to just swim in it. The urge to dive would be irresistible.

I shake my head. "I don't have my bathing suit."

Billy's eyes almost pop out of his face. "That's, uh, not a problem for me if you . . ."

I chuck a pebble at him, and he rolls away and almost falls into the pool, which is almost a shame because then I'd have to jump in and save him, even in my clothes, and then maybe I'd swim out just a little bit to feel that cool bliss on my skin. I'd poke my head underwater for just a few seconds to see what's down in that blue hole.

"What time is it?" I ask.

Billy checks his watch, a chunky digital contraption. "Almost six."

"Already? Ugh, I have to be back for dinner."

His face droops a little, but he picks up his backpack and machete and stands. "Maybe another time."

"Yeah." It's hard to drag myself away from the stunning blue pool, but part of me is relieved that the torture of looking but not diving is over for now.

The forest path is completely overgrown with vines and weeds and flowers again—it's impossible to tell that we ever hacked our way through to get here. The pollen is fainter, at least, and I don't feel dizzy or sleepy this time as Billy swings and swipes his way through the dewy, crawling plants.

"So your parents are pretty strict about dinnertime?" he says.

"Only one of them is technically my parent," I say.

"Sorry." He flashes a rueful look over his shoulder. "This must be super awkward for you."

I brush a branch with delicate, fringe-like leaves out of the way. "Yes."

"You can always come hang out with me when things get weird," he says. "No pressure, but the lighthouse is pretty nice and you can use the internet."

And Sean is there too.

"What's your brother up to today?" I say.

"Probably sleeping." Billy scoffs. "He's like a vampire. Sleeps all day and then plays video games and trolls people on our crappy internet all night. I don't know why he bothers. It takes like eight days for a single page to load."

I can't picture that beautiful boy with the ash-blond hair huddled over a computer, harassing random strangers for fun. But I guess it's hard get an accurate impression of someone when you meet them on a moonlit, tropical beach.

Aa-dee-dee-dee, trills the bird.

"It's calling your name," says Billy.

"Thank you!" I say, relieved that somebody else finally noticed it.

"You're . . . uh . . . welcome?"

We reach the bottom of the steps leading back to my house, and Billy shuffles his feet and starts twirling his machete in a way that make me nervous. "So, maybe I'll see you tomorrow?" he says.

"It's not like I have anywhere else to go." His face falls, and I wish I could take it back. It's not Billy's fault I'm stuck here, practically crawling out of my own skin because I can't dive. "Sorry, I didn't mean it like that. I'd love to hang out."

He snaps back into his usual grin. "There's more of the island you haven't seen yet. I could take you on another un-official tour?"

"That'd be great." I lean in to take the flower crown off his head, and his eyes widen for a second before he realizes what

I'm doing. "Thanks, Billy," I say, setting the crown on my own head.

"No problem. See you tomorrow." He spins around, machete swinging, and disappears into the forest.

As I head up the steps, my lungs grate and burn, and I have to stop to cough. Doubled over, abdomen contracting and eyes streaming, I watch scarlet droplets spatter onto the step above my feet. It seeps into the stone and disappears.

Then, seconds later, a vine sprouts from the exact spot. It unfurls and a pink bud appears at its tip.

I blink hard, then rub my eyes. There's no possible way that just happened. I stare at the flower, willing it to disappear— like it would if it were a hallucination caused by dehydration and ruined lungs and a long day in the heat—but it stubbornly remains, bobbing gently in the breeze.

Maybe it was just a coincidence. Or maybe, as gross as it sounds, there's a species of fast-growing plant here that sprouts when it comes into contact with anything water-like. Blood is mostly water, after all.

Or maybe I'm losing it.

The flower bud tips in my direction. Its petals begin to unfurl, but it's just a coincidence that it's blooming at me like this, like it's thanking me for my blood. It has to be a coincidence. Stomach churning, I step around the plant, careful to not let it touch my ankle, and then dash up the steps.

Chapter
9

"YOU LOOK BETTER this evening." David holds the wine bottle out in my direction, but I wave it away. "Doesn't she look great, Carrie? Like she's got her color back or something. This ocean air must really agree with you, Addie."

I gulp down another glass of water, along with a comment about how I'd be getting even more ocean air in Dahab if I hadn't accidentally died. I'm tempted to ask my mom whether they would have buried or cremated my body, but that would ruin dinner.

"Thanks," I say. "I feel a little better."

My mom gazes at me, and I worry she can sense all the fascinating and unsettling things that have happened to me today. But then she smiles. "There definitely is a little more color in your cheeks, hon."

"Maybe," I say, because she looks so hopeful and I don't have the heart to tell her that none of my exercises seem to be helping, no matter how many times I do them. I also don't have the heart to tell her that I might have hallucinated a vampire flower on the steps. "You really don't have to worry about me so much," I say. "I'm fine, and Billy's a nice kid, so I can hang out with him if you want to go off and do things on your own."

David waggles his furry eyebrows. "You two didn't waste any time."

"Um, no," I say, infuriated on both Billy's and my behalf. "He's like fifteen."

David laughs, and a piece of lettuce falls out of his mouth and lands on his T-shirt. "Ah, to be a worldly seventeen again."

"Oh, stop it," says my mom, but I stand and start clearing up my dishes. I'm too tired after last night's interrupted sleep and today's long list of bizarre events to put up with David's mock-fatherly teasing.

"I'm going to read for a while," I say. "Thanks for dinner, Mom. The fish was perfect."

She beams at me. "Ken said he'll take us out on the boat tomorrow to catch some more."

"You go without me," I say. "I promise I'll be fine."

She purses her lips. "We'll think about it. Oh, and Melinda brought over that book about the island if you want to check it out. It's on the coffee table in the living room."

"Thanks," I say. "Good night."

Even though my eyelids are so heavy that I don't think I'll actually manage to read, I grab the paperback book and head to my room. *A Brief History of Eulalie Island*, it says, the title overlaying a watercolor painting of a crescent-shaped beach flanked with palms. At the center of the beach stands a figure in a green dress with long white hair that reaches the backs of her knees. I squint at the picture, hoping to make out the details of Eulalie's face, but they're too tiny.

With a yawn so big it makes my jaw ache, I set the book on

my bedside table. Tomorrow I'll read about the island. For now I'm going to sleep—without my video, but that feels slightly easier than it did last night. Maybe by the time this trip is over, I won't feel compelled to watch it anymore. Maybe I'll also be able to stop obsessing over where I went in those eight and a half minutes, though that seems less likely.

Halfway through my second round of breathing exercises, I notice that the flower crown at the foot of my bed is leaking sap onto the blanket. Holding the wilted wreath carefully between two fingers, I bring it outside and drop it into the bushes. As I head back to my room, I listen for the distant strains of a harp, but the only sounds are the insects, the waves, and the wind in the trees.

I dream I'm in a rowboat, drifting in a black sea under a night sky. A dark-haired girl in a long white dress sits on the bench across from me. Her skin is pale as bones. She inclines her head toward the water, where shapes are drifting up from the depths. Faces, hundreds of them, slick and white like fish bellies, eyes closed.

Bodies.

The girl stretches her hand out toward them, and the boat lists.

"Don't!" I snatch her wrist, which is only bones, no flesh or skin. With a gasp, I let go, and she smiles. Her teeth are shards of broken glass. A thick length of rope is wrapped around her waist. The bodies are gently bumping against the underside of the boat.

"Where are the oars?" I whisper.

She reaches back and pulls something out from behind her. But it's not an oar; it's an anchor, attached to the same rope that's looped around her waist. Before I can react, the girl heaves the anchor overboard. As the rope plays out, she looks deep in my eyes and mouths a single word.

Help.

The anchor yanks her over the side of the boat.

Chapter

10

I WAKE NOT in my bed but the middle of the forest, the dirt path warm under my bare feet. It's been years since I've felt this panic jolt of not being in my room, of having done something I don't remember. My hand goes to my medallion, sliding it back and forth on the chain as I try to get my bearings in these dark, whispering woods.

Aa-dee-dee-dee, calls a bird that should be sleeping, eerie and muted.

Moonlight makes deep pockets of shadows and distorts the shapes of the trees. The air is just as hot as it was during the day, and sweat coats my skin. As the jungle exhales its rotten flower breath, something tickles my knee. With a screech, I swipe it off. A beetle lands with a buzz and a crunch in the dirt; it flashes blue and crawls away.

Terror flares in my gut. I have no idea how to get back to the house.

Don't cough. Just breathe.

I'm no stranger to panic—it's a normal human reaction to danger, and freediving is an inherently dangerous sport. But over the years, I've learned to live with my fear, to dissociate myself from it as I dive. To move forward despite it, but also with it. *Let your fear come along for the ride*, Mia once told me, and that's what I need to do now.

More blue flashes appear in the bushes, pulsing together in a slow rhythm.

"Addie." A whisper floats on the breeze.

"Who's there?" I start toward the sound but stop when I realize the flashing blue beetles are following me.

In the safe daytime, I was fairly certain Billy was pulling my leg about ghosts, but now I'm not so sure. Anything seems possible in this moonlight. I'm trying not to think about the fact that Billy's family doesn't come out here at night and why that might be. With a shudder that rattles my teeth, I turn back the other way, but the beetles shift direction too. Crossing my arms over my burning chest, I run down the path, and the beetles dart above and around me, skimming my hair, my bare shoulders and arms with their hard little bodies.

The path shifts uphill, and something tall looms ahead that might be the stairs to my house. I almost don't dare hope. Swatting the bugs away from my face, I dash forward, but a root catches my foot and I fall. Pebbles and dirt rip into my knee. The burn in my chest is threatening to become an explosion, but I stagger upright. I can't stop now. I am moving forward, despite my fear. The moonlight grows brighter, whiter. Faintly, almost inaudible in the distance, a harp's eerie melody is playing.

There aren't any stairs, just a sloping face of rock. This isn't the way to my house. The beetles land all at once and begin crawling up the hill, forming a single file. I've never seen beetles act like that, and Billy's words echo in my memory: Nothing about Eulalie Island is normal. Not the bugs and not the plants, which I desperately hope are not sprouting in the dark where I can't see them.

Breathe, Addie. Just breathe.

I have two choices: I can follow the creepy blue beetles, or I can turn back into the dark forest filled with that broken harp music. Obviously that isn't really an option. The island isn't that big—if I keep going in a straight line, I'll eventually hit the ocean, and then I can follow the beach until I reach the house.

I am terrified, but my fear and I climb the hill. The stone is dry and dusty, and pieces of it crumble away in my hands. The air begins to cool, and I suck down greedy, painful mouthfuls. From the other side of the incline comes a soft lapping sound, and as I reach the top, the clouds fall away from the moon.

I'm standing above the cenote, which is smooth as a mirror and glowing green-blue like it's lit from deep inside. The harp music has faded to nothing. My feet shuffle forward; my toes curl over the edge of the cliff. It's a short dive, only about fifteen feet, and I know the water is deep enough. But if I dove, I might not ever want to come back up. Sweat prickles the corners of my eyes, and when I shut them, I can feel the coolness of that beautiful water kissing my skin.

Aa-dee-dee-dee.

Even the birds want me to.

I shouldn't.

Aa-dee-dee-dee.

I stretch my arms out like wings and jump.

The forest drops away and the moonlight smears as I break the surface of the cenote. Down I plunge, bubbles streaming up my skin and through my hair, and everything is blue, blue, blue, and the sense of belonging is so pure it hurts. At about two meters, my descent slows and buoyancy begins to take hold, but I fight it with my arms, needing to stay for just a little longer. The bubbles tumble up without me.

Thirty more seconds and then I'll go up. Hovering suspended, I watch the silvery surface ripple. The pulsing throb I felt in the water this afternoon is still present—it's even stronger now as it surrounds my body—and I imagine this is what it feels like to be in a womb. With a gentle shift of my jaw, I equalize pressure. It's so easy. Nothing hurts. I'm safe.

Thirty more seconds.

I don't want to go back to cloying air and broken lungs and horrible honeymoons, but I need to be gentle with my body or I'll never get better. Dropping my arms, I let the world pull me back.

The breath I take is the first truly clean one I've had in weeks. It feels accidental, but I inhale again, and still nothing hurts. I'd forgotten what this felt like, this simple act that used to require no thought whatsoever and has now taken over my entire life. Treading water, I breathe and breathe like it's this amazing new thing I've just discovered, then burst into giddy laughter.

Someone clears their throat behind me, and I whirl around. Standing by the water's edge is a tall boy with ash-colored hair and an amused, almost embarrassed smile. Sean is wearing the same dark pair of shorts, and moonlight gleams on his wide shoulders, which I'm trying not to stare at.

"How's the water?" he says.

"Incredible." My skin is humming with the beauty of this pool, the dreamlike heartbeat of its water, the perfection of this night.

"I looked for you on the beach." Sean's voice is low, all the ragged emotion from last night smoothed away. He steps into the water, and as hard as I try, I can't keep my mouth from grinning. He wanted to see me again.

"I kind of ended up here by accident," I say.

He nods like that's a normal thing to happen in the middle of the night. The glimmering waterline reaches his flat stomach and I really need to stop staring, so I roll onto my back and watch the stars instead. Maybe this isn't going to be the worst two weeks I've ever had.

I hear the tiny lapping sounds as he moves closer, but I float, letting the pool's gentle thrum carry me, until everything is quiet again. When I finally flip over, he's treading water beside me. Shining droplets fleck his cheeks, and I wonder if he looks this good in sunlight. I'm certain he does.

"Do you feel a kind of . . . pulse in the water?" I say, opening my hands flat to absorb the sensation.

Sean nods. "It's another one of those strange things about the island. I kind of like it."

"Me too," I say.

"Did Billy tell you about this place?" he asks.

"He brought me here this afternoon." I pause. "I know nobody's supposed to dive, but I only went under for a couple of seconds. A minute tops. Okay, maybe ninety seconds at the absolute maximum."

Sean laughs. "Don't worry, I'm not going to tell on you."

"It's amazing," I say. "I *feel* amazing here. I have this . . . lung injury and I shouldn't be able to hold my breath for even a minute. But I just went under and I didn't mean to stay, but nothing hurt, so I did, for just a little while, and when I came back up, I felt like a new person. A healed person. Nothing seems real here, like this just can't be actually happening. Sorry, does that sound completely weird?"

"Not at all," he says.

"Well, it feels completely weird." I drag in a massive lungful of air and gust it out. "I haven't been able to do that in weeks."

Sean drifts closer, his treading arms weaving around mine. "Do you know why people aren't allowed to dive in this pool?"

"Billy told me there are tunnels and caves down there," I say. "I don't know a ton about cave diving, but it's dangerous because people can get stuck. And sometimes even if there's air in the caves, it's poisonous."

"That's part of the reason," he says. "The other part is that nobody feels pain in this water."

"How?" It doesn't seem possible, but when I touch the cut on my knee from when I fell, I realize he's right. The skin is still torn, but it doesn't hurt at all. Again, I'm flooded with the sense that I'm dreaming, but I can't even pinch myself to check because I wouldn't feel it.

"The island has a lot of secrets nobody knows the answers to." Sean's face darkens for a second.

"You're not kidding," I say, drifting closer. "I coughed some blood onto the stairs near my house earlier, and I swear a vine grew right out of the spot in about three seconds."

As soon as the words are out, I feel ridiculous. That was a borderline-insane thing to admit to someone I just met. But the corner of Sean's mouth turns up.

"The island must like you," he says.

A shiver races across my skin at his borderline-insane response.

"Anyway," he continues, "you can see why people aren't allowed to dive here. It's not safe if they can't feel when they're running out of oxygen."

"Some of us know our limits," I mutter.

He laughs. "I've been diving in it since I moved here, and nothing's happened to me."

"Billy never mentioned you were a freediver," I say, wondering why he'd keep such a significant detail about his brother from me.

"I don't know if I'd call myself a freediver," he says. "I've done some spearfishing, but I bet I'm nowhere near as good as you."

It's arrogant of me to agree, but it's probably true. Or used to be.

"How is it down there?" I ask, unable to keep the raw longing out of my voice.

Sean's dark eyes sparkle. "Amazing. Absolutely perfect visibility. It's like another world."

Peering down into the glowing depths, I'm sure he's right. "Maybe I'll go under again, just for one more minute."

My doctors said I wasn't allowed any long breath holds until the bleeding stopped, but a minute isn't that long for me. And even if it's a problem, I'm willing to deal with the consequences if it means diving into that glow again.

Sean's smile widens. "Want me to be your safety diver? I can resuscitate you if there's an emergency."

The thought of his mouth on mine makes my face go hot. "There's no way I'm going to need CPR after sixty seconds."

"Of course not." He drifts closer still. "A minute is nothing."

I shouldn't do this. I really, truly should not dive, even if nothing hurts and my entire body is singing from the beauty of this otherworldly place. I should say good night to Sean and walk back to the house, but his fingers brush mine under the surface and my skin goes hot, despite the water's chill.

"Okay," I say. "Let's go."

Chapter
11

THE WATER THROBS in a steady rhythm as we swim down into the glowing blue. My arms and legs move at a languid pace, much more slowly than I'd normally go, but I need to take it easy, and I'm not sure how far Sean can make it either. The light should be dimming as we descend, but instead it brightens, flooding my eyes with a gentle radiance as we follow the craggy walls of the cenote down.

Sean's upside-down face is serene in the blue light. He flashes an *okay* sign that I return, even though I know we need to go back soon. The pulsing drum of the water has become even more like a heartbeat, vibrating deep inside my skull.

Negative buoyancy takes hold as the walls open up and we sink into a soaring cavern. The sandy floor drifts closer, a wide hole in its center continuing down even farther. Silt runs down the sides of the hole, pouring into the depths like a sandy waterfall. There's nothing I want more than to swim down into that second chamber, whose pulse is drawing me nearer, deeper.

But it's time to go back. If I want to come here again, I need to protect my lungs. As if sensing my hesitation, Sean slows too. We freefall for a few more seconds before I finally hold my hand up, palm out, making the sign for *stop*. He gives me a thumbs-up, the sign to go back to the surface, and we turn in synchronicity, slowly rising.

Kick, stroke, kick, stroke. It's harder work going up, and a heavy sense of loss fills my chest as the floor disappears beneath us. The thrumming heartbeat fades as the surface nears, and I want to cry, which is absurd because I should be thrilled by what I've just done. And I am thrilled—ecstatic, in fact. It's just that I never want to stop.

As we break the surface, night air rushes into my lungs, and I'm amazed all over again by the smoothness. I should be coughing up blood, but a sweet softness coats my tongue and throat. It's pure magic. There's no other explanation. I cannot believe David Donovan, of all people, is responsible for bringing me to this place.

Treading beside me, Sean wipes his eyes. "What did you think?"

My laughter rings out over the water and stone. A bird echoes it back. "I think I might still be dreaming," I say.

He gives me a look that muddles my insides. "You're not."

I glance at the sky, which is no longer black but a deep blue. Dawn is coming and I need to get back, but I want another few minutes with him, with this water. "Have you ever thought about training to become a freediver? With the right coach, you might be able to compete."

Sean drifts backward, his brow furrowing. "It's just a hobby. And I can't dive that deep anywhere except this pool. It helps when you can't feel pain."

"We must have gone down at least fifteen meters," I say, kicking toward him, "and you're not even winded. Seriously, you should look into it when you get back to college. There might be a program nearby. If you want, I can ask around?"

He frowns again, and I'm not sure what's so upsetting about the idea.

Aa-dee-dee-dee, calls a bird, and Sean's gaze goes hazy before snapping to me and softening. He brushes a droplet from my cheek with his thumb, and the water's pulsing thrum fills my head again. I wonder if blushes are visible under moonlight.

"I'm guessing Billy didn't tell you about me because he didn't want us spending time together," he says.

Considering how I'm feeling right now, I also suspect that Billy wouldn't like it. Another bird begins to warble, a song full of broken notes cast into the lightening sky. I dip my head under one last time, and the heartbeat is still there, faint but steady.

"I have to go," I say reluctantly. "Can we do this again tomorrow . . . I mean tonight?"

Sean's face sinks in the water until only his eyes are visible, and I'm seized with a sudden fear that he'll say no, that he's realized my awkwardness out of water is even worse than a seal's, or that I've screwed everything up by pushing him to compete. But then his mouth emerges and curves into a smile.

"Sure."

Chapter

12

THE SUN IS all the way up by the time I wake, luxuriating in the softness of my bed. It was surprisingly easy to find my way back here in the early light of dawn. The path hadn't grown back at all since Billy and I hacked our way home yesterday. Not a single branch caught my clothes, not a single insect landed on me. My lungs still hurt—the ache hit me as soon as I stepped out of the cenote—but it's no worse than yesterday, so it seems I didn't injure myself by diving. Maybe I've even healed a little.

I roll over, glance at the clock beside my bed, and gasp. It's eleven thirty. My internal alarm always wakes me by six o'clock, no matter how late I've been up the night before, but it seems that a lot of my internal stuff isn't working anymore. With a sigh, I wiggle my toes under the sheet and stretch my arms overhead, replaying last night's dive in my head over and over: the cool resistance of the water on my arms and legs, the welcoming pressure, the glowing lights, the strange and beautiful heartbeat. The stillness inside me matching the stillness of the water. The complete lack of pain. Sean's fingers brushing mine.

A sudden breaking pop in my lungs sends me rocketing upright, and I cough and cough, gasping between the hacks.

Flecks of red land on the perfect white of my sheet, and I clasp both hands tight over my mouth. My nose and eyes are streaming, and I'm choking for air. As the attack slowly subsides, reality sinks in. I'm not better. Not even a little bit. And in the light of day, it seems almost impossible that I ever made such a deep dive with these burning, sticky lungs. Maybe it was all a dream.

But my pillow is still damp.

Once I'm able to get oxygen into my body again, I wipe my face with three tissues, spit a mouthful of blood into the toilet, and flush it away. Then I head for the kitchen to get some water.

Outside, the pink of the flowers has deepened to fuchsia and even plum purple in some places. Butterflies in matching colors flit from blossom to blossom, and I wonder if they all hatched from their cocoons at the same time. Somehow, the scent of the flowers has gotten even stronger, more syrupy, though still slightly rotten.

Aa-dee-dee-dee, call the birds.

A raspberry-colored butterfly lands on my bare shoulder, and an inexplicable chill slithers over my skin. Gently, so as not to break its fragile wings, I brush it off, and it swoops away into the swaying woods.

There's a note on the kitchen table, written in my mother's looping cursive:

> *Out sailing with Ken. You told us to go without you,*
> *but I'm not sure you were actually awake when you*

said that. Can't believe you slept so late! We'll be back
before dinner, hopefully with fish. Love you!

Underneath, she's drawn a stick figure lady with a heart for a torso. It's cheesy, but it makes me smile and takes the chill off my skin.

After a few yoga asanas, some breathing exercises, and a cold chicken sandwich, I change into my bathing suit and shorts. Then I fill my water bottle, throw a towel over one shoulder, and tuck the book about Eulalie Island under my arm. The breeze dances across the glittering ocean as I follow the steps down to the beach. It's a little cooler today, a perfect day for sailing. I scan the horizon, but there's no sign of my mother and David. I hope they're having fun, and I hope they stay out there for a while still.

The ocean whispers and lures, but my lungs need to rest after last night. After laying my towel in the shade of a palm tree, I open the book and skim through the early chapters about the brutal colonization and trade history of the Caribbean. It's painful to read about the genocide, the atrocities that were done to the native populations and the slaves on so many of the nearby islands, especially considering they were committed by people we learned about in school like they were heroes.

Because of its small size, or perhaps because of ships' difficulty in navigating to its shores, Eulalie Island was never colonized, and there are no historical or archaeological records of Indigenous people living there.

I'm surprised that over so many thousands of years, nobody ever settled this island, with its sheltered beach and its cenote full of clean, fresh water.

Scientists discovered odd, constantly changing magnetic fields in the waters surrounding the island, which affected navigational instruments and sent ships spiraling off course. Combined with strong currents, erratic weather patterns, and unusually large waves, this made accessing the island extremely difficult.

Just like Billy told us yesterday: it's almost like the island didn't want people to come. If someone had said that to me a week ago, I'd have laughed in their face. It still makes no sense objectively. Of course an island—a lump of rocks and sand and plants in the middle of the ocean—doesn't get to decide who steps onto its shores.

But for some reason I can't quite explain, Eulalie Island feels like more than just a lump of rocks and sand and plants. Last night, Sean told me the island likes me, and even though I know it's irrational, I can't help but hope it does.

Or maybe I'm getting dehydrated again. With a sigh, I unscrew the lid of my water bottle and chug half the contents before returning to the book. A few pages later, there's a hand-drawn picture of a white-haired girl who resembles the one on the cover. She sits on the branch of a tree wearing a loose white shirt and a pair of cropped men's pants. The sailors must have given her clothing when they arrived. Her face is dainty and sweet, and she can't be older than seventeen, despite the color of her hair.

Portrait of Eulalie by J. Burke, circa 1762.

Something small bounces off the back of my head and lands on my towel. A shiny black nut. Tucking Melinda's ribboned bookmark into my page, I sit up.

"Billy?"

The ferns rustle and shake, and a child's giggle wafts out.

"Wait!" I leap up and hop into my shorts. "Don't go!"

"You're the *it*," calls a reedy voice.

"No, I don't want to be the—I just want to talk to you." Grabbing my flip-flops and abandoning my towel and book, I run to the edge of the bushes, which have gone still.

"Little girl?" I call. "Are you there?"

Nothing.

"Please don't go." I shove my feet into my flip-flops. "Okay, I'll play, I'll play. I'll be the *it*. How high do you want me to count?"

A lemon-colored lizard emerges from a cluster of lilies and darts up a tree trunk.

"Twenty?" I call. "Thirty?"

"Twenty eleven!" she yells, crashing away through the bushes.

"You got it." I lean against a tree and put my hands over my eyes. "One . . . two . . . three . . ."

When I get to five, I peek over my shoulder. Even though there's not a breath of wind, the bushes are swaying in a much wider swath than a girl running through them would make. It's like the island is playing too, helping her to hide.

"Eighteen . . . nineteen." I push off the tree and shove my way into the green. Wet leaves make saliva trails down my arms as I pick up speed.

"Twenty-nine . . . twenty-ten." In a clearing, I scan the forest floor for her footprints, then peer up into the treetops. Butterflies in a hundred different berry hues flit in lazy spirals. "Twenty-eleven. Ready or not, here I come!"

From somewhere deep in the woods comes a feral shriek. I surge forward, shoving the plants out of my way, dodging the butterflies, beating my way toward the center of the island.

"I hope you've got a good hiding spot!" I yell. "Because I'm pretty good at this game."

Her giggle drifts through the forest, and I follow it until I find the narrow road that we took the golf cart down yesterday. "Ready or not! Ready or not!" I call.

"You shan't never find me!" she squeals.

Sweat trails down my neck in sticky streams by the time I reach the valley and the crumbling Wells house. I skid down the hill, and as I clamber through a window framed by roots, the air bathes my skin in a moss-scented chill. A muffled squeak comes from the back of the house.

"Darn, I guess you must not be in here," I call.

The squeak becomes a giggle, high-pitched and delighted. Slightly inhuman. My stomach lurches, and I'm hit by the sudden urge to run back to the beach. Then a flash of gray and rags shoots through the kitchen and out the open doorway. As I dash after her, a root I'm certain wasn't there a second ago catches my foot and sends me sprawling.

"Careful," she calls, her tone suddenly flat, and I freeze.

Aa-dee-dee-dee, sing the birds.

Standing, I ease around the root, which is as thick as a man's arm, and then step out of the crumbling house. The shrill little giggle is coming from somewhere to my left, but I can't see her anywhere in the bushes and rubble.

"You're not very good at this game," she whispers. My eyes snap down to a gray face, its chin resting on the ground and a long-legged spider on its forehead. There is something very, deeply wrong with this face.

It looks like a corpse.

The black mouth stretches into a smile, and I gulp down a shriek. It's completely impossible, but I've never been more sure of anything in my life: this is not a living person. I am not dehydrated or hallucinating. Billy wasn't pranking me. I'm playing hide-and-seek with a dead child.

"V-Violet?" I say, sinking to a crouch before I pass out.

"Yes?" Her gap-toothed smile widens.

"How are you doing that?" I gulp down the bile in my throat. "It looks like you . . . took off your head and put it on the ground. You can't do that, can you?"

She howls with laughter, and then her head lifts and her shoulders appear. The rest of her body is just as corpselike, with dirt-covered, slightly bloated skin and dark bruises everywhere. She's the exact same size as my cousin, which makes it somehow more horrifying. I never want to think of Grace looking like this, and it's taking every ounce of my strength to not run away. If I'd seen Violet up close before, I never would have followed her into the woods.

"I was hiding on the stairs," she whispers, pulling the spider from her forehead and tucking it into the pocket of her dress. "Look!"

She points to something on the ground, but my feet won't let me move any closer.

"It's all right," she says. "Mama doesn't like us to play on the stairs, but if you're careful, you won't fall in."

My spine goes rigid. "Is your mother on the island too?"

"No." Violet gives a wheezy sigh. "Mama's been gone for a long, long time. I'm almost all alone."

I edge closer, unable to shake the mental image of her disembodied head but feeling sorry for this undead, motherless child. Next to Violet's dirty bare foot, there's a square opening in the ground, hidden by thick underbrush. Moldering stone steps lead into blackness. Before I quite realize what's happening, Violet dashes down the stairs and disappears.

"Wait!" I yell.

The hole breathes out a gust of mildewed air that smells inexplicably like a nightmare. Somewhere deep down, I hear water lapping.

"The game's over," I call. "I found you. Please come back."

"You haven't tagged me." Violet's singsong voice is nearly lost in its own echo.

I rub my eyes until spots swim behind my eyelids, unable to understand how this is real. For the next two weeks, I'm stuck on a haunted island. Violet is more creepy and gross than she is scary, but that doesn't exactly make it all okay. Sometime right before my diving accident, I must have veered onto the strangest, most *wrong* timeline of my life.

"Addie-dee!" she calls. "Come on!"

Ignoring every impulse in my body, I lean over the rotten-smelling hole. "How do you know my name?"

"I like to eaves-dot," she says. "Mama says it's a frightful habit, but Mama isn't here now. Do you know how I can find her?"

Violet's voice sounds even farther away, and I bend low, straining to hear. "No, I'm sorry," I say. "But if you come up here, maybe we can talk about it?"

"The game isn't over." Violet is just as stubborn as my cousin too. "You haven't tagged me."

I peer into the festering hole and cringe. "How about we just declare you the winner? I don't need to tag you, because you're so good at this game."

A long silence, then a splash.

"Violet?" I call.

No answer.

"Violet, did you fall in?"

Still nothing. Swearing, I ease down the damp stairs until the ground is level with my shoulders. The inexplicable, nightmarish terror builds with each step. This is absurd and dangerous. Violet is already dead, and nothing worse could happen to her than that, but she reminds me so much of my cousin, and I'd never want someone to let Grace go into a pit like that, dead or alive. I don't have a flashlight; I don't even have my phone. But still, I can't bring myself to leave her down there.

"Hang on, I'm coming!" I say.

Panic wells in my chest, and I have a sudden urge to start packing air and hold my breath like I'm diving. But I'm not in the cenote and that's not possible on dry land, not with these ruined lungs. Instead, I focus on slowing my breath and calming my pulse as I slip underground and the world goes dim. Something furry scampers over my toe, and I scream.

In the dark below, water drips and sloshes.

Fists clenched, I force my feet to keep moving down, and down, and down until the black swallows me up and there's no difference when I close my eyes or open them. Finally, there are no more steps, and the world lightens to gray. I'm standing on a narrow ledge beside glimmering black water.

"It's crawly and creepy in this hole." Violet's voice is startlingly close; I can just make out the edges of her crouching body a few meters away on the ledge. She didn't fall in after all. "You're much more braver than Billy," she says in an approving tone.

"Of course I am." As I slide closer, the shapes of things become clearer. We're in a low-ceilinged cavern, and across the water on the opposite side, there's a jagged little tunnel. The heavy, sinister energy I felt on the stairs is unbearable down here.

Frigid fingers close around my wrist, and I bite my lips shut to keep from screaming again. "Jesus, Violet." I fight to keep my voice even. "*I'm* supposed to tag *you*."

Her distended, gray arm wraps around my knee, and a shiver crawls up my spine. "Mama says we mustn't take the Lord's name in vain," she says in a grave voice.

"I'm sorry."

"It's all right." Her face is dusty and cold against my leg, and it's all I can do to not shove her off me. "Nora says we only have to try our best. It reminds me of her down here."

"Is that your sister?" I say. "Lenora?"

Violet whimpers, her frigid breath raising the hair on my skin.

"Do you know where Lenora is?" I ask. But if this cave reminds Violet of Lenora, maybe I don't want to know anything about her sister.

"No."

"When's the last time you saw her?"

Violet lets go of my leg and swings backward. Instinctively I reach out to stop her from falling into the water, but she slips through my fingers, coating them in dust.

"I don't have to tell secrets just because you founded me," she says. "And you haven't won the game anyway."

"Well, I did offer to let you win, but you said no and then I found you," I say.

"That's not me and Billy's rules." She lets out a huff that

smells like rotting meat. "This is me and Billy's game."

I laugh. "You two didn't invent hide-and-seek."

"Did so."

"Can I ask how old you are?" I say. "That's not a secret, right?"

Her cold fingers crawl like an insect down my forearm. "Three and eight-sevenths."

"Did you know I have a cousin who's almost the same age as you?" I try not to gasp as her tiny hand closes tight around my wrist again. "Her name is Grace, but she doesn't know fractions yet. You're a very smart girl."

"Nora was teaching me about fractions before she swam away." Violet punctuates her sentence with a sad little hum. "Now I am alonely, and no one can notice me."

"I'm here," I say. "For a little while, anyway. And Billy is here too. He sees you."

"Billy isn't Nora," says Violet quietly. "And he isn't my mama."

Her words make my stomach hurt. I can't imagine what it must be like to be eternally three years old and stuck on an island all alone. As gruesome as Violet looks, she's just a little kid who didn't ask for any of this.

"How did Nora swim away?" I ask.

From across the cave comes a small blue flash, then another. They seem to be coming out of the tunnel. Violet and I watch silently as they float across the water toward us.

"Violet," I try again. "How did your sister swim away? Where were you when it happened?"

She doesn't answer, transfixed by the lights, which are floating up out of the water now, casting their blue glow onto the ceiling and illuminating us. Wisps of blond curls frame Violet's dead, doll-like face. Her eyes are sunken, her lips crusted and cracked. She's staring hard at the lights, her body shaking.

Suddenly the lights disappear, plunging the cave into darkness. By the time my eyes readjust, she's gone.

"Violet?" I fumble back to the stairs and dash up them, which is a mistake. As I reemerge into the sunlight, dust fills my lungs and I bark out a cough, then another. Each scarlet droplet that hits the ground sprouts into a tiny, twisting vine, and I watch in horror as they writhe like worms toward each other. I still don't understand how this is happening, but I just spent half an hour with a dead kid, so apparently anything is possible on Eulalie Island. Violet doesn't scare me anymore, but something about the vines does. I'm torn between wanting to stomp them to death and not wanting to touch them.

"Stop it," I whisper, and the vine closest to my foot rears up like a tiny cobra and sprouts a fuchsia bud. The other vines begin to blossom too.

Aa-dee-dee-dee, call the birds.

"Leave me alone. I don't like this," I say, though I don't think the birds or the vines care whether I like it or not. As I back away from the crawling plants, I notice something damp and scratchy tied around my wrist. It's a clumsily braided bracelet made of red string and grass.

A gift from Violet.

Chapter

13

WHEN I GET back to the house, David is gutting a large, silver-striped fish on the patio table. Iridescent scales litter the flagstone, and oozing innards are piled up on a plate by his elbow. He wipes his forehead with the back of his arm and smears blood into his eyebrows.

"I caught us a *waa-hoo*!" he yells, and I trip out of one flip-flop. My nerves are still completely shot.

"You what?" I say, retrieving my sandal.

"A waa-hoo!" He jabs his knife into the side of the fish and lifts it up, floppy and dead, as my mother opens the screen door.

"He's been doing this all afternoon." She tosses an indulgent smile at David. "The fish is called a wahoo. Addie, are you all right? You look . . ."

She tips her head, and I wait for her to say it. *Like you've seen a ghost.* If she says it, I'm going to start laughing, and I don't think it will be the good, normal kind of laughter.

". . . like you fell into a ditch," she finishes.

"Awesome." I rub my stinging eyes and wish I had a plausible explanation for looking like this. It's not like I can tell her about Violet. I'd never be able to convince her. Billy's probably right that only he and I can see her because we died. And if David thinks my mental health is slipping, he'll use it as leverage to convince my mom to ban me from freediving.

"Can we actually eat that?" I ask, nodding at the mangled fish. The flat gray eyes in its disembodied head remind me of Violet.

"We certainly can." David stabs the creature's spine, and I flinch. "Ken's setting up a grill on the beach, and we're going to have a dinner cookout."

"With the Carpenters?" I say.

"Who else would we have it with?" David sends a shower of scales across the patio.

Not Violet, that's for sure. I desperately need to talk to Billy, tell him what happened this afternoon. And if we're having dinner with the entire Carpenter family, Sean will be there too. My stomach flutters.

"How was sailing?" I ask.

"Just magnificent," says my mom. "I can't get over how clear and beautiful the water is."

That comment would sting if I hadn't been diving in even clearer and more beautiful water last night. She gives me an apologetic smile and pulls me into a hug. "How are you feeling?"

"Fine." The braided cord twists on my wrist, and I think of lonely little Violet with her frigid fingers and her family gone, and I let my own mother hug me longer than usual.

"You're all dusty," she says.

"Must be sand." I pull away. "I'll go take a shower before the barbecue."

"Be quick," she says as I slip away to my room. My beach towel from this afternoon lies neatly folded at the foot of my bed, along with the book about Eulalie Island. I wonder if my mom brought it back, or if Melinda or Ken did.

After a shower, I ponder my array of clothing. It's silly to worry about what to wear, because Billy probably won't notice and his brother has seen me twice now in soaking wet pajamas, so I grab a T-shirt and shorts, weave my hair into a loose braid, and head back outside, where my mom is helping David pack up what's left of his mutilated wahoo in a Tupperware container.

"Is that the only fish?" I ask, praying the answer is no.

"Ken caught a red snapper, and I made quinoa salad." My mom pats another Tupperware on the table. "We won't starve." She plants a kiss on David's shoulder and smooths her blue sundress. It's similar to the one she wore the day I died, but with tiny leaves instead of flowers. The old dress was dry-clean-only, and it didn't survive the saltwater-and-blood bath it got.

Proudly clutching his container full of fish, David leads us down the cliff staircase. About halfway between our house and the lighthouse, not far from the spot where I first met Sean, a barbecue smokes. Billy sprawls on a camping chair beside a folding table where Melinda is busy mixing up drinks in various pitchers.

"Lovely to see you again, Addie." She holds out a cup full of ice and brownish liquid. "Would you like some banana-turmeric kombucha?"

"Um, thanks." I sit in the empty chair beside Billy and take a careful sniff of the drink. The yeasty, spicy banana aroma makes me sneeze.

"Careful," he says, wrinkling his nose. "People have died from drinking that shit."

"William Henry Carpenter," says his mother.

"Sorry." He rolls his eyes. "People have actually died from drinking that stuff."

"Not from *my* kombucha, thank you very much. I've been honing the recipe for years." Melinda jabs a spoon in the direction of the barbecue. "Why don't you keep an eye on the fish until your father gets back?"

"Where is Ken?" asks my mother.

"He's just taking care of a few business things that came up, but don't worry, he'll be here in a couple of minutes." Melinda slices a lime in half and squeezes it over the rest of the cups, which she's already filled with rum and what looks like mango juice. Billy sips a can of soda, and I guess I'm the only one stuck with kombucha.

As the grown-ups have their drinks and my mother marvels at the quality of the late-afternoon sunlight on the ocean, I join Billy at the barbecue. He's trying to wiggle the spatula under a fillet that's about to crumble into pieces.

"Let me." Taking the spatula and nudging him out of the way, I quickly flip the fish.

"Did they teach you that at freediving school?" he says.

"I cooked a lot when my parents were getting divorced." Forgetting that I'm supposed to be wary of my drink, I take a long swig. The sour banana-turmeric fizzes on my tongue, and tears fill my eyes as I fight to gulp it down. Billy watches, the corner of his mouth twitching.

"If you need 911, I'll have to go back to the lighthouse to get the satellite phone, and it'll take them at least an hour to get here," he says.

"Stop." I wipe my mouth on the back of my hand and take shallow breaths until the need to cough passes. "Look what I got today," I say finally, holding my wrist up.

Billy eyes the bracelet dubiously. "Did you make that?"

"Violet gave it to me. We played hide-and-seek."

He breaks into a grin and lowers his voice. "So do you believe me now?"

"I want to say no, but . . . yeah." Just thinking about Violet with her chin on the ground and that spider on her forehead sets my teeth on edge. "I honestly thought you were pranking me."

He waves his hand dismissively. "I'm used to nobody taking me seriously. I'm just glad you came around."

"But Violet's not really a ghost," I say. "She has a body, so doesn't that make her more like a zombie or something?" My stomach wobbles at the thought.

Billy shakes his head. "She doesn't lurch around moaning and rotting and eating brains, so I ruled that out a while ago. Violet's something we don't have a word for, but she's probably closest to a ghost."

For some reason, this eases the gelatinous feeling in my gut. A three-year-old zombie is too horrible to consider.

"Where did she hide?" asks Billy.

"There's a trapdoor in the ground behind her house," I say. "I almost didn't see it, but then she——"

"Wait, you went into the hole?" Billy's jaw goes slack. "That place has horror movie vibes."

"It definitely does," I say with a shiver. "And so does Violet. I didn't want to go down there, but I was worried something happened to her."

He laughs, incredulous. "Um, she's dead. What could possibly happen to her?"

"Yeah, yeah, I know." I twist my medallion on its chain. "This whole thing is just . . . too much. I don't know what to think or believe anymore."

"I hear you," says Billy. "The island takes some getting used to. I'm still finding new weird stuff all the time. Violet's a good kid, though."

"Underneath all those horror movie layers, she's kind of sweet." I can't believe I'm agreeing with his assessment of an actual dead person, but it's true. "I wish I knew why she's stuck here."

"There he is!" calls Melinda, and for a second, I think she's talking about Sean and my pulse jumps, but the figure striding down the beach toward us is unmistakably middle-aged and wearing a Hawaiian shirt.

"Where's your brother?" I ask Billy.

He shuts the barbecue lid and waves away the smoke. "Probably in our room, sleeping."

I start to bring the cup to my lips again but stop just in time. "Isn't he coming for dinner?"

94

"Nope." Billy kicks a coconut half-buried in the sand. "I told you, he's like a mole person."

It shouldn't sting this much that Sean isn't coming. We barely know each other, and he has no obligation to show up at a parent-organized barbecue just because I'm here. But it really did seem like there was something between us last night. He even went looking for me.

"Why doesn't he ever leave the lighthouse?" I ask.

Billy crushes his empty can, then sidles over and reaches for one of the cocktails on the table, but his mother swats his hand away. Ruefully, he opens a cooler, pulls out two more sodas, and hands one to me. "Sean hates my parents for making him come here all summer instead of staying on campus with his stupid frat bro friends. I don't know why he hates hanging out with me, but that's not new."

"Sean's in a frat?" It seems so unlikely, even more so than him being an internet troll.

"Delta Kappa Epsilon." Billy cracks open his drink and takes a long gulp.

"Oh" is all I can think of to say, so I open my soda too. Clearly Sean has layers I haven't even begun to peel away. So far I know that he's secretly good at diving, he hates his family, and he enjoys trolling and frat parties. Yet he's always seemed so sensitive and intelligent every time we've spoken. He's like one of those people with different personas for different situations. I don't know which version I'm seeing.

"How's the snapper coming?" Ken lifts the barbecue lid, and David rushes over with his container of mangled wahoo parts. Melinda starts lighting tiki torches, and Billy and I drag our chairs farther away from the grown-ups.

"What was down there in the hole behind Violet's house?" he asks as we watch the sun sink toward the horizon, streaks of deep pink bleeding up through the sky.

"It was a cavern full of water," I say, twisting my medallion on its chain. "And there was a tunnel at the back. I'm guessing it connects up to that network of caves you were talking about?"

"Probably." Billy burps at the stunning gold-and-fuchsia sky, then waves his hand in front of his face.

"How come nobody is allowed to dive in them?" I ask.

"We had some guys staying here last year—a man named Roland and his nephew—who decided they wanted to map the caves under the island," he says. "My dad wasn't thrilled about it, but they said they were expert divers and they had all these certifications and stuff, so he let them."

The tone of Billy's voice is getting softer, and the slight edge in his voice makes me dread where the story is going. The sun's rays dim, and a sour breeze slithers out from the edges of the woods.

"I used to wait at the cenote to time them and make sure they came back," he says. "Not that we could have rescued them if they didn't."

I cringe at the thought of getting stuck somewhere in a web of tunnels so deep underground that nobody could find me. The torches flicker as the wind gusts again, slithering over my skin and whispering in my ears.

"At first, they were really excited," says Billy. "They found all kinds of caves down there, and they showed me pictures. It looked amazing, but there was no way I was going down there to see it in person. They had to take off their scuba tanks to get through some of the narrower tunnels. My dad *really* didn't like that."

"Sounds dangerous." It wouldn't be a problem for me, though. I wonder how far the other caves are from the cenote.

"Yeah, we'll get to that part," says Billy with a grimace. "The nephew, Zach, was in his twenties and was going to grad school for history or something, I don't remember." He yanks the tab off his soda can. "Really nice guy. He used to play horseshoes with me sometimes. Anyway, his uncle, Roland, got really into mapping the caves. He was taking thousands of pictures and staying up all night drawing diagrams of the tunnels. He was completely obsessed."

I can see how someone could get obsessed with that glowing water, that strange, pulsing beat. "The maps sound like an interesting project, though."

"I guess." Billy flicks the soda tab into the air and catches it. "But he was diving like eight hours a day, and Zach kept saying it was dangerous and he was going to get sick."

"He's right." I'd never let myself dive eight hours a day, no matter how alluring the water was. That's just asking for trouble.

A black shape flits out of the woods and darts over our heads, then another. My mom and David cover their drinks and peer up nervously.

"Bats," says Ken. "Don't worry, they won't hurt you."

"They keep the island's insect population in check," says Melinda. "And did you know they're nocturnal pollinators?"

"All part of the ecosystem." My mom smiles, but her hand goes to her hair like she's worried they're going to make a nest in it.

The bats keep coming, one after the other, and we watch them wheel in the watercolor sky, each finding its own hunting path and zooming off across the beach or back into the woods. From this distance, they could be birds, but I don't think I'd like to meet one up close. Those leathery wings make me squeamish.

"How far down do the tunnels go?" I ask Billy, forcing my attention away from the bats.

He shrugs. "Pretty deep. Roland brought a bunch of scuba tanks with him, but he ended up having to go over to Tortola to refill them. Zach was getting pissed off because his uncle just wouldn't stop diving. My dad finally put his foot down and told them they couldn't do it anymore."

"Good. What did Roland say?"

"Not much." Billy sighs. "I thought he'd be madder, but he just sort of accepted it. We didn't realize he'd started diving all by himself at night."

I rub the goose bumps off my arms. I can't imagine a more dangerous thing than cave diving alone. At least when I dove last night, I had a buddy and I knew my limits.

Another gust of wind sets the palm trees swaying. The last

of the bats flap away into the sky. The barbecue fills the air with the mouthwatering scent of charcoal and cooking fish, but underlying that, drifting out from the woods, is something earthy and dank, like old mushrooms.

"Zach woke up alone one morning," says Billy. "Roland's stuff was down by the cenote, but he wasn't there. My dad took his own gear and went down looking for him, but he wasn't willing to take his tank off to get through the narrowest tunnels. We called the police and they sent a recovery team over, and they finally found his body wedged inside a tunnel with his tank still on. It took them two days to get it out."

"Oh God," I say. "That's horrible."

"I saw his body when they finally brought it up," says Billy. "He was all bloated and blue, but he had this huge smile on his face. I know it sounds weird, but it was like he'd just seen the most beautiful thing you could imagine."

My foot taps a nervous rhythm in the sand. To be very honest, that cenote was one of the most beautiful things *I* could ever imagine. I wonder what's down in those caves beneath it.

"At least he died doing something he loved?" I offer.

Billy chews his lip. "Seems more like he died doing something he couldn't stop doing."

A chill seeps under my skin. That's how I feel about diving too. But there's no way I'll dive as much as Roland did. There isn't enough time anyway.

"Food's ready!" calls Ken. Beside him, Melinda is dishing out quinoa and green salad onto plates laden with grilled fish.

Even David's mangled wahoo smells amazing. We all take a plate and find our seats, and for a while everyone is silent, sucking air into our mouths as we wolf down the scalding fish. The air slowly darkens around us, the wind stills, and the torches flare and spark. It's surprisingly peaceful, and I find myself wanting to slow down and preserve this moment, even though I've got bigger plans for tonight.

Once we've had seconds and thirds and Melinda has passed around a container of whole wheat pecan carob cookies, the grown-ups settle into pleasantly dull conversation, and Billy and I are left to ourselves. The sunset's colors are gone, and stars slowly fill the sky.

"Violet told me that Lenora swam away," I say. "I wonder if it was down in that cave behind their house. Maybe Lenora drowned somewhere underground like Roland?"

"It's possible," says Billy. "Nobody except Roland has even been through most of those caves, but he didn't mention finding any bodies."

"Why do you think Violet's stuck here but Lenora isn't?" I say, spinning my medallion. "Why didn't she move on to the afterlife or wherever it is that dead people go?"

"You mean the one we didn't go to?" Billy's mouth quirks up.

"But we didn't come back as ghosts either," I say. "Why did that only happen to Violet?"

This feels like an important piece of the big picture I can't see. Did Violet fall into the same nothingness I did, but then wake as a ghost? Did she make a choice somewhere in the process? Or did a completely different series of events happen to her?

Something else is bumping around in the dark recesses of my memory too. A hand in my hair. A long-haired girl sitting on my bed in the dark. A girl who I may have also dreamed about in a rowboat.

"Violet's never seen her sister since she died, right?" I say. "She told me she's been all alone since Lenora swam away."

"I think so?" Billy shrugs. "Good luck getting her to tell you anything even close to understandable. I've been trying since we moved here."

"I want to figure this out," I say. "She's just a kid. If that was my four-year-old cousin and we were all dead, I'd want somebody to help her too."

Maybe there's a way to help her move on, free her from being trapped on this island all alone. But if the alternative is just nothingness, like what happened to me, is that necessarily better? Even if Violet did move on to some kind of afterlife, we'd never know. But this can't be right for her, this endless, lonely wandering.

"Okay." Billy yawns. "No pressure, but you've only got eleven days."

I laugh. "Not that you're counting."

He hitches in his breath, and I'm grateful for the darkness because I don't think I want to see the expression on his face right now.

"So do you want to help me?" I say, quickly changing the subject before this gets any worse.

He pauses. "Sure, but how?"

"I'm not exactly sure yet." I twist the bracelet on my wrist. "Let's find Violet tomorrow, play hide-and-seek again, and ask her some more questions."

"Sounds like a plan."

"All right, Bill-ster," calls Ken. "Time to start packing up."

"God forbid we stay out past eight o'clock," mutters Billy as he folds up his camping chair. Now that everyone's stopped talking, the nighttime sounds of the forest are surprisingly loud. Buzzes and hums, chirps and croaks, all blending together in a droning chorus that vibrates way down inside my ears.

"You're not exactly bothering the guests if we're out here with you," I say.

"Tell that to my dad," says Billy. "God, I can't wait to go away to college like Sean. No wonder he never wants to come back."

"You've only got a few more years," I say, but I know that's no consolation. I can't even stand the prospect of not diving for a few months. We stuff the chairs into their carrier bags and gather up all the trash, and Melinda hands us flashlights for the walk back. Deep in the trees, I think I spot a blue flash, but then it's gone. I wish I could slip away to the cenote right now and float in that pulsing glow.

"See you tomorrow," Billy says, and the eagerness in his voice gives me a twinge of guilt.

When I get back to the house, I plug my dead phone into

the charger and set an alarm for midnight. I tell myself I don't care if Sean shows up at the cenote tonight, since he didn't care about seeing me earlier. I'm only going there so I can swim again, and maybe take a few short dives.

I mostly believe that.

Chapter
14

I DREAM THAT I'm at the bottom of a hundred-meter dive, about to grab the tag from the plate at the end of the guideline, the one that proves to the judges that I've made it all the way down. As my fingers close around the plastic rectangle, a hand reaches out through the shadowy water and closes around my wrist. It's pale as bones, and the fingernails are long and gnarled. A face looms up in the cloudy darkness, and if I weren't focusing so hard on not breathing, I'd gasp.

It's my own face. But it's my face from the video of the accident, gray with dead-fish eyes and blood trailing out of my slack mouth.

I scream, and as all the air comes bubbling out of me, I realize I'll never make it back to the surface now. Water floods into my mouth, my throat, my sinuses. I pull and yank and twist and squirm and kick, but my dead self won't let go. We're sinking deeper, deeper into dark nothingness, and I need to breathe, I just need to breathe, even though it will kill me.

I suck in a massive breath of water that becomes air as I wake.

Someone's still tugging on my wrist.

A black-haired girl is in my bed, and she's trying to rip Violet's bracelet off.

"Stop it," I gasp, but she doesn't respond. One of her bony hands grips my elbow and the other is latched around my wrist, and I realize this is the person I mistook for my mother sitting on my bed the other night. She's the girl I dreamed about in the rowboat. And it's sickeningly clear that she hasn't been a living person for quite some time, just like Violet.

This has to be Lenora.

Violet may be a creepy little dead girl, but her older sister is terrifying. Her face is little more than a skull with thin, nearly transparent skin stretched over it. Her broken-glass teeth flash as she tries to bite the bracelet loose, and I shriek and roll away. Briefly, she lets go, but then she's on top of me again, reeking of rotting seaweed and brine. If this were a month ago, I'd have kicked her off easily—I'd have kicked her halfway across the room—but now I'm weak and slow and my lungs are sticky.

Before I can scream again, her thumb finds a hollow at the base of my throat, and everything dims. She bends until her forehead is almost touching mine. Her eyes are like marbles, too small for their sockets.

"Where did you find that bracelet?" she whispers in a voice that sounds like dead leaves.

I jerk my head sideways and sink my teeth into her hand, but it's dusty, rancid bone, and I gag. She doesn't even flinch.

"Or did it find you? Did it slither like a snake onto your wrist?" As she tilts her head, her long curls fall around both of our faces, and I'm not sure they're actual hair. They might be seaweed.

"Violet gave it to me," I say, cringing back into my pillow.

"You're lying," she hisses. "Violet would never give that to anyone."

"We were playing a game," I say. "Why don't you ask her?"

Lenora laughs, a broken croak that makes her bones clack. In a flash, her hands are on my shoulders, pinning me to the mattress. "Where is she?" Her putrid breath makes me cough, flecking her cheek with red.

"I don't know," I choke out. "If you'd just listen to me—"

She shakes her head, and a clump of seaweed hair lands on my pillow. She stares it for a moment, and then her bones clack again as she shudders.

"I haven't got time for listening," she whispers. "If you like games so much, let's play."

There's a snap at the back of my neck, and then she darts away through the french doors, the tattered shreds of her once-white dress whirling. As the doors swing wide and she disappears into the dark, my hand goes to my throat. My medallion is gone.

"Get back here!" I yell, even though the last thing I want is for that horrible creature to come back into my room. Not bothering to find my sandals, I leap out of bed and tear after her. A flash of white disappears around the corner of my bungalow, and I follow it into the woods, charging through branches and brambles.

"Give it back!" I call.

The moon casts everything in eerie black and white, and somehow it isn't as hard to shove through the bushes as I expected—they're practically parting in front of me as I run. Ahead, there's a flash of weedy, long hair and a rasping laugh. I skid around a massive tree trunk, and I swear the bark groans when I touch it, but it's hard to hear anything but the pulse thundering in my head. I have to stop running before I cough up a lung, but I *need* that medallion.

"Stop!"

Lenora stands on a boulder in a small clearing, her tattered dress billowing. Beetles crawl up her torso and neck, casting their blue glow on her sunken skull face.

"Don't come any closer," she hisses.

"Please." My voice shakes, and my breath comes in wheezing gasps. "Just give it back."

The forest floor is strangely spongey. Not wet, but soft like moss. Lenora holds the medallion up by its chain, swinging it back and forth, and I freeze. Then, without warning, she hurls it over my head and into the woods behind me.

"No!" As I whirl around, the ground falls away in the spot where I was just standing. A hole opens up, black and yawning and just wide enough for a person to fit inside. The stench of ammonia and sulfur pours out, and I back away, coughing.

Lenora is gone.

Still hacking and gasping, I skirt wide around the hole to the boulder where she stood, but there's not a single branch or leaf out of place. The surrounding bushes are still, but the chorus of nighttime insects is earsplitting.

Something crunches under my heel, and I stoop to pick it up. It's a filthy, rolled-up scrap of paper. Inside is a bone that looks like it came from someone's finger. With a yelp, I drop the gruesome little package, but as it lands on the ground, I notice there's a message scrawled on the paper. Shuddering, I find a stick to nudge the bone away and unfurl the paper.

Stay away from Jonah.

"Jonah?" I mutter.

Something brushes my shoulder, and I scream and lurch sideways.

"It's okay—it's just me." Sean eases closer, palms up. He's wearing a dark T-shirt with his shorts tonight, a towel slung over one shoulder. "Sorry to scare you, but I was on my way to the pool and I heard yelling. What are you doing?"

My hand goes to my neck, where the medallion is supposed to be hanging, and I'm not sure how much to tell him. Billy said nobody else could see Violet, which means they've probably never seen Lenora either. I don't know how Sean would react to a story about seeing ghosts, considering he never believed Billy. I shouldn't care what he thinks about me, but I do.

"I . . . uh . . . almost fell into this hole," I say. "I must have gotten lost on the way to the cenote."

Sean peers over the edge. "I'd scream too."

"What do you think is down there?" I say.

He glances at the paper on the ground and rubs his jaw. "Maybe the elusive Jonah?"

"Do you think he's another ghost?" As soon as the words are out, I regret them.

"*Another* ghost?" His eyebrow quirks up, and I can't tell if he's intrigued or making fun of me. "Has Billy been telling you stories?"

Tomorrow I'm the one who's going to tell Billy some stories. But right now, I need to change the subject before his brother decides he doesn't want to hang out with me anymore. And ghosts or no ghosts, there's no way I'm giving up on diving in that cenote tonight.

"Do you still want to swim?" I say.

Sean's smile sends a charge through my body. "Why do you think I came looking for you?"

Chapter
15

THE MOONLIT PATH takes shape on the other side of the bushes, and as we head deeper into the forest, I peer into the shadows, wondering if Lenora is out there, watching us. I'm still not sure if she tried to kill or save me, but it did seem like she threw the medallion to keep me from stepping into that sinkhole.

"Why didn't you come to the barbecue?" I say, trying to keep my mind off gruesome dead girls. "Are you afraid to go out in daylight? Or just completely antisocial?"

Sean laughs, and something darts through the trees overhead, sending down a shower of chilly droplets. I try not to visibly cringe.

"I'm not antisocial," he says. "I just hate Ken."

"Why?"

"Because he's Billy's dad, not mine." Sean pulls me off the path just as the moon slips behind a cloud. In the sudden darkness, I stumble, and when he turns to catch me, our feet tangle and his free hand brushes my side. His body is so close I can feel its warmth, and I think, *This is it*. We both draw in our breath.

Then, with a quiet laugh, Sean turns away, and the space around me feels briefly empty, though the earthy, mineral smell of him lingers. He holds open the curtain of Spanish moss, and there is the cenote, mirror-flat and ringed with glowing blue. It's straight out of my dreams—if all of my dreams weren't nightmares.

I walk straight into the water, my chest aching like I've just come home after a long journey, even though it's been less than a day since I last came here. My nerves are still on edge after the encounter with Lenora, but the water's lulling pulse is slowly easing the tension, draining it away. I can't explain why, but here I feel safe.

Still at the cenote's edge, Sean removes a few things from his pockets, then pulls off his dark T-shirt. His skin looks like marble in the moonlight, his chest and stomach smooth and flat as a statue's.

"I didn't know about Ken," I say, kicking backward toward the center of the pool. "Billy never mentioned it."

Sean lets out a dark laugh. "Why am I not surprised?"

"Stepdads are the worst," I say. "David wants me to stop freediving, like he somehow gets to decide that because he and my mom signed a piece of paper. *I* didn't sign any paper."

"I completely understand." Sean opens his hand, and a beetle lands in the center of his palm, flickering in a steady rhythm.

"Those bugs are beautiful, but I can't stand the feeling of them on my skin," I say.

He nudges the insect, making its wings flutter. "They're not so creepy once you get to know them."

I laugh, but he doesn't, and then I don't know what to say.

Giving the beetle a gentle flick that sends it buzzing toward the stars, he wades into the water. "Is your real dad still around?" he asks.

"No, not really," I say, hating how my voice breaks.

"What happened?" He drifts closer.

"It's a long story," I say. "You don't want to hear all the sordid details."

"I've got time." He gives me that ruinous smile again, and even though I usually hate telling people about my dad, right now it doesn't hurt to think about him. Maybe this water makes everything better.

"My parents fought all the time," I say. "It's one of the reasons I started diving, just to get away from all the noise and chaos. We had a pool, but it just wasn't deep enough, so I started going to the ocean, if that makes any sense?"

"It does," says Sean.

"Out of the blue, my dad emptied the bank account he shared with my mom and left," I say. "He didn't care how we ate, paid our rent, nothing. Then like a year later, he decided he was sorry and wanted to talk to us again. Not move back. Just, like, chat on the phone and act like what was happening was normal."

Sean's eyes soften.

"My grandmother died not long after that," I say.

"Were you close?"

I nod, unable to say more about that. She's one of the many reasons I can't stop dwelling on my own death. I thought I might see her. "She was his mom, so he had to come back for the funeral. He asked if he could stay at our house for a couple of days, and my mom said yes. So he slept on the couch and my mom and I were walking on eggshells the whole time, and she was being so, so kind to him . . . because I guess we both thought maybe he'd stay."

I roll onto my back so Sean won't see the tears about to leak out of my eyes. A warm current drifts up from the depths, and the water's pulse is slowing, lulling.

"But he didn't stay," I continue. "He got on a plane and flew back to Seattle."

"I'm sorry," murmurs Sean.

I give up on holding the tears back and let them slide down the sides of my face. "He literally couldn't get farther away from Florida without leaving the continental US. He didn't even know anybody out there. He had no reason except to escape us."

"Look." Sean's mouth is inches from my ear, and I thrash upright, swiping at my cheeks and wanting to submerge my entire face. He points to the water, where tiny threads of silver swirl like smoke. "Those are your tears."

"I didn't—I mean, I'm not." I wipe my nose and blink hard.

"It's all right," he says, cupping his hand around the silvery swirl. "The island doesn't mind sadness."

I half laugh, half sob in response, but there's something about the water turning my tears to swirling silver that makes me feel secure and connected. Loved. My heart has slowed to the same rhythm as the pulsing beat.

I splash some water onto my stinging eyes. "So, do you

want to tell me something depressing about your dad?"

"No, thanks." Sean laughs. "How about we dive instead?"

I nod, grateful for a distraction, and start pulling air into my lungs. It still feels incredible to breathe like this. Ten minutes ago, it would have been agony, but now it's like I'm a new person. Or rather, the person I used to be before the accident. I miss that person so much. Sean draws in the same slow, gulping breaths, and soon we're both ready.

I hold three fingers up, and he nods. Two fingers. One.

Taking a last sip of night air, I flip upside down and dive.

Chapter

16

SEAN STAYS BESIDE me, not quite touching, as we descend into the blue. Out of habit, I equalize, but once again, there's no pain. The pressure is always present and deepening, but nothing hurts. As we hit negative buoyancy and begin to drop, Sean brushes my wrist, and I flash him the *okay* sign. I tuck my arms flat against my body, and we fall like stones. The rhythmic beat of the water reverberates through my bones, steady and mesmerizing, and I disappear into it, let my entire self drop away as my body falls. The water shimmers and wavers, and the hole at the bottom takes shape.

Nothing hurts. I don't need to go back up. We can keep diving for at least another minute. I point to the hole and Sean flashes an *okay* sign before kicking ahead and disappearing inside. My brain gives a tiny flicker of warning, but the droning beat of the water, its soft caress on my skin, cancels out the warning, and then I'm propelling myself through the opening too.

Instead of another wide column like the one we just passed through, I find myself in a horizontal corridor, just wide enough to stand in and shimmering with indigo light. The water's thrum is louder down here, vibrating through my every cell and urging me farther along. Sean points down the tunnel, and again I give him the okay, even though we should think about turning around soon. I just want to see what he's pointing at first.

Three slow kicks, alternating strokes with my arms, and the beating rhythm is so deep inside me, it makes me want to sob. Ahead, Sean stops, plants his feet, and springs upward. Then he's gone. I swim to where he was and discover a hole at the top of the tunnel, with beams of violet shining down. Kicking upward, I shoot through the hole, and the surface wavers overhead. Once my head breaks through, I suck in a deep, clean breath—and then another.

"What do you think?" Sean flashes a radiant smile, and it's the first time I've seen him so elated, so unguarded.

"I have no words." I gaze up at the cave's ceiling, a black dome shot through with streaks of lime green and turquoise and electric pink. It's like looking at the northern lights in a midnight sky.

"Are you sure this is safe?" I ask. "The air could have dangerous gases in it, and nobody would be able to find us if something happened."

Sean wades over to a tiny beach made of smooth stones. "I've been coming here for ages, and Roland tested the air when he came down here too. It's totally safe."

It's not *totally* safe, but my curiosity is stronger than my fear. The stones slide under my feet as I follow him onto the beach. "Are all of the caves like this?" I stretch up to touch the ceiling, and there's a slight beating pulse in the stone.

"They're all different," he says. "They all feel different too."

"This one is so calm," I say.

Sean nods. "I've been coming here a lot lately. When every-thing feels like too much, I can breathe down here."

Even though I'm fully out of the water now, there's still no pain in my lungs. I trail my hand along the wall of the cave, letting the soothing energy flood down my arm and into my torso. It reminds me of the meds they gave me when I couldn't stop having middle-of-the-night panic attacks after my acci-dent. When I kept waking up thinking I was still dead.

"Can I ask you a personal question?" Sean sits in the center of the small beach, letting the stones run through his fingers.

"Maybe?" I lean my cheek against the wall and shut my eyes as all the tension and worry leaches away.

"It's about your accident," he says.

"I'm listening."

A pause.

"What did it feel like?" he asks. "When you died? If that's something you're okay with talking about, I mean."

"It felt like nothing," I say. "One minute I was there, under-water, and then the next minute, I just . . . wasn't."

The silence stretches out as I try to frame what I mean to say.

"It wasn't like falling asleep, where you can feel your-self slowly dozing off. It was just like a switch." I snap my fingers. "Dead. Everything didn't go black; I didn't feel a sudden nothingness. Because I wasn't there anymore to feel anything."

When I look up, he's staring at me with such raw longing, it's a little unsettling.

"I don't know if there was supposed to be more to it," I say. "You read all these stories about people who have died and come back, and a lot of them talk about similar things they experienced. Maybe I wasn't dead long enough for any of that stuff to happen."

"Do you ever think maybe that those things just weren't going to happen to you?" he asks.

I let my breath out. "All the time."

"Sometimes I think it would be nice to let it all go," he says. "To never have to be myself again."

"I like myself." As soon as the words are out, though, I wonder if they're true. I've spent a lot of time hating myself lately. It's entirely possible that I only like myself when I'm succeeding at something.

A shadow crosses Sean's face. "Lucky you."

I don't know how to answer that. *Don't hate yourself* is an incredibly trite thing to say, and much easier said than done. Maybe he has reasons for not liking himself. Clearly there's another side to him, one Billy knows but I'm not seeing. Not yet, anyway.

Stones clatter as Sean gets to his feet. "There's another cave close by. Do you want to see it? We don't have to dive to get there."

"What time it is?" I ask.

He checks the chunky black watch on his wrist. "One thirty-eight."

"You and Billy have the same watch," I say.

"Ken gets us the same exact present every Christmas." Sean rolls his eyes. "At least it's waterproof."

"I should go back before it gets too late," I say. "I didn't even wake up until eleven thirty today."

His eyebrows lift. "I sleep later than that all the time."

"Well, I never do. Billy says you're like a mole person, and I don't want to be a mole person."

I worry that I've just insulted what might be a symptom of his depression, but Sean's laugh rings through the cavern.

"Come on, just one more cave," he says. "Then I promise we'll go back." He takes my hand and clutches it to his chest, his gorgeous eyes dancing, and I'm clearly the biggest push-over of all time because as my fingertips brush his wet skin and find the pulse of his thrumming heart, I find myself nodding.

"Just for a few minutes."

"I'll set an alarm for half an hour," he says, poking at the buttons on his watch. "I think you're going to like this one. I call it the cathedral."

"Twenty minutes," I say, but he just pulls me over to a low opening in the wall.

"It's narrow and hard to see at first," he says, dropping to a crouch and pointing inside. "You're not scared of the dark, are you?"

"No," I say. "My mom says I'm missing all the usual human fear instincts, but it's not technically true. I have them; I've just gotten really good at doing stuff in spite of them."

He flashes a grin. "I like that about you."

I want to tell him I like a few things about him too, but I keep my mouth shut and crawl inside the tunnel. The floor is slick, covered in about an inch of water, and the passageway curves, growing wider and brighter with a greenish-silver light.

"Do these tunnels ever flood?" I ask.

"Sometimes if there's a lot of rain," he says. "But don't worry, I haven't seen this one flood in years."

"Hasn't your family only been on the island for two years?" I ask.

He laughs. "It feels like at least two hundred."

"At least you get to go away to coll—" My train of thought disappears as I duck under an overhanging boulder at the end of the tunnel and emerge in a cavern. Sean wasn't wrong to call this place the cathedral. It's easily the length of a football field, and at least twice as high, with a stone path cutting across its center and twin pools of shallow, silver water on either side. Looming stalactites connect with stalagmites to create enormous pillars throughout the space, and green light filters in from somewhere overhead.

"How is this real?" Even though I'm speaking quietly, the cave takes my words and whispers them back in a looping echo.

"It's hard to believe, isn't it?" Sean's voice answers from a hundred directions as he gestures for me to go first. I step onto the path and start toward a raised area at the opposite end that looks like a stage. Or an altar, if this is a cathedral.

As we continue down the path, I feel my mood shifting, sobering. It's not a sadness, exactly, that fills me as I walk. It's more like I'm missing something. Or remembering something lovely and beautiful.

"Nostalgia." I peer over my shoulder, and Sean nods, his eyes a little glassy.

"It's intense, but I thought you'd like it."

"I love it," I say. "Thanks for convincing me to come."

Something like embarrassment flickers across his face. "It's nothing."

"It's the farthest thing from—" I freeze.

There's a girl standing in an alcove at the back of the altar.

Chapter
17

"THERE'S SOMEONE there," I say, putting my arm out to stop Sean.

He laughs. "Who, the statue?"

"The . . . what?" I squint at the alcove, where the girl remains motionless.

"Look closer," he says.

My legs tremble as I climb onto the altar. He's right. It's a statue of a girl with white hair that cascades in waves to her knees. She wears a garment that's somewhere between a dress and a long shirt, made entirely of leaves and white flowers. Her bare limbs are long and lean. Her eyes are so blue, they're nearly purple, and there's a small nick in her nose. One of her hands is slightly outstretched, and the other holds a heart. Not a pretty Valentine heart—an anatomical one that looks human. Her fingers are red with blood.

"Eulalie," I whisper.

"How do you know it's her?" asks Sean.

"There's a portrait of her in your mom's book about the island," I say. "One of the crew members of the *Fortuna* drew it."

He tips his head. "Really?"

"Yeah. Have you not seen the book?"

"I never bothered reading it." He reaches out like he's about to touch Eulalie's outstretched fingertips, then changes his mind.

"I'll give you the book when I'm done reading," I say. "Who do you think made this?"

"Maybe an artist came here and never told anybody?"

"They must have come recently or they wouldn't have read that book and seen the illustration," I say. "But this statue looks old."

Sean shrugs. "The drawing must be from the seventeen hundreds. Maybe it was published in other places too. Or maybe it was passed down through a family or a secret society."

The idea of a secret society devoted purely to Eulalie gives me a delicious, shivery feeling. "What's in the water over there?" I ask, pointing to the shallows near the other end of the altar, where a large object lies.

"It's . . . another statue." The hesitance in Sean's voice is strange. I cross the altar and peer into the silver water, which just barely covers the statue's body. It's another girl, the same size as Eulalie, but with its decapitated head lying beside the body. I recognize that face, those black curls, even though the face looks like a skull now.

"Lenora," I whisper.

She is heartbreakingly beautiful, with sweeping brows and hazel eyes and a full, curving mouth. Lenora wears a simple white dress that reaches the tops of her bare feet, and like Eulalie, one of her hands is slightly outstretched. The other holds a knife with a thin, curving blade.

"I heard she killed her sister," says Sean.

"How does anybody know that if they never found the bodies?" I ask. "Where did you hear that?"

"I can't remember. But look at her. There's something sinister in those eyes."

Not nearly as sinister as they are now.

"I guess the mysterious artist must have had some strange fascination with the girls of this island," I say. "Do you think there's a statue of Violet somewhere?"

Lost in thought, Sean doesn't answer. I lean in and bump his shoulder with mine. "Penny for your thoughts?"

He drags his gaze from the statue. "Does anyone actually say that anymore?"

"I'm pretty sure nobody under eighty does," I say. "And, well, me."

"Are you secretly an old lady in disguise?" He eyes me with pretend suspicion, and I grin.

"I'll never tell."

"Somehow I doubt you are." Sean's gaze drifts down to my legs, and my cheeks go hot. He catches himself and flushes too. "Anyway, what would I do with a penny?"

"I don't know," I say. "Throw it into the water and make a wish?"

He ducks his head. "There's a lot of things I'd wish for."

"Like what?" I bump him again with my shoulder, and this time he stumbles sideways, catching my waist and taking me with him. Then there's no space between us, his arms are around me, and I can't tell if it's my heartbeat or his that's thudding against my ribs. It might be both. His breath is warm in my hair, just above my ear.

Something starts to beep. It's Sean's big, clunky, moment-ruining watch. With a ragged laugh, he pulls away and presses several buttons before it finally stops. I want to smash that thing against the wall.

"I guess we should get you home," he says.

"Yeah, I guess so," I say reluctantly. "Can we come back tomorrow night and explore more caves?"

His dark eyes gleam. "Absolutely."

We're just about to start down the stone path when a sudden impulse makes me double back and wade through the shallow water, pulling Violet's bracelet from my wrist. Bending low over Lenora's ruined statue, I slide the bracelet over the fingers of her outstretched hand.

"Here, you can have it," I whisper.

The hazel eyes of her decapitated head stare blankly up.

Chapter
18

THE REVERSE DIVE to the surface of the cenote is beautiful and pain-free, and when we emerge in the cricket-filled night, Sean and I tread water for a few moments, gasping and smiling like fools. It might not have been safe to dive in those caves, but it's been so long since I've felt that thrill of danger, that burst of adrenaline singing through my veins. I missed it so much.

"I don't want to go home yet," he says.

"Me neither." I'm tempted to ask him to meet me later this afternoon, but Billy will be around and it would be awkward. And we wouldn't be able to dive.

Aa-dee-dee-dee, calls a bird as we swim to the shore, and Sean repeats the call in a gently mocking tone.

"Do you think it's doing that on purpose?" As soon as I step out of the water, the sticky ache in my lungs returns. Still, the dive doesn't seem to have made it any worse.

Sean hands me his towel. "I told you the island likes you."

I don't know how to respond. Part of me wants to laugh, and part of me is starting to think maybe this island does feel certain ways, as absurd as that seems. The Spanish moss that leads back to the path ripples, and the prospect of walking back through the woods alone, with Lenora lurking out there somewhere, sets my teeth on edge.

"Want me to walk you home?" asks Sean.

"Sure, if you want to." I mostly succeed at sounding nonchalant.

Sean dries himself with his T-shirt, gesturing for me to keep the towel. As we walk through the woods, glowing beetles line the path. On impulse, I hold out my hand, and one lands on my open palm. The flashing pulse of its blue light reminds me of the water's heartbeat, and the same serene calm washes over me.

"I guess you were right about getting used to these things," I say.

There's a slither and a crack in the woods, and my hand snaps shut. The beetle makes a papery crunch.

"Shit," I whisper, unfolding my fingers. "I'm so sorry."

Gently, Sean takes the crumpled insect. He cups it between his hands and blows inside. Faint blue glows in the gaps between his fingers, growing brighter. When he opens his hands, the beetle zips out and zooms away.

"How did you do that?" I'm not sure I believe what just happened.

"It wasn't dead." He shrugs. "Why are you so jumpy? You said you weren't afraid of the dark."

"You'll laugh at me if I tell you," I say.

Sean holds a branch up so we can both duck underneath. "Is that the worst thing you could imagine happening? Me laughing at you?"

"Okay, fine," I say. "So you really don't believe in ghosts, right?"

He groans. "Like Billy's stories about Violet running around the island?"

"Something like that."

"No."

Now it's me who's laughing. "You live on an island with glowing zombie beetles and magical water that makes pain go away and . . . and cathedral caves with inexplicable statues of dead girls, but ghosts are just one bridge too far?"

Sean shrugs. "What can I say? I'm an enigma."

"What if I could prove it to you?" I stop to peer into the dark trees. Even if he can't see Lenora, he'd have to see the movement of the things around her.

"Hey, isn't this yours?" He stoops and picks something up off the path. A medallion.

"Yes!" I practically snatch the necklace, feeling a twinge of guilt that I left Violet's bracelet down in the cave. Now I'll definitely have to go back and get it. As if I weren't already counting the minutes until I can dive again.

"How did it get out here?" asks Sean.

"It's a long story."

"Does it have to do with ghosts?"

I want to wipe the smirk off his face. "Actually, it does. How did you even see it?"

"I have good night vision."

I bet Lenora has good night vision too. I wonder if she's been watching us this whole time, if she's lurking somewhere right beside the path. My fingers shake as I try to open the necklace's clasp, but it's broken. The urge to cough claws up through my chest.

"Need help?" Sean edges closer, and as much as I want to let him touch me again, I'm about to lose the battle against my lungs, so I shove the necklace in my wet pocket, wave him away, and cover my mouth with both hands. I cough and cough until the black woods spin and I couldn't care less what ghosts are out there, because I feel like I'm about to join them in death.

Sean's hand rests lightly on my back, and he murmurs quiet nothings until I'm spent and slowly coming back together.

"Sorry," I say, turning away to spit into the bushes.

A snakelike vine slithers out beside my foot, then tips upward, offering a single white orchid that's shaped like a skull. We both stand there, staring at it.

"I, uh, don't know how that happens," I say. "It's kind of freaking me out."

Sean bends and plucks the flower off the vine. "You're fascinating, Addie Spencer."

He holds the blossom out, and I don't want to touch that ghostly thing, but as soon as my fingers close around the stem, the petals darken and unfurl, changing the flower's shape from a skull to something halfway between a lily and a rose. I can't tell what color it actually is, but under the moonlight it looks black.

Aa-dee-dee-dee, calls the bird.

The flower's blood-warm sap drips onto my fingers as Sean and I continue down the path. The forest is as still as a black-

and-silver tapestry, and if Lenora is out there, she's leaving us alone. Hopefully her game is over for now.

We reach the bottom of the stone steps and stop.

"I can meet you here at midnight if you want to walk together again?" he offers.

"Sure," I say, trying and failing to keep the ridiculous grin off my face. "I'll see you then."

"Try not to fall in any sinkholes while I'm gone." Sean sweeps a strand of hair from my cheek and leans in to brush his lips across the spot. He smells like the caves, like stone and fresh water. The buzzing of insects around us becomes a roar, then subsides as he pulls away.

"Good night," he says.

"'Night." I manage to make it sound casual, but a million neurons are setting off fireworks inside my head as I climb the stairs.

Chapter
19

I WAKE JUST after noon to the sound of birds calling my name. It's stiflingly hot, and my sheets are damp. On the bedside table, beside my medallion with its broken chain, is the flower Sean gave me. It's the same deep purple as a ripe eggplant, and its petals haven't even withered. The phantom sensation of his lips still lingers on my cheek.

I roll out of bed but stop as soon as my feet hit the ground. There's a trail of ants crawling from the french doors to the center of my floor. They're all carrying flower petals. The petal closest to me is a nearly white shade of lavender, and the purple hues deepen as the line goes back, darkening to an almost black.

I told you the island likes you. Sean's words echo in my memory. It feels almost like the ants are bringing me a gift. One I didn't ask for.

The line inches forward, and on the floor on the other side of it, half-hidden under the dresser, something glints. A silver safety pin. The perfect thing to fix my broken necklace with. Carefully stepping over the ants, I pick up the pin, poke it into the broken clasp of my chain, and hook it together at the back of my neck. When I glance at the floor again, the ants have dropped their petals in a ruler-straight line of ombré colors and are slowly making their way back out through the crack under the french doors.

"Thank you," I whisper, feeling more than a little bit unhinged.

Aa-dee-dee-dee, call the birds outside. *Dee-dee.*

After showering and dressing, I slip out the back door in search of food. In the time I was sleeping, the island has exploded in a riot of purple. Mauve and plum and violet and magenta, the flowers cover the trees, spilling down over the roots and twining through the dirt. Vines climb the outside walls of the house, sprouting buds in the palest shade of lilac, and once again, I can't stop thinking that this is all for me, somehow. I'm almost . . . flattered.

My mother and David sit at the poolside table, eating spinach salad dotted with walnuts, goat cheese, and apples. She's wearing her hat again, and I hope it's clean.

"There's my little sleepyhead!" She grabs an empty plate and starts doling out more salad from the bowl on the table. "This is two days in a row, hon. Are you all right? Do you think we should call the doctor?"

"No, I actually feel great." Technically, my lungs still hurt, but I'm humming with a jittery energy. Taking the chair across from them, I pour myself a glass of water from the pitcher and down it in seconds.

"Sleeping until noon and feeling great, eh?" says David with a knowing grin. "You sure you aren't coming down with a case of puppy love?"

I resist the urge to tip my chair backward into the pool. "I already told you there's nothing between me and Billy."

His brother, on the other hand, I can't stop thinking about.

My thumb slides over the back face of my medallion.

"Can you believe the flowers today?" My mother gestures at a flotilla of purple water lilies that have appeared in the pool overnight. "I've never seen anything like it."

"The island has a lot of secrets," I say with a small smile.

"I suppose so." She chews for a while, staring thoughtfully at the flowers. "I wonder if I'm allergic to all of them or just that one I picked the other day."

"Better not to find out," says David. "I'll buy you all the flowers you want when we get home."

"Oh, don't worry about it." She waves her arm dismissively, and I notice a light pink rash trailing down her forearm.

"You know, Addie," says David. "I've been thinking about your injury, and I have the perfect solution."

Great. I stuff a wad of salad into my mouth.

"Why don't you join a swim team?" he says. "You're obviously a strong enough swimmer to kick some serious butt."

I swallow, then refill my water glass. "Because I'm a free-diver, not a swimmer. It's an endurance sport, not a race."

"Sure, sure, I get it." David absolutely does not get it. "But it wouldn't hurt to give it the old college try, would it? Let me see if I can pull some strings and get you into a good training program. Pools are a lot safer than the open ocean."

Not some of the pools I've been in recently.

"I appreciate the offer," I say. "But you can't just pull

strings or pay a bunch of money to make me good at a totally different sport."

David jabs his fork in the direction of the stone stairs. "Look, there's Prince Charming now!"

Billy's blond head bobs into view. "Sorry to bother you while you're eating," he says, pulling out his inhaler. "I can come back."

"No, no, come on over. Please, have a seat." David smiles indulgently and gestures at the chair beside me. As if it weren't bad enough that he's trying to destroy my life, now he's playing matchmaker. I stuff half the salad into my mouth so I won't say anything horrible. A fuzzy black caterpillar the length of my finger is inching up the leg of the table, heading toward his knee. It would be polite to warn him, but I don't.

Billy stays where he is. "My dad wanted to know if you still want to go snorkeling at the reef this afternoon?"

"That'd be lovely." My mother pats David's knee, inches from the caterpillar. *Not her*, I think as hard as I can, and the caterpillar pauses, swiveling its head around, and I swear it looks at me through the glass tabletop.

"What do you think, Addie?" says my mom.

I force the pulpy lump of salad down my throat. "No hard feelings, but I'd rather not float around on the surface of water I can't dive in."

Her smile crumbles as she lets go of David's leg. The caterpillar's fuzzy back humps up as it resumes its journey. "Oh, hon, I didn't even think of that."

"You could practice your crawl stroke," offers David, and I bite down on my tongue.

"No, it's really fine," I say. "My back is a little sore, and I want to do some yoga this afternoon."

And my mind is whirling with all the things that have happened to me recently, the beautiful and the terrifying. I need to calm down, center myself, do some breathing exercises before I go looking for Violet.

The caterpillar is millimeters away from David now. It could nibble his leg hair if it wanted.

"You can't hide from us forever, Addie," says my mom. "I know this isn't how you hoped to be spending your summer, but maybe if you just got out a little, you might have fun."

"I *am* having fun." Despite all the weird and scary things on this island, that is absolutely true. I haven't felt this alive since before my accident.

Suddenly David yelps. He leaps up, knocking his chair backward, and slaps his leg. I hide my mouth in my napkin as the caterpillar hits the patio and curls up in a fuzzy ball.

"Are you okay, Mr. Donovan?" Billy rushes over to help David, along with my mom, and my shoulders shake with silent laughter.

"I'm fine, I'm fine." David waves everyone away. "A little spooked, that's all."

"Are those poisonous?" My mom points to the caterpillar, which has uncoiled from its ball and is inching toward David's foot again.

"I don't think so," says Billy.

"Do you want me to get your heart pills, hon?" says my mom.

"No, no, I'm fine. He just gave me a little tickle." Flashing everyone a broad, healthy smile, David kicks the caterpillar into the swimming pool.

Sorry, I think as it sinks like a stone.

"Okay, so I'll go tell my dad you still want to go." Billy edges backward awkwardly. "What time should I tell him?"

"As soon as he's ready." David starts collecting plates and utensils. "Maybe while we're out, I'll catch us another *Waa-hoo!*"

Billy ducks his head and presses his lips together. "Yeah, okay. Just come down to the dock whenever you're ready."

"Bye, Bill-ster!" I call, and he rolls his eyes before leaping down the stairs.

Chapter
20

AN HOUR LATER I stand on my yoga mat, facing the woods in case any ghosts are thinking of surprising me. Melinda's book about the island lies on a lounger by the pool. After David and my mom left, I skimmed through it, searching for some evidence of Sean's claim that Lenora killed her sister. But the author just repeated Ken's theory that they drowned and their bodies were swept out to sea.

I'm balancing in utthita parsvasahita, standing on one foot while holding the big toe of my other foot with my leg extended to the side, when Billy comes bobbing up the stairs.

"Mind if I join you?" He grabs a towel from a lounger, lays it out beside me, and grabs his own big toe. He tries to stick his leg out to match mine, but yelps in pain and lets go. With a tiny sniff of a laugh, I swivel my leg to the front, and when I let go, my foot hovers high in the air.

"Damn, I'm usually great at this pose," says Billy. "I just didn't, like, have time to warm up beforehand."

"Uh-huh." I set both hands on my hips and slowly float my leg down while Billy hops around holding his other foot. Coughing lightly, I wipe my forehead and sit with my legs outstretched, then reach forward to grab my feet. Billy sits cross-legged beside me.

"I saw Lenora last night," I say. "She came into my room."

"What?" yells Billy. "Did you seriously just make me do *yoga* before revealing this gigantic piece of news?"

"Sorry," I say. "I was going to feel lopsided if I didn't finish doing that pose on my left side."

"Did she have her harp?" he asks.

"No, she did not drag her harp all the way up to the house to play me a concert," I say, folding my right leg sideways and leaning forward again. "She was incredibly scary, in actual fact."

"I bet," says Billy. "Violet's already pretty scary, and she's only like three."

"Violet's nothing compared to her sister," I say with a shiver.

"So, what happened?" asks Billy. "What does Lenora look like?"

"She jumped on me in my bed while I was sleeping." Just thinking about it makes my skin prickle everywhere.

"She *what* on your *where*?" Billy's freckled face turns pale.

"It was terrifying." I glance into the woods and lower my voice. "She's practically a skeleton, and instead of hair she has seaweed, and I think her teeth are glass. It's like she put herself together with whatever pieces of things she could find."

"Guhh." Billy crosses himself, though he does it backward. "I'm so glad that was you and not me. I would have wet the bed."

I burst out laughing, and some of the nervous tension in my shoulders eases. Only Billy could make me laugh about one of the most horrifying things that's ever happened to me.

"What did she want?" he asks.

"Violet's bracelet. But I wouldn't give it to her, so she took my medallion and ran into the woods, and when I followed her, I almost fell into a sinkhole."

"You have to watch out for those," says Billy.

"Yeah, I get that now," I say. "And then I . . . lost the bracelet, but"—I swallow Sean's name—"I found my medallion later on the path."

Billy holds up his bare wrist. "I lost my watch too. Do you think Lenora took it?"

"Why would she want your watch?" I say.

"Because it's awesome?"

I laugh. "If you say so. But I still don't understand why she'd want her sister's bracelet if she killed her."

"Wait, what?" Billy scrunches his face up. "Where did you hear that?"

"I, uh, read it in your mom's book," I say, taking a gamble that he hasn't read it.

Billy's face scrunches even tighter. "My dad never mentioned that."

"Probably because he doesn't want to scare the guests," I say. "Remember how mad he got when you talked about the harp music?"

Billy groans. "I hate how he's so obsessed with making everything perfect. I mean, I know it's a bunch of rich people paying a shit-ton of money to be here, but—" He stops, cheeks reddening. "Uh, sorry, was that rude?"

I shrug. "It's not my money." But now I'm wondering if Billy's dad knows more than he lets on, not allowing the family to leave the lighthouse at night.

"Lenora also left me a note," I say. "Well, I think it was her that left it. A rolled-up piece of paper with what looked like a finger bone inside."

Billy shakes his arms and legs like bugs are crawling on them. "I'm *so* glad this was you and not me."

"The note said to watch out for Jonah," I say.

Billy stops shaking off the imaginary bugs. "Who the heck is Jonah?"

"Maybe another ghost?" I say. "Maybe somebody who used to live on the island?"

"I don't like this at all," says Billy.

"Me neither," I say. "But I'm kind of invested now. And I'm pretty sure Lenora wasn't trying to murder me. Like eighty percent sure." I'm trying to keep my tone light, to keep hold of the humor. It makes it easier to talk about these terrifying things if I'm laughing.

"I shouldn't be surprised you're not scared, considering you do deadly sports for fun and profit," says Billy.

"There's not much profit," I say, but he waves his hand dismissively.

"Look, it's David's little buddy."

A fuzzy caterpillar head pokes over the edge of the swimming pool, turning one way and the other like it's looking for something. Or someone.

"How is that thing not dead?" As much as I appreciate the caterpillar scaring David, I don't want it near me either. I stand and roll up my yoga mat.

"Must be an amphibious caterpillar."

"That's not a thing," I say, and Billy shrugs. "Anyway, let's try to find Violet. I know it's hard to get a straight answer out of her, but maybe now that I've seen Lenora, it'll help us get some answers."

"Can't hurt." Billy pulls off his backpack and starts rummaging inside.

"Violet!" I step into my flip-flops and head for the woods. The caterpillar also starts scuttling in that direction, so I skirt wide around it. "Violet, do you want to play hide-and-seek again? Billy's here, and he can be the *it*!"

Aa-dee-dee-dee, calls a bird, but the bushes remain still.

"Violet?" I try again, but again there's no answer.

"Let me." Billy holds up an orange package and gives it a shake. "Violet, I have Cheezy Crunchies."

A twig snaps.

"Come on, Violet!" Billy stuffs a handful of Cheezy Crunchies in his mouth. "It's the spicy kind!" he yells, spraying orange powder into the flowered bushes.

"Can she actually eat them?" I whisper, but before Billy can answer, a little gray hand shoots out of the bush, and I jump. The hand opens and turns palm up, and Billy shakes several Cheezy Crunchies into it. Then the hand disappears, and the bush crunches and smacks and shakes. Billy points under the bush, where orange crumbs are falling like snow.

"Not technically," he whispers. "But she likes how they taste."

"Those are very spicy!" Violet's face pops out, cheese dust coating her gray cheeks and chin, and I can't decide if it's funny or disgusting. "Give me more!"

"Can we talk to you for a little while first?" I say.

"No! Talking is boring. Spicy, crunchy treats are better."

"How about we do both?" I say, pulling an orange snack from the bag and holding it just out of her reach. "Can you come out of the bush?"

"No!"

"Oh well, that's okay." I pop the Cheezy Crunchy in my mouth and make sure to crunch it extra loudly as I saunter toward the pool. "I'm pretty hungry, so I'll probably want to eat all of these anyway."

Violet is on me in a flash, clutching my arm with those bloated, cold hands. "Don't eat all of them! You have to share!"

"Come on, Addie, sharing is caring." Billy waves the bag, then sits on a lounger and pats the cushion beside him. Violet lunges for the spot like I was about to steal it, then snatches the bag and stuffs a fistful of orange snacks into her mouth.

"Addie-dee is greedy-dee," she says, giggling at her own rhyme and stuffing her mouth again. In seconds, the cushion is covered in orange crumbs. Something wispy and black is poking out of her ear, waggling back and forth, and I'm trying not to look too closely at it.

"Can you tell us something about your sister?" I say, perching on the lounger beside them.

"Nora is all gone." Violet sadly stuffs another Cheezy Crunchy in her mouth, and her jaw bones click as she chews. A second thin, waggling thing emerges from her ear, and then an entire spider crawls out. The food in my stomach threatens to make its way back up my throat.

"When's the last time you saw Nora?" asks Billy.

"Ooh, these are so, so spicy!" yelps Violet, waving a hand at her mouth. The spider scurries down her neck and inside the bodice of her dress. "May I please have some water?"

I hand her my water bottle, and as she gulps greedily, a puddle forms on the lounger and I make a mental note to wash the bottle before using it again myself. The rim is now coated in an orange-cheese paste.

"Do you remember the last time you saw Nora?" I try, once she's done gulping and leaking.

"She swam away." Violet's lower lip juts out just like Grace's does when someone has disappointed her.

"Where did she swim?" I ask. "The ocean? The cenote?"

Violet's gray eyebrows knit. "What's that?"

"That round, deep pool in the woods," I say, but Violet just shrugs like she's never seen it before, which seems unlikely. Another skinny appendage wiggles out the edge of her nostril, and I'm going to be sick.

"What if I told you she's still here?" I ask. "And she's looking for you."

Violet rolls her neck in a spineless, uncanny way that sets

my teeth on edge. "Why hasn't she found me? I've been here such a very long time. Nobody holds me when I'm scared or when I have bad dreams. Nobody ever gives me hugs or toys or even talks to me."

My heart sinks to somewhere down around my stomach.

"Hey, I'm here," says Billy.

"But you only just came here," sniffs Violet. "And you never give me hugs."

Billy stammers an excuse, and my eyes prickle with sympathy. It hurts to even look at poor Violet, as horrifying as she and her ear-spiders are. Although she's hundreds of years old, she still has the heart and mind of a little kid, and even if she didn't, no one deserves to be left alone for this long.

"I don't know why Lenora can't find you," I say. "It doesn't seem fair."

"Can't *you* help her?" Violet asks, grabbing my hand.

"I really, really wish I could." I force myself not to snatch my hand away, even though hers reminds me of a rotting fish. "And I promise I'm going to try."

"Nora should try harder too." Violet sighs out a puff of dusty air. "Sometimes I think she cares more about Jonah than me."

Billy gives me a sharp look, but before either of us can say anything, Violet yanks my hand upright.

"Addie-dee, where is my bracelet?"

I hiss in my breath. "Oh, it's . . . I . . . took it off."

She stands, and the empty Cheezy Crunchies package floats to the ground. Thunder rumbles in the distance. "Where did you put it?" Her voice has lost its singsong quality, gone low and flat.

I glance at Billy, who shrugs helplessly. I can't tell the truth because I don't want him to know where I was last night. Of course I should tell him, but he'll be upset, and that's the last thing I feel like dealing with right now. "I put it in a safe place so it wouldn't get lost," I say. "It's so important and special, I didn't want to take any chances."

Violet drifts backward, her ragged dress tangling around her legs as a gust of wind whips in from the forest. "I want it back now, please."

"You're taking back your present already?" I try, hoping to appeal to her sense of manners.

"I never said it was a present." Her little face darkens, and so does the sky. If this were Grace, there would be tears already. Violet's lack of tears is far more ominous.

"I can't get to the place where it is right now," I say. That, at least, is the truth. Billy narrows his eyes, and I pretend not to notice. "But I promise I'll get it for you later and I'll give it to you tomorrow, okay?"

Thunder reverberates, much louder now, and rain begins to fall.

"If you did lost it, I will never, ever forgive you." Violet's tiny hands clench into fists.

"No, I know exactly where it is," I say as her fists start to shake. "Don't worry, okay? Everything will be fine, and I really appreciate you lending me such a beautiful bracelet."

Thunder crackles and roars as she fixes her sunken, black

eyes on me, and in that moment, both of us standing in the pelting rain, Violet is no longer a child. She's ancient and weary and angry and inhuman.

Lightning flashes so bright it fills my vision, and then she's gone.

Chapter
21

"COME ON!" I yell to Billy, dashing for the main bungalow.

He hesitates, water dripping off the brim of his hat. "I'm not supposed to go inside."

"Oh, please." I hold the door open and beckon. "I'm not going to tell on you."

He hovers on the doormat, bare feet shuffling back and forth. Thunder roars again, rattling the dishes and setting my teeth on edge. It's almost as dark as night outside, so I flick on the lights over the kitchen island and then grab some dish towels from a drawer.

"Will the parents be okay out on the boat?" I say, tossing him a towel.

"Oh, sure," says Billy. "We get micro storms like this pretty much every day, and they can just go belowdeck until it's over."

Another shattering crack of thunder makes us both jump. The lights flicker but stay on.

"Want a snack?" I mop my shoulders and the back of my neck. "Since Violet ate all of yours?"

"No, that's okay." He bumps the screen door with his shoulder, then mutters an apology to it.

"Don't be silly." I pull a package of chocolate chip cookies from the cupboard. Normally when I'm training, I don't eat processed foods and sugar, but there's no point in following those rules now. After ripping open the package, I hold one out toward Billy and wave it coaxingly. "You know you want some."

It's borderline inappropriate, and I didn't mean for it to be, but Billy wipes his feet about eight times, leaps across the kitchen, and snatches the cookie. "Thanks," he says, stuffing the entire thing into his mouth. Outside the open window, rain streams in a curtain off the thatched roof.

"So it sounds like Violet knew Jonah," I say.

Billy nods, mouth full of cookie. "But there were only four people in the Wells family—the parents and two daughters—so who was this extra guy?"

"Someone else who ended up on the island?" I say. "Maybe he got shipwrecked or came here on his own?"

Billy gazes longingly at the package of cookies, and I slide it over. "Probably shipwrecked," he says. "You couldn't sail a big ship here all by yourself, and it's way too far to come in a rowboat or something."

Thunder rumbles again, but softer. The oppressive darkness outside is slowly lifting.

"I wish we had internet," I say. "We could look up shipwreck records from the eighteen hundreds."

"I can look it up at the lighthouse," says Billy. "But even if you find some guy named Jonah who got shipwrecked, what's that going to prove or explain? Do you think he's a ghost here that nobody's ever seen? Or is that an old note from when the girls were alive?"

"I don't know," I say. "But I feel like these are all pieces of the same puzzle. Do you think we'll see Violet again today?"

"Probably not." Billy wipes his chocolaty mouth with the back of his hand. "She's pretty mad."

"I didn't mean to upset her." I rub my thumb over the back of my medallion. It was careless to leave the bracelet on Lenora's sculpture like that, but for some reason, it felt right to give it to her. And I was so distracted by Sean that I wasn't really thinking straight. Even now, my thoughts keep drifting to him, to those wide, dark eyes, the way he looked at me after kissing my cheek. I'm counting the minutes until tonight.

Billy's loud chomping drags me back to the present. "Storm's over," he says.

Water is still dripping steadily off the roof, but the sky is blue again. The mossy smell of rain on hot stone floods in through the window.

"Can we go to Violet's house?" I say.

Billy grimaces. "Do we have to?"

"Even if we don't find her, maybe we'll find some clues." I turn on the tap to wash the cheesy orange paste off my water bottle, scrubbing it three times with soap before rinsing.

"Okay, but I'm not going inside the house," says Billy.

"Have you ever seen the flowers turn this color before?" I step around a bush that has collapsed under the weight of its dripping purple blossoms. The stems all bend in my direction like I'm the sun, which is unsettling.

"Nope." Billy leads the way down the path into the valley. "They've never changed color, but the island is always doing something weird, and I think we're sort of used to it at this point."

"What else has it done?" I ask.

Billy leaps over a rock and slips in the mud, almost wiping out. "There were centipedes everywhere when that guy Roland and his nephew were here. Some of them were longer than my hand."

Shuddering, I scan the bushes for any sign of centipedes and then bump into Billy, who has stopped in the middle of the path.

"Look," he whispers.

Crouched in the shade of a tree is an iguana chewing on a scrap of paper. Its squinty eyes swivel toward us, devoid of all emotion. Billy eases closer and I want to pull him back, but he knows the animals here better than I do. We have iguanas in Florida, but they're half the size of these. Unfazed, the iguana keeps chewing, and I wonder if it's eating another cryptic note about Jonah or just a piece of trash.

"Drop it," Billy says in a stern voice like he's talking to a dog. Not being a dog, the iguana doesn't obey. As Billy inches closer, it hisses and lashes its tail. The branches overhead sway and groan. I want to tell Billy to leave it alone, but there's a drawing on the paper and I'm seized by the need to see what it is.

"*Drop* it." Billy picks up a stick, his bare feet silent on the ground. The iguana rears onto its back legs. A gust of breeze flutters the paper, and I spot part of a face, a strand of long hair drawn in thick black.

"Drop it," I whisper, and the iguana lands on four legs again. It opens its mouth, and the paper falls.

Staring up from the ground is a rough but unmistakable drawing of my face. The top of my head has been chewed off. Still chomping, the iguana stares at me with its fathomless eyes.

"Did . . . did you draw that?" I ask Billy.

"No way," he says, picking the paper up. "I can't draw to save my life. This is really good. It looks just like you."

Aa-dee-dee-dee, calls a bird.

I crowd in next to him, desperately curious but not wanting to touch the paper. With just a few strokes of charcoal, the artist has perfectly captured the sweep of my eyebrows and nose, the line of my jaw. "Is anybody in your family this good at drawing?" I ask.

"No way. Sean failed art class twice," Billy scoffs. "Who the hell fails art class? Literally all you have to do is show up and make something."

I file this away as yet another thing about his brother that makes no sense. "My mom can't draw. I'm pretty sure David can't either—and I definitely don't think he'd be drawing me. That leaves Violet, who's way too young, and"—I gulp— "Lenora. It's got to be her."

Billy nods. It's the only feasible explanation, and the word *feasible* is a stretch. But why is she drawing me? This drawing feels intimate in a way I can't explain. It's got something to do

NICOLE LESPERANCE

with how close up it is, the unguarded expression on my face. I can't imagine Lenora caring enough about me to draw this. And yet, here it is.

"You look sad," says Billy.

"In the drawing or in real life?"

"Both." Billy looks from me to the drawing, then back to me. "Were you always like this? Or is it just because of the accident?"

I blow my breath out, triggering a cough. I was going to say it was only because of the accident, but that's not quite true. For years I've been pinning my happiness on numbers of meters. On how far I can push myself and succeed. Take all of that away, and there's just the sad girl in that drawing.

"I . . . don't really know," I say.

"That's okay," says Billy. "I won't put it in the written exam for our club."

"I appreciate that," I say. "Now let's hurry up before the parents get back."

"Want this?" He holds the drawing out, but I shake my head.

"You keep it."

Chapter
22

INDIGO BUTTERFLIES FLIT out of the Wellses' roofless house as we approach, bobbing and floating in the dappled sunshine. With its mossy walls, the house looks like something out of a dark fairy tale. The birdsong grows louder as I approach the opening that used to be a door. Each bird is screeching its own melody, like some chaotic orchestra, and I realize that I have no idea what any of them look like. Despite their constant racket, I'm not sure I've seen a single bird in three days.

"Billy, are the birds here normal?" I ask.

"What do you mean?" He peers at me curiously, then trips over a root.

"I don't know," I say. "What do they look like?"

"Like . . . regular birds?" He laughs. "Feathers, wings, beaks—they like to poop on stuff sometimes?"

"Huh." I rack my brain, thinking back to the beach, but there weren't any seagulls. No birds on our patio, not even when we left crumbs on the table. They all stay high in the trees, watching and calling my name. Another weird change since I got here, apparently.

Leaving Billy outside, I step into the ruins. The temperature drops, and the musty air makes me cough. As I wipe the bloody flecks onto the leg of my shorts, a vine slithers out from a crack in the foundation, and I stomp on it, crushing the leaves and stem before it can blossom. It's unbearable that those flowers are growing from my blood. The island is taking pieces of me and making them part of itself. As gorgeous as it is, I don't want to be part of this island.

"You okay in there?" asks Billy.

"Fine." I grind my heel into the vine and keep moving.

Lenora's harp lies in the same position, and I feel slightly guilty for having broken its last surviving string. There's nothing else in the room, but Lenora's presence lingers, just barely perceptible, like the traces of someone's perfume.

It's hard to get the half-rotten harp upright with a tree growing through its center, but I manage to get it diagonal, and then I sit on the ground and slide my shoulder underneath. Time and nature have taken their toll on the instrument, but it's somehow even more lovely with the real vines intertwined with the carved roses. I've got no idea how to actually play it, so I'll just pretend. As my fingers drag across the invisible strings, I feel a shuddery vibration go through the harp, through the ground, through the walls and the trees and even the humid air around me.

"Whoa," whispers Billy outside.

Aa-dee-dee-dee, call the birds, like they want me to play again, but something about it feels wrong. Like I'm summoning things I shouldn't be.

"What's that near the bottom of the harp?" Billy pokes his head through a former window. "It looks like writing."

Gently, I set the instrument down, then find a stick to clear away the leaves and dirt. Twining among the roses is a line of hand-carved text.

J, may this music bring me your love.

I read the words out loud.

"Nope, I don't like that," says Billy.

"J has to be Jonah, right?" I say.

"I hope you didn't just summon his ghost by pretend-playing the harp," says Billy.

It's obviously a joke, but I grit my teeth because I just had the same thought about summoning. "You don't think that could actually happen, do you?"

"Considering I've lived here for two years and I just heard of the guy today? Seems unlikely," says Billy.

"But you've never seen Lenora either."

"True."

My chest clenches up suddenly, and then I'm coughing so hard I have to hold on to the mossy black wall of Lenora's house to stay upright.

In seconds, vines sprout from the earth, spiraling in a semicircle around me, trapping me against the wall, and all I can manage is a half-hearted kick to get them away, but more take their place. Still I cough, my lungs on fire and my head spinning, as tendrils slither like snakes over my arms, my shoulders. Flowers bud and blossom, their petals turning from white to pink. They yawn open like they're breathing me in, like they want to eat me, and I'm coughing too hard to pull them off.

Billy rushes into the room and stomps a vine with his bare foot, then yelps in pain. He starts ripping away the plants, whose flowers are deepening to red, then purple as they spiral higher around me, crowding in closer, closer as I gasp for breath.

"Don't move," he says, as if I could do anything else. Finally, I manage to draw in a full breath of air, then another, and I yank the rest of the vines off my torso, my legs, my neck. My gaze snags on something sticking out of a crack in the mossy wall.

"Come on!" Billy pulls me through a path he's cleared, but I lunge back and shove my hand into the crack. A narrow object tumbles out, and I barely manage to catch it before it falls into the swarming vines. We race out of the house and up the dirt path, not slowing until we're far from the valley.

"Stop," I gasp, crouching and breathing as shallowly as possible. I will not cough again. I cannot.

"You're okay," says Billy, panting. "Everything's okay. Look, no more vines." He's wide-eyed, his face pale, and if he's anything like me, his heart is almost beating out of his chest.

"What . . . was that?" I gasp.

"I have no clue," says Billy. "Hold still." He pulls something from my hair. A tiny, perfect flower the color of blood. We both stare at it for a long moment, and then he throws it into the bushes.

Aa-dee-dee-dee, trill the birds.

I hold up the object I pulled from the crack in the wall.

It's a slim pocketknife about six inches long. The curved handle is made of ivory, and its silver-black blade is nearly rusted shut, but I manage to pry it open. The blade is also curved, and wickedly sharp.

"This is Lenora's," I whisper.

"Makes sense if you found it in her room," says Billy.

"Yeah, but I've seen her—" I pause, remembering that Billy doesn't know I dove in the cenote with his brother and found her statue. "I've seen a photo of her holding it. In that book your mom lent us."

I'm going to have to hide that book from Billy until we leave this island, which is starting to sound like a better and better idea with each passing minute. Or I could just tell him everything. It's the right thing to do, but he'll be hurt, and I'm not sure I can cope with that right now, on top of everything else that's happening.

"I wonder if she carved those words into her harp with this," I say. The thought makes me want to drop the knife, or bury it, or throw it into the deepest part of the ocean. At the same time, the handle fits perfectly into the curve of my hand, and there's something oddly soothing about it.

"Maybe." Billy eyes the blade but keeps his distance. "So, uh, are you okay after that whole . . . vine thing?"

"I think so." I check my feet and ankles for scratches or rashes, but the only thing on my skin is a light film of dirt from the path. "Have you ever seen that happen before?"

He shakes his head. "I know I've said a bunch of times

that this island is weird, but that's weird even for here. I was honestly a little scared for you."

"I think it's my blood," I say. "Those plants seem to like it."

"I wish I could say you're wrong, but I saw it too." Billy chews his lip. "You want to go home now, don't you?"

"I've wanted to go home since I got here," I say, and his face falls. "But that's not exactly true. I want to go back to my old life where I never came here in the first place."

Billy nods, his face like ashes. "I can't believe somebody cool finally came here and the island is fucking it all up."

I laugh, although my hands are shaking so hard I'm afraid I'll cut myself with the knife. "I'm not leaving yet. Remember how my mom said I'm missing the usual fear instincts?"

Billy cocks his head, and then I remember that was a conversation I had with his brother, not him. "No, but that definitely makes sense."

"It's not that I'm *not* scared," I say, trying and failing to snap the blade back into the handle. "Because I absolutely am. I'm just really good at doing scary stuff."

Billy breaks into a beaming grin. "I guess you couldn't swim miles underwater if you weren't good at that."

"Exactly," I say. "And right now, I care more about figuring out this Violet and Lenora thing than I care about being scared."

A sharp whistle cuts through the trees, startling us both.

"Bill-ster! You out there?"

"Hey, Dad!" calls Billy.

"Is Addie with you?"

"Yes, I'm here too!" I yell.

"To be continued," says Billy.

I snap Lenora's knife shut and tuck it into my pocket as we hurry back through the forest.

Chapter
23

AFTER ANOTHER AWKWARD dinner with my mom and David, I'm back in my room, writing postcards.

> *Dear Evie and Mia,*
>
> *Hope the diving is still great and you're getting some breaks! The weather here is perfect and I can't believe I'm actually telling you about the weather when so much other stuff is happening.*

> *Hey Mia and Evie,*
>
> *Miss you both! Today I hung out with a small ghost who loves spicy Cheezy Crunchies and playing hide-and-seek. Then some vines tried to strangle me!*

> *Hello from Eulalie Island,*
>
> *Hope training is going well! I'm still ridiculously jealous of you both, but it turns out I have a ghost stalker here, so maybe it's you who should be jealous.*

> *Greetings from "paradise,"*
>
> *Everything here is beautiful and scary. I'm diving again, even though I shouldn't be. With a boy who is so hot it almost hurts to look at him. Don't tell anyone.*

Of course I can't mail any of these, especially the last one, and I feel bad for wasting Ken and Melinda's postcards as I rip them up. After two rounds of breathing exercises, I flick off the lights and climb into bed.

I wake in the dark, halfway out the french doors that lead to the cliff.

Where was I going?

Was it the stairs? The woods? Straight off the side of the cliff? It's a long, long way down to the beach below. I can almost feel the crunch my bones would have made as I hit the sand. Cold tendrils of fear slither up the back of my neck as I lock the doors and back away from them.

Sitting on the bed, I start the meditation routine that I always use to calm my nerves before dives, but this terror is rooted so deep inside me that I can't separate myself from it. It sits like a boulder on my chest, crushing the life out of me.

Where was I going, all alone, with my eyes closed?

Breathe, Addie, just breathe.

But my breath is a series of short gasps punctuated by coughs. I hate that I can't force myself to calm down. I hate that I'm still coughing after all this time and hard work. I hate that I'm not better at any of this, and I hate that I'm still letting useless emotions like fear control me. It makes no sense that after everything that's happened to me recently, *sleepwalking* is the thing that triggers a panic attack.

It's not just the sleepwalking, though. It's a lot of things I've been shoving under the rug because I don't want to think about them. Number one being the shifty, intensifying *wrongness* of this place, despite its dazzling appearance. And the fact that something has changed inside me. Something that makes plants grow from my blood. Something that makes me wander at night.

Swearing quietly, I shake out my hands, my arms, my legs. Then I step into the center of my room, and even though I don't have my yoga mat, I do five rounds of surya namaskar A, then B. It's hard to balance in the darkness, but I pull all my focus into trying, and gradually my pounding heart slows.

My phone is dead, even though it's plugged in and nothing seems wrong with the socket. Swallowing another itchy cough, I glance at the clock. 12:17. I'm late to meet Sean. I shouldn't be meeting him at all, and I definitely shouldn't be diving to those underground places where no one can find us. Still, the cenote is impossible to resist. That enchanting, glowing water that will soothe me with its heartbeat, take away all this pain and fear.

Besides, I promised Violet I'd get her bracelet back, and I can't break that promise.

A quiet rap on the french doors makes me jump, which unleashes another coughing fit. If that's Lenora come to finish me off, it'll be easy work for her. But Lenora isn't the kind of person who knocks. I slide closer, wiping my mouth, and peer though the black pane.

Sean's moonlit form takes shape outside, tall and lean. His

gorgeous face is so hopeful and unguarded, it's like darts going through me. In less than two weeks, I might never see him again. Maybe even sooner if things get worse on this island. I unlatch the door, and salty air rushes in.

"Sorry I'm late," I say. "Give me a second to put on my bathing suit."

"No problem." He turns away toward the ocean while I dash into the bathroom, pull on my black one-piece and a pair of shorts, and grab a towel. His smile widens as I step out into the night, still shivering with nerves and fear.

"I was starting to wonder if you even owned a bathing suit," he says.

"Didn't you know competitive freediving is always done in pajamas?" I manage a shaky laugh, even though the darkness is swallowing me up and the floral stench is triggering memories of those vines curling around me. Deep in the forest, a harp is playing a sinister, looping waltz.

"Can you hear that?" I whisper.

Sean cocks his head. "Hear what?"

"The music."

"What music?" he asks. "Addie, are you all right?"

"No, actually." There's no point in hiding the truth. "A lot of strange things happened today and I'm still kind of . . ."

terrified, panicking, squirming

". . . dealing with it."

"What happened?" He drifts closer, his arm brushing mine, and I want to take his hand but I'm sure mine is a clammy mess. We reach the stairs, and I still don't want to go out into that quietly creeping forest, but I don't think I can stop myself from doing it anyway.

"Do you remember when I coughed and a vine grew out of the spot where my blood fell?" I say.

"Of course."

A tiny blue light flashes in the bushes, then another in the branches overhead.

"Billy and I went to the Wells house this afternoon," I say. "And the same thing happened with the vines, except this time they were swarming around me, getting taller and taller and I felt like they were trying to choke me or . . . eat me or something."

"The island loves you, Addie." Sean sounds surprisingly unconcerned.

Aa-dee-dee-dee, calls a bird from somewhere deep in the trees.

"I don't think you're taking this seriously," I say. "It was scary."

"I'm sorry," he says. "It's not that I'm not taking you seriously. But I've lived here a while, and I don't think you're in any actual danger. The island just has disturbing ways of showing its love sometimes."

The shudder that washes over me is like insect legs on my skin. Sean keeps saying things like this—things that make no sense, even though it feels like they somehow make perfect sense.

"Has it ever done that to you?" I ask.

"Something like that . . ." He trails off. "Why were you at the Wells house?"

"Just looking around."

"Did you find anything?" Sean holds a branch out of the way, and the flowers, gray in the faint light, crane toward me. The harp pauses, then begins another waltz.

"We found words carved into the bottom of Lenora's harp," I say. "They said 'J, may this music bring me your love.'"

He scoffs. "That's melodramatic."

As a ghost, Lenora is the very embodiment of melodrama. Apparently she was like that when she was alive too.

"We also found a knife inside a crack in the wall," I say. "With an ivory handle, just like the one Lenora's statue is holding."

"Hmm," says Sean, and I wait for him to continue, but he doesn't.

"Do you honestly still not believe me about there being ghosts on the island?" I say. "Because that's a pretty strange coincidence."

Something rustles in the undergrowth, and I suck in my breath, but Sean keeps walking. I wonder if in addition to not seeing ghosts, he also can't hear them. Or maybe he's just not afraid of these woods at night like I am.

"How does that prove the existence of ghosts, though?" he says. "All it means is the person who sculpted her knew she had that knife and it's been stuck inside that wall ever since then. Maybe there's a portrait of Lenora where she's holding it."

"I think it's all related," I say. "And eventually you're going to find out I'm right."

There's a strangeness to his laugh, and I worry I've gotten too metaphysical and weird, but then again, he's the one who just told me about the island expressing its love for people.

"Do you still have the knife?" he asks.

"Not on me," I say. "I left it in my room."

We skirt around the giant boulder and push through the curtain of Spanish moss, and after the day I've had, the cenote's glowing perfection makes me want to cry. I want to dive in and never come back. I want to drink it and fill myself with that dazzling blue.

Sean runs for the water, tugging his shirt over his head as he goes. I almost lose my balance as I hop out of my shorts and dash after him. As soon as my feet hit the water, every speck of pain in my body dissipates, and I don't care about ghosts or bloodthirsty vines. I don't care about ruined dreams or wasted summers. I only want to dive.

Chapter
24

AS WE TAKE our last breaths and descend, the pressure smooths away all the tiny wrinkles of my lingering nerves until there's nothing left. The rolling beat fills my sinuses, and it feels almost like the pieces of a melody are coming together, like the dawning of some new understanding I can't quite put my finger on.

This time Sean follows me as we descend through the hole at the bottom of the cenote and down the underwater corridor, and when we emerge under the northern lights dome, we both burst into inexplicable laughter.

"Easy, right?" he says, and I shrug because it really was nothing. I feel like I could dive here forever. I *want* to dive here forever. Moments later, we're crawling through the next passageway, and as we step out into the vast space of the cathedral, I can't resist shouting.

"Echo!" My voice bounds over the water and stone, growing fainter until it fades away. I grin at Sean, then tap his shoulder.

"Tag!"

As the word reverberates through the cavern, I dash down the path that splits the cavern in two. With an outraged laugh, Sean takes off after me, our wet feet slapping the stone. It's

unbelievable that I can run again—and even more unbelievable that a boy who looks like this is chasing me. I almost
let him catch me, just to see what might happen, but I really
want to get Violet's bracelet first.

As I wade into the silvery water beside the statue of her
sister, my elation fades.

"Shit," I whisper. The statue's wrist is bare.

Sean stops at the end of the pathway. "What?"

"I put a bracelet on this statue's arm," I say, crouching low
to search the shallows around it. "I needed to—I needed it
back, but now it's gone."

"What did it look like?" Sean jumps in to help me look.

"It was braided grass and red string," I say, and he gives me
a funny look. "It wasn't mine, but it was really important to
someone else."

"I'm sorry." He lifts Lenora's head to check underneath,
which makes me inexplicably queasy. He doesn't put it back
on her neck when he sets it down, like I would have done.

"This can't be happening," I mutter as I search the floor of
the altar, but it's not like the bracelet could have traveled anywhere on its own, and there's no wind down here to blow it.

"It'll turn up," says Sean.

"You don't know that," I snap, and he holds his hands up in
a surrendering gesture.

"You're right," he says. "I don't know for sure, but lost things
have a habit of turning up in unexpected places on this island."

"Because ghosts take them?" I can't help retorting. And
maybe that's not unreasonable. Maybe Lenora came down

here and took it back. Maybe that's why she didn't visit my room tonight.

"Usually, the less hard I'm looking for something, the more likely I am to find it," says Sean. "Trust the island, and it'll turn up."

"I trust you, island!" I yell, slumping down against the wall. "I am definitely not looking for any bracelets!"

Sean laughs. "It's not going to work that fast."

"Figures." Shutting my eyes, I blow out a heavy sigh. Violet is going to be so upset if I don't give that bracelet back tomorrow. The poor kid has absolutely nobody she can trust, including me. She deserves so much better.

Wait. My eyes pop open. "Do you think the caves might have flooded in that rainstorm earlier today? Maybe the bracelet got washed away to another place?"

"It's possible," says Sean. "Let's keep going, and maybe we'll find it. You're not ready to head back yet, are you?"

"No." For a variety of reasons, I'm not.

His mouth curves into that sliding smile that turns my insides to mush, and I let him pull me up to standing.

"There's another underwater tunnel up ahead," he says. "It's a little narrower than the ones we took to get here, but we'll be fine."

"How narrow, exactly?" I say.

He runs his hands up my shoulders, and it's so hard to keep my face neutral while my heart is rocketing like this. He lets go, fingertips hovering a few inches away from me on each side. "Maybe like this?"

"That's not very wide," I say. "Especially for you."

"Don't worry about me." His voice goes a little raspy as he takes both my hands. "I swim through it all the time. I just want to make sure you're okay with it."

We're so close, I can feel his body heat, the gentle beat of his pulse—or maybe it's mine—in our intertwined fingers. All of this is a bad, dangerous idea, but it's hard to think rationally when he's looking at me like this.

"I promise, what comes after the tunnel is worth it," he says. "And maybe you're right about the bracelet getting washed down through there."

I hate the thought of going back to Violet without her bracelet. Still, I hesitate.

"Last year I swam through some really narrow tunnels with my friend," I say, remembering the trip to Hawaii with Evie and her family. "I'm not exactly claustrophobic, but tight spaces aren't my favorite."

"Mine either," says Sean. "But it's really not that bad. Do you want to check it out and see what you think?"

"I guess it wouldn't hurt to look," I say.

The smile on his face almost makes me forget the nerves jangling under my skin, but not quite. He pulls me a little closer, and my breath catches, reality stutters for a moment, but then he lets go and gestures to a narrow opening at the opposite end of the altar.

"After you," he says.

As I slip into the passageway, I can hear him breathing, slow and even, and I imagine what that breath would feel like on my skin. I'm grateful for the darkness, which hides my face and my thoughts.

The floor slopes downward. Ahead, there's a rustling, rushing sound I can't quite figure out. My gut is telling me this is a bad idea, but I don't want to leave Sean and go back to the surface, back to my room, back to the house with my mom and David. Plus, I haven't found Violet's bracelet yet.

The rustling grows louder, and I start to make sense of the sound. Whispers. A hundred different whispers, all at the same time. Each voice is a single, unintelligible word. I stop, and Sean bumps into me, grabbing my waist to keep us both from falling. I can feel his heart thudding against my spine.

"I think I want to go back," I say.

"Are you afraid?" He's still holding me, his mouth in my hair. I could turn around and put my arms around him too. It would be so easy.

"What's that sound?" I say.

"It's just the water." He pulls away, and I curse myself for being such a coward. "It's not scary. Come on, I'll show you."

Sean edges around me in the tight space and leads the way through the corridor. The whispering gets louder, a sizzling, plinking sound that fills my head and makes my teeth ache. Then the passage opens up, revealing a pool of steel-colored water. There's no sky down here, but it's raining. The falling droplets make radiating pinpricks all over the pool's surface, and each drop is a single whisper adding to the eerie chorus.

Addie, I think I hear among the whispers, and my skin crawls.

"Do you hear voices?" I ask. This is a million times worse than the birds calling my name, because I can't tell if it's real or not.

Sean cocks his head. "No, do you?"

"I don't know. Maybe." I might just be losing my mind.

"There's definitely something a little . . . unsettling about this cave." Sean drifts closer, pointing to the flat wall at the opposite end of the cave. "The tunnel is right over there, and then I promise it gets better."

There's no sign of Violet's bracelet floating anywhere. I wade into the pool, which is startlingly cold compared to the rest of the water on this island, although the pulsing beat is still present. The whispering raindrops patter onto my skin, fizzing with a static-like energy. It's not painful, but there's something unbearable about it.

Addie.

I still can't tell if I'm imagining the words.

Ours.

Sucking in a breath, I dive under, and the whispers vanish. The deepest part of the cave is about four and a half feet, and there's no sign of the bracelet anywhere. In the center of the wall at the opposite end, there's a round black hole just below the surface.

As soon as I stand, the raindrops coat my scalp in barely audible whispers.

Ours. Love.

I sink under again, letting the heartbeat lull me, pulling myself together before reemerging.

Soon. Soon.

"I hate it here," I say. "Can we go back?"

Sean wades into the pool. "We can do whatever you want, but trust me. The next cave is worth it. And there's no rain on the other side."

It's so narrow in that tunnel, though. I'd have to kick all the way through without using my arms. But it's not the swimming that scares me—it's the tightness of that space. And these nonstop whispers are making me question my hold on reality.

Soon.

I swipe the rain off my face. "How long is the tunnel?"

"About thirty feet."

Nine meters. That's nothing, even without my arms. But still, my brain is firing off a million alarm bells about this cave, and that tunnel feels like an even worse idea. It's one thing to dissociate from my fear when I'm doing things I know I can handle. It's another thing to ignore my instincts about safety.

"Is this the spot where Roland got stuck?" I drop low in the water, leaving just my eyes, forehead, and the top of my head exposed to the whispers.

Ours.

Sean pauses. "If I say yes, will that change your mind about going?"

"Possibly." I drop all the way under again. Faint amber light gleams at the end of the tunnel. It's a straight shot through, but the idea of passing the spot where a dead man was trapped for days makes my skin crawl even more than it already is.

"The guy was an idiot," says Sean when I reemerge. "He should have taken his tank off and pushed it in front of him. I've swum through there hundreds of times and never gotten stuck."

It feels wrong to speak ill of the dead in the spot where they made a terrible mistake, but Sean is right. No experienced scuba diver would ever attempt that tunnel with a tank on their back.

"He must have been desperate to get to the next cave," I say. Or maybe those whispers got into his head too and he lost his mind.

Soon.

"When you get there, you'll see why." A mysterious smile plays at Sean's lips. "The other caves are nothing compared to this next one."

He hasn't been wrong about a single cave so far, and all I want to do is get away from these horrible whispers. We may as well keep moving forward.

"Okay," I say. "But you have to promise me it's worth it."

"I promise," he says, dark eyes solemn. "It's more than worth it."

As the water closes over me, panic clenches like a fist around my heart. I could make so many bad decisions right now. Swimming through that tunnel. Getting stuck. Coughing. Breathing in.

No.

My fear doesn't control me. I position myself at the mouth of the cave, letting stillness fill my head, my jaw, my shoulders.

As I kick into the tunnel, the water's beating rhythm drowns out the jolts of terror. The heartbeat echoes deeper inside me as I move farther and farther inside, and for a moment I drift, suspended in the spellbinding rhythm. Every emotion in my body disappears. It's so light, so exquisitely weightless. Then my back brushes the top of the tunnel, and I jolt back to reality.

Pushing off, I skim forward again, toward the dappled light at the end. I wiggle out of the tunnel, and as my face breaks the surface, giddy relief soars through me. I'm waist-deep in a pool the color of dark caramel. A set of steps hewn into stone leads up.

Sean emerges beside me, startlingly close, and I want to wipe the gleaming droplets off his cheekbones.

"It's better now, right?" he says.

"So much better." It was almost worth the awfulness of the last cave, just to let it all go and feel this incredibly light afterward. My head feels so clear and still. I wish I could do that with my entire life.

"Do you have any idea how ridiculously"—he searches for the right word—"*badass* you are, Addie?"

I shrug. "You said you've swum through that tunnel hundreds of times."

"It took me days to work up to it." A shadow passes over his face. "I kept panicking as soon as my shoulders went in."

"Yours are wider than mine." I trail my finger over his shoulder, and goose bumps break out on his wet skin. His gaze meets mine, his pupils dilate, and the unmistakable understanding that passes between us makes my legs tremble. Tiny ripples of water radiate from his body to mine.

Wordlessly, he takes my hand and leads me to the stairs. Everything is slow and dreamlike as we ascend. The beating rhythm shivers up through the stone, and I don't think I could stop now if I tried.

Chapter

25

AN ARCHWAY LEADS to a round chamber with walls of white crystal bathed in pale pink light. The space isn't huge, but the ceiling feels miles away. From its center, a thin stream of shimmering water falls, continuing down through a round hole in the floor. There's no splash, no sound of the water hitting anywhere beneath us, and I can't imagine how far down the hole goes. The beating rhythm under my feet slows to a hypnotic pace, and my last hope of finding Violet's bracelet dies, but I'm too mesmerized to be upset.

Sean sits at the edge of the hole, legs dangling, and gestures for me to join him. I move slowly on the slick floor, not wanting to find out just how deep the hole is.

"Put your hand in." Sean gestures to the silver stream of water.

Something stops my fingers inches from the water. "What will happen?"

Sean trails his hand through the gleaming water, breaking the stream into droplets that cast tiny rainbows on the floor and my bare legs.

"Nothing bad," he says. "Just try it."

The water is body temperature. As it rushes over my fingers, everything fades away: the stone under my legs, the cave around me, even Sean. There's nothing but me and the slowly beating pulse. Colors dance in my vision: fuchsia and sapphire, gold and green and flame. A deep feeling of understanding—of pure, unbounded love—fills my body, and I wonder if this is what dying was supposed to feel like, but didn't.

A gentle tug on my wrist brings me back to reality, to Sean's beautiful face bent close to mine. His expression is unfathomable, his dark eyes filled with a conflicted emotion I don't understand.

"What was that?" I say, blood pounding in my ears.

"It's the island's heartbeat," he says. "Do you see what I've been trying to tell you all this time, that it's not something to be afraid of?"

"I think I might still be afraid of that—just a little bit," I say.

"Don't be." Sean trails his fingers through the water again and stands. "You don't need to be afraid of any of this." With a broad stroke, he swipes his hand across the wall of the cave, and a blue line appears. He returns for more water, cupping it into one hand and using the other to make a curving blue slash, then another. The urge to touch the silver stream again is strong, but I'm afraid of those overwhelming emotions, afraid I might never be able to stop, so I tuck my knees up and wrap my arms around them, watching Sean paint.

Slowly, the lines come together, and a girl's face appears. Long hair. Sweeping eyebrows and sharp jaw. Sean steps back to inspect his work, then adds a final curve to the chin.

It's me. He's the one who made that drawing we found the iguana eating. He draws me when we're not together. He thinks about me.

He turns back toward me, his face full of uncertainty, of hope, of something that floods my lower abdomen with warmth. I stand and dip my hand back into the water, letting the burst of euphoria wash over me. Sean remains motionless as I reach up and trace my fingers lightly from his broad cheekbone to his jaw, leaving two faint lines of blue.

Then his mouth is on mine, his hands tangling in my hair as he drinks me in, tipping my head back until I'm almost falling. I wrap my arms around his waist and pull him closer, tighter, but it's not enough. The island's heartbeat throbs through my head, my body, my own heart, but this time as everything drops away, Sean is still there, his body pressed against me as the colors swirl. His tongue slides against mine and a full-body shiver washes over me. We kiss like we're drowning, like we're each other's oxygen.

It's almost too much—no, it *is* too much. I'm consumed by the booming rhythm of the cave, of Sean's heart, of mine all becoming one, and I'm starting to lose the edges of myself. I break the kiss, gasping for breath, dizzy, still clinging to him like he can save me from floating away.

Sean leans his forehead against mine. "I've been wanting to do that for a long time."

"Me too," I say, and he leans in again, his lips barely brushing mine, and this time there's no throbbing sound or waves of color. Just the warm rush of his breath mingling with mine.

On the wall beside us, my portrait has faded almost completely.

"Billy said you failed art class," I say. "Twice."

Sean laughs. "Why were you talking about me in art class?"

"We found one of your drawings in the woods," I say. "I asked if anybody in your family could draw, and Billy said no. How did you manage to fail art if you're this talented?"

His mouth twists in a wry expression. "I'm not very interested in following directions."

"I guess that's not always a bad thing," I say. "But how does Billy not know that you can draw?"

Sean shrugs. "Maybe he just doesn't care enough to notice."

"I doubt that," I say. "It sounds like he wishes you'd pay more attention to him. Even if he'd never admit that to you."

Sean's watch beeps the hour, and he lets me go with a rueful sigh. "We should get back. And you're probably right about Billy."

"Maybe you could hang out with us this afternoon?" I say.

He traces the faded line of my painted jaw on the wall. "I'll think about it."

There really shouldn't be much to think about. Spending time with his brother and the girl he's just been kissing shouldn't be a complicated decision. But before I have time to spiral into second thoughts, Sean catches my hand and presses the delicate inside of my wrist to his lips.

"Of course I'll hang out with you. What time?"

There's no hiding the goofy smile that bursts onto my face,

and I don't even try. "How about three o'clock at the beach? Is that enough time to catch up on your mole-person sleep?"

It will also give me and Billy a chance to do some more research on Lenora and Violet, and for me to figure out what to do about Violet's missing bracelet. Maybe by the time Sean gets there, Billy and I will have collected enough evidence to convince him to believe in ghosts. Maybe we can all come clean about everything and work together.

"I guess it'll have to be," says Sean. "Now let's hurry up before you get caught and your mother doesn't let you hang out with us anymore."

As soon as I step out of the cenote, my lungs feel like they're full of rocks, but there isn't time to dwell, because the sky is the same pale pink as the inside of a seashell and the elusive birds are all awake, chirping and screeching and calling my name.

Sean and I duck through the damp curtain of Spanish moss and cut down a different path, one I hadn't noticed before. It's so overgrown, I'm not surprised I didn't see it, but as we weave along it, the plants sway and lean out of the way to let us pass. Sean brushes his hand over a deep purple blossom, and it darkens to red. A rustling shiver passes through the bushes, and all of the flowers begin to change, turning scarlet and crimson and almost-black cherry.

"What's happening?" I whisper.

"The island is happy," he says, and there's an unspoken meaning in his words. The island is happy because of us. I'm not fighting these wild, impossible ideas anymore. I know deep down that they're true. As we passed back through the whispering cave, the voices were all repeating the same word.

Love.

The hushing of waves grows louder, the trees stretch taller, and the path opens onto white sand. The ocean is grayish blue in the dim dawn light. At the far end of the beach, I spot the wooden stairs that lead to my house.

"This is where I was sitting that night you crawled out of the ocean," says Sean, pulling me close and wrapping his arms around my waist. "I thought I was dreaming."

"And you were . . . crying," I say.

A shadow passes over his face, and I regret bringing it up, but he leans in and kisses my temple, then my cheekbone, then my jaw.

"Do you still wish you didn't exist?" he asks.

"In this exact moment, no."

His lips taste like water and minerals. He pulls away with a groan. "Are you really sure you have to leave?"

I reluctantly untangle myself from him. "Yeah, and I should probably go alone from here, in case anybody's looking for me."

He brushes a strand of my hair from my face. "Sleep well. I'll see you later."

Standing on tiptoe, I pull him close, and as our lips meet once more, I hear faint fragments of the island's heartbeat.

Chapter
26

ANOTHER LATE-MORNING wake-up, another note from my mother saying they're out on the boat. I'm glad she's stopped inviting me, and I hope she's having fun with David, not worrying. I've got enough things to worry about for the both of us. Number one is the fact that I've only got nine days left with Sean. Number two is Violet's missing bracelet.

The heat is oppressive, the stench of flowers nearly unbearable, though the array of red hues throughout the forest is stunning. I wipe sweat off my upper lip as I rummage through my mother's carry-on, searching for the travel sewing kit she always carries. Luckily, it's still there, and there's red thread inside. I'm not sure what kind of grass Violet or Lenora used to make the bracelet, but it can't be that hard to find something similar in the woods.

As I shove through the screen door, Billy leaps out of the way with a startled yelp.

"Sorry, didn't see you!" I say.

"Want a muffin?" Billy holds up two berry-studded pastries, one half-eaten. "You almost smashed them with the door, but thanks to my catlike reflexes, they're okay."

"You mean they *were* okay." I grab a muffin and sink my teeth into the top. It's fresh out of the oven, and the blueberries and raspberries are still gooey. With a happy groan, I lean against the shady side of the house, chewing and taking in all the red flowers. "Thanks. I didn't realize how hungry I was."

"Do you want the rest of this?" Billy holds up the other muffin, and when I shake my head, he stuffs it in his mouth. "Thank God," he says, spraying crumbs onto the patio. "This is my fourth one. I could eat the whole tray."

"So, I've officially lost Violet's bracelet," I say.

Billy swallows. "She's going to hate that."

"I know." Polishing off the last of my muffin, I pull the coil of thread from my pocket. "I'm going to make her a new one and hope she doesn't notice."

Billy glances at the trees. "You better hope she's not listening."

I gulp. "Didn't think of that."

"Oh sure, I'd love some Cheezy Crunchies! Are those the spicy kind?" he says loudly, and we both wait.

Silence.

"I think we're safe," he says. "What do you need for the bracelet?"

"Some long grass about this wide." I hold my thumb and forefinger half an inch apart. "My thread is a little thinner than the original string, but hopefully if I double it, she won't notice."

Billy looks dubious.

"Come on, she's like three," I say. "My little cousin would never notice the difference."

"Your cousin hasn't been roaming the earth for a hundred and eighty years," says Billy.

"True," I say. "But she'll be mad either way, so I may as well try."

We find some long grass growing by the stone staircase, and Billy holds the ends as I braid it together with the red thread.

"It's too neat," he says. "And it looks brand new, not like a thing a little kid has been wearing for centuries."

With an exasperated huff, I dunk the bracelet into the pool, then scuff it against the cement edge. "Is this better?"

He squints at it. "A little?"

I roll the bracelet around on the ground under some bushes, then use my fingers to work dirt into the grass and loosen the braid. "This is getting better. She'll never know."

"Who will never know?" A gray face pops out from the bushes, and I topple out of my crouch. With a hissing giggle that sets my teeth on edge, Violet crawls out and sits cross-legged beside me, arranging the shreds of her once-white dress in a circle around her like the petals of a dead flower.

"You startled me," I say, crushing the bracelet inside my fist in a last-ditch attempt to make it look worn and then stuffing it into my pocket. Hopefully she'll forget all about it.

Violet edges closer and plucks at a strand of my hair that's fallen out of my ponytail. "You look pretty, Addie-dee."

"Thank you. So do you." I resist the urge to cringe away from her freezing fingers on my neck.

"Can I make your hair into a braid?" Without waiting for

an answer, she plops down behind me and yanks my elastic out, along with a sizable chunk of my hair.

"Ouch!" I yelp. Hairstyling is another one of Grace's favorite hobbies, and it's always painful, but never quite this bad.

"Nora always hurted me when she brushed my hair," says Violet. "I would scream very loud when she tugged on the knots, and she didn't even say sorry."

"That sounds awful." I clench my teeth as she rips the knots in my own hair, dividing it into sections.

"Nora wasn't always very nice to me," sniffs Violet. "Sometimes she would wait until I was having my nap, and then she would sneak away with Jonah."

"Oh, really?" I sit up straighter.

"They didn't think I knowed, but sometimes I wasn't all the way sleeping." Violet tugs and twists my hair. "I can be very sneaky when I decide to be."

"That's an understatement," mutters Billy.

"Who's Jonah?" I ask.

"Jack and Jill went down a hill, into a cave of water," she sings in an eerie, off-tune voice. "Jill fell down and broke her crown, and I went tumbling after."

A chill washes over me as I picture me and Sean wandering through the underground caves. Wading into dark pools, slipping through impossibly narrow, water-filled tunnels.

"Did Jonah and your sister go into a cave together?" I ask.

Is that song going to repeat itself with new characters?

"Sit still," hisses Violet, wrenching my braid so hard my head tips back.

I grab my hair out of her icy fingers and turn to face her. "Did something bad happen to them?"

"You ruined my braid!" she wails, startling the furry brown spider on her shoulder, which dashes into her hair.

"I'm sorry," I say. "But can you answer my question?"

Violet's head drops sideways at a ninety-degree angle. "Do you have my bracelet?"

I can feel Billy cringing from across the patio. Reluctantly, I pull the bracelet from my pocket, and Violet gives a harpy-like shriek. As I tie the strands around her tiny wrist, she ducks her head to inspect it. Stringy strands of her hair slither over my fingers, and the spider wanders down to look too.

"There you go," I say, quickly finishing off the knot and sliding away from her.

"This isn't mine's," she says. "This is somebody else's."

"What . . . I mean, no it's not!" I widen my eyes at Billy, but he makes an "I told you so" face.

"Where is Nora's hair?" says Violet.

"Where is what?" My voice has risen about three guilty octaves.

"Nora's hair." Violet's sunken eyes fill with rage. "She braided it into my bracelet, but now it isn't there. Where did you put my bracelet with Nora's hair in it?"

Even though she's sitting perfectly still, the shreds of Violet's dress are levitating off the ground, rippling in a non-existent wind. I gulp hard, all excuses disappearing from my paper-dry tongue. I'm used to toddler tantrums, but something tells me this is going to be on another level entirely.

"I . . . couldn't find it," I say.

Billy rushes over and tries to take Violet's hand, but she snatches it away.

"Addie feels terrible," he says. "So she made you a whole new bracelet."

"I do *not* want a different one!" shrieks Violet. The crimson flowers on the nearest bush wither and fall to the ground. "Where did you put mine's? You promised you'd give it back! You promised."

I did promise, and I failed. I can't stop failing, no matter how hard I try. Violet has no one at all. She trusted me, and I screwed it all up. They're both staring at me, waiting for an answer, and my only answer is that I'm a horrible human being.

"I left it on a statue in one of the caves." As soon as the words come out, I want to swallow them back.

"A statue?" says Billy. "What are you talking about? What cave?"

"It's just a cave I found," I say. "I was going to tell you about it later."

His eyes narrow. "Really."

"No, she wasn't!" yells Violet. "Addie-dee is a nasty, horrible liar. Ask her who she was going to the beach with today."

Billy's brow furrows. "Ask her who she *went* to the beach with or who she's *going* to the beach with?"

"Assssk her," hisses Violet. "But she will lie, because they are both rotting liars."

"Hey, that's not very nice," I say. But it's true. I should have come clean to Billy yesterday. There was no excuse for lying to him when he's been so kind to me all week.

Violet lets out an earsplitting shriek that fades into a howl, lifting all the hair on my arms.

"I'm so sorry," I say, but she floats to her feet in a way no living human could.

"I gave it to you for safekeeping." Her whisper is a razor blade. "I thought you could help me, but you are not my friend anymore, Addie-dee."

Dread pools in my stomach. Violet might look all of three years old, but the last thing I want is to end up on the bad side of a toddler ghost. There's no telling what she's capable of.

"I promise to keep looking for it." I reach for her but end up pulling away a ragged shred of her dress.

"You are the horriblest snake of a liar." Violet whirls away into the bushes, which barely move as she disappears.

Aa-dee-dee-dee, sing the birds, and this time it sounds like a reprimand.

I bury my face in my hands. "That went well."

Billy says nothing.

"I swear I was going to tell—"

"I don't get it," he interrupts. "Who did you go to the beach with—or are you planning to go with? Who else is here besides me?"

I'm done lying. Billy deserves to know the truth, even if it hurts his feelings.

"Sean," I say.

"My *brother* Sean?" Billy's freckled face is a whirl of confusion.

"Yes," I say. "We've been meeting up at night and exploring some of the caves. I'm so sorry I didn't tell you."

"Sean snuck out at night?" Billy is yelling now. "He actually left the lighthouse? And went in caves? With you? But why would he—" He catches sight of my mortified expression, and understanding dawns in his eyes. "Oh no. No, no."

"I'm so sorry."

"Addie, why?" Billy rips a fistful of leaves off a nearby tree and throws them on the ground, where they immediately shrivel. "I know you think I'm too young, but Sean? He's such an asshole."

"He's not that bad," I say. "He said he wanted to hang out with you this afternoon."

"Not that bad?" He rounds on me, as furious as Violet was—maybe even more so. "You're going to tell me all about my own brother now? The guy who's been shitting on me for my entire life? That's hilarious."

"It's not . . . I'm not." I can't believe what a huge mess I'm making, first with Violet, now with him. "Billy, I'm really, really sorry. I didn't mean to lie to you, I just . . ."

He waves me off, heading for the stairs. "I have a bunch of rat traps to check before my dad gets back. Hope you and Sean have fun at the beach."

"I wanted you to come too," I say, but it sounds pathetic, and he doesn't bother answering.

With a heavy groan, I lie back on the patio and stare up through the shifting branches. I've ruined my chances of finding out anything more about Violet or Lenora. I've ruined my friendship with Billy. And now I dread seeing Sean again, because I have to tell him Billy knows about us sneaking out, even though I promised to keep it secret. I've betrayed every single one of them. I am a horrible person. I want to run into the forest and all the way to the cenote. I want to dive into that clear, clean water and let it take away all these hideous feelings, but I deserve every last bit of pain right now.

For a long time, I lie there on the stone tiles, sweating and stewing in self-hate, until the heat makes me feel like I'm going to be sick. Then I go inside to check the time. Still only two o'clock. Maybe I'll go float in the ocean for an hour. If I'm lucky, I'll float away and never be seen again.

I drag myself to my room. Someone tidied up my scattered clothing while I was asleep and hung my bathing suit up to dry, though it's still damp. The lilies in the vase are the same color as the blood I still keep coughing up, even after all this time, and I'm so utterly exhausted. I'd crawl into bed and sleep away the rest of the day if it weren't so sickeningly hot.

After pulling on a dry bathing suit and tossing a towel over my shoulder, I let myself out through the french doors and into the merciless sunshine. I'm halfway down the stairs in an overheated daze when I hear screaming.

It's coming from the lighthouse.

Chapter
27

I THUNDER DOWN the stairs as the screaming continues. It's a woman's frantic voice, although I can't make out the words. Far down the beach, a plume of black smoke billows from one of the lighthouse's lower windows. My first instinct is to pull out my phone and call 911, but I don't have it with me because there's no cell service in this ridiculously isolated place.

The sand is loose and unstable, and I keep stumbling as I race toward the burning lighthouse. I hope Billy didn't go back there after our fight. My foot sinks into a hole, and I crash to my knees. There's no time to wipe away the blood or sand; I stagger up again, coughing and running and feeling like my heart is about to pound straight through my ribs.

Melinda stands on the jetty outside the lighthouse, her orange caftan billowing. "Sean! Wake up!" she's yelling.

The water surrounding the lighthouse is shallow and full of huge rocks. If Sean jumped out one of the higher windows, he'd break his legs. Of course, that'd be better than burning to death.

"Sean!" I shout, coughing into my hands and breaking into an agonizing sprint.

As I near the jetty, the lighthouse door flies open. A person staggers out, engulfed in a cloud of smoke. As it billows away,

I spot short, blond hair. But it's not Billy. This person is taller and wider, with slumping shoulders and pale skin.

It's not Billy. It's not Sean. Who else could be in their house?

Melinda wraps the boy in her arms and sobs. "Where's Billy? He's not inside, is he?"

He shakes his head, and I don't understand why she's asking this stranger about Billy when it was Sean she was worried about only seconds ago. Then my whirling brain screeches to a stop. Slowly, sickeningly, it all comes together.

This is Sean.

I can see it now—he's definitely Billy's brother. They have the same bushy, blond eyebrows, and Sean's cheeks are just as round as his brother's. But if this is Sean, that means the other boy—*my* Sean—isn't.

The person I've been hanging out with is not Sean.

The person I kissed last night is not Sean.

The person I've been dreaming about, sneaking away with every night, trusting my life with, is not Sean. I flash back to his arms slipping around my waist, his skin warm and smooth under my fingertips, his heart beating against mine. His breath whispering in my ear, his lips on mine.

It

wasn't

Sean.

I want to scream.

Violet's song loops through my brain as I clamber onto the jetty: *Jack and Jill went down a hill* . . . There's blood smeared all over my hands, and I've given up on stifling my coughs at this point. If that person wasn't Sean, who—or what—is he? I fight the urge to pinch myself to see if I'm dreaming; my lungs hurt so much that I know I'm not. I wish I were, though. This is too awful.

The real Sean peers at me over his sobbing mother's shoulder and frowns like I'm interrupting something that's none of my business.

"Why didn't you come when I called you?" cries Melinda. "The frying oil was on fire and I couldn't get the fire extinguisher to work, and then the curtains went up and I didn't know where you were!"

"I was getting the other fire extinguisher." Sean disentangles himself from his mother and rubs his bloodshot eyes. "I put out the fire, Mom. The curtains are burned, but the rest of the kitchen is fine. You didn't have to panic like that."

Melinda pulls him into a hug again. "Oh, thank God."

"Yeah, no thanks to you, though," he scoffs, and I want to smack him. "How did that even happen?"

"I have no idea." Melinda wipes her runny nose, and I wish I had a tissue to give her. "I filled the pan with oil to fry some eggplant fritters, and then I went out to pick basil. You didn't turn the stove on?"

"Uh, no?" Sean scoffs. "Why would I do that?"

"Violet," I whisper. She was mad enough to set a fire, and nobody but Billy or I could see her doing it.

Sean blinks like he'd forgotten I was here. Then he gives my swimsuit-clad body a thorough up-and-down. I glare back.

"Is this Billy's new girlfriend?" he says.

"Sean!" says Melinda. "This is Caroline and David's daughter, Addie. Don't be rude."

Caroline's daughter. Not David's.

"Hey," he says, jutting his chin upward in the universal frat-boy greeting.

"Nice to meet you . . ." I can't make my mouth form his name, not after I've been using it for the wrong person all this time. It doesn't feel like it belongs to him. I clench my hands into fists, nails digging into the meat of my palms. How could I have been this stupid? How could I not have realized that other person wasn't Billy's brother? And if he's not Billy's brother, who on earth is he?

Jack and Jill went down a hill, into a cave of water . . .

Sean's still leering at me, and I want to throw something at his wrong, wrong face. He turns to his mom. "I'm going back to bed. Try not to burn anything else, okay?"

"Can I help you clean up?" I ask Melinda as he heads inside.

"Oh, honey, that's very kind, but no." She gives me a weary smile. "I just can't believe I couldn't get that fire extinguisher to work. When Ken comes back, I'll send him over to your house to check all of yours."

With a jolt, I realize Violet might be on her way to my house next. A coughing fit blasts up through my chest, and I turn away, doubling over. Melinda rubs my back until it passes, which makes me inexplicably teary.

"Can I get you a cup of tea?" she asks. "I promise I'll microwave it instead of using the stove."

"No, thanks," I say, hiding my bloody hands. "I think I'll go back to the house and take a nap."

And make sure Violet hasn't burned it down.

Halfway down the beach, I stop to wash the blood off my hands. A wave rushes in, leaving behind a line of golden shells that look like teeth. Another wave brings another row of shells, larger and pointier this time. They glint in the sunlight like an offering, another creepy gift I didn't ask for. I leave them lying there and continue down the beach.

There's no smoke coming out of the house up on the cliff, and I suspect Violet's random act of arson was more about revealing the truth than it was about destroying the Carpenters' home. Still, she could have killed someone with that fire. Three-year-olds should never be left to their own devices, even when they're ghosts. Especially when they're ghosts.

Jack and Jill went down a hill . . .

"Why didn't you tell me that wasn't Sean?" I yell at the woods.

Aa-dee-dee-dee, answer the birds. My brain feels gluey in the tropical heat, unable to process everything I've just learned. Or maybe not wanting to process everything, because I know there's more to this story. That person I kissed wasn't Sean, and both Lenora and Violet have warned me about a person named Jonah.

. . . into a cave of water . . .

Ignoring the stab of pain in my lungs, I sprint down the tideline, feet slapping the wet sand as the ocean brings more and more toothlike shells. I hurtle up the steps, coughing open-mouthed and not caring where my blood lands. Those vines will have to catch me first. Gasping and hacking and covered in sweat, I shove the french doors open and grab the Eulalie Island book from my bedside table. It falls open to the bookmarked page, to the drawing of Eulalie sitting in the tree.

Portrait of Eulalie by J. Burke, circa 1762.

It's not the same style as his other drawings—this one is more detailed, more photorealistic—but the curve of her jaw and the sweep of her eyebrows are unmistakable.

"Jonah Burke," I whisper.

Outside, the racket of screeching birds goes silent.

There was nothing eerie or undead about him, though. He looks nothing like Violet or Lenora. I felt his warm skin, his heart beating in his chest. He was very much alive, and it makes no sense. The one thing I do know for sure is that he lied to me.

I rack my brain, trying to recall the details from the night we met. I crawled out of the ocean and asked him his name. No, I asked him if he was Sean, and he said yes. What a sinister thing to do. He let me believe he was someone else for days. He took me to dangerous caves where no one could find us. He showed me all these secret places that no one else knows about, except for two dead people: Lenora and Roland.

My skin turns to ice.

I have to find Billy and tell him everything. Even if he still hates me for lying, he needs to know what's happened, and I need help making sense of this. There's no way my mom or David would ever understand—I can just picture the look on their faces if I told them I've been sneaking out at night with a boy who may or may not be from the eighteenth century. It's beyond absurd. I'd laugh at this story if I heard it from anyone else.

The clock reads 3:15. I wonder if Jonah kept his promise and went to meet me at the beach. But how could he have? Of course he wasn't going to walk up to Billy, introduce himself, and explain why I thought he was Sean. He would have stayed away, then met me tonight with another excuse that I would have bought. I wonder how long he thought he could keep up this twisted little game. Given how gullible I've been, it might have lasted the whole trip. Nine more nights of sneaking out, of diving, of kissing him. I probably would have let it lead to more, which is equally mortifying and devastating.

I shove outside, smashing the screen door against the side of the house.

"You'd better not be out here, Jonah Burke," I mutter as I head down the stairs and into the woods.

Chapter
28

AS I HIT the bottom step, the golf cart comes skidding around the corner. Hot pink and orange pool noodles poke out of its sides, dragging through the plants along the sides of the path.

"There you are!" My mother climbs out, taking an armload of pool noodles with her. Her hat is crooked, her face is flushed from the heat, and her smile is radiant. She leans into the passenger side to give David a kiss.

"Have fun, you two!" she says, and Ken waves before slamming the cart into reverse and executing a three-point turn at terrifying speed.

"I'm . . . where's . . . what?" I watch the golf cart disappear into the leafy forest.

"We're spending the afternoon together, just me and you." My mom hands me two of the noodles and straightens her hat. "I told David we need some girl time."

"What's he going to do all afternoon?" My heart is still thundering, but it's hard to stay furious while holding pool noodles.

"Ken's giving him a lesson on gutting and filleting fish." She laughs. "It's a gift to all of us in many ways."

"True." I scan the trees, searching for some sign of Billy or Violet or Jonah.

"Pool or ocean?" my mom calls from halfway up the steps.

"Huh?" Something is rustling far off in the red-blossomed bushes, but I can't make out what.

"Pool or ocean?" She hops down a few steps and tugs on my pool noodle. "It's too hot to do anything but swim."

If I could, I'd choose the cenote, but that's the last place we should go. I can almost hear its gorgeous, lapping water calling me. Whispering through the trees. Promising to take away all my pain.

"Ocean," I say, swallowing a cough and following her up the steps.

I'm floating on my back, cradled in noodles and wondering how I've gotten myself so impossibly tangled up in a mess that I can't tell my mother about. She's coached me through a thousand dilemmas over the years, and I've never hesitated to ask her for advice, even on things she doesn't fully understand, like freediving. But right now, the gap between what's believable and what's actually happening is so wide, I don't know where to start. I couldn't possibly start.

"Did you and Billy have a fight?" she asks, lifting the brim of her hat. "We saw him on the way back and he seemed upset."

"Sort of." I stretch out my legs and tip my head back. The warm, undulating water is nothing compared to the cenote, but it still works some of its old magic, clearing a few pockets of calm in my whirling mind.

"Be careful with that boy's heart," says my mom. "I know you think he's just a kid, but it's pretty obvious how much he likes you."

"I don't just think he's a kid," I say. "I genuinely like him as a friend."

"Sounds like you two need to have a serious talk."

We do, about many things.

"And I owe you a huge apology," she says. "I've been so caught up with David all week, I feel like you and I have barely spoken."

"What? No." I paddle closer to her. "I'm honestly happy that you two are spending all this time together. I'd feel terrible if you wasted your honeymoon on me."

"That would never be a waste," she says. "You're my daughter, Addie. Nothing means more to me than you."

"Thanks," I say. "But it makes me feel worse when you make a big deal about me. I promise I'm okay."

That's a lie, but this particular not-being-okay has nothing to do with her.

"Well, you shouldn't be okay," she says. "Your entire life plan has just exploded, and I just want to make sure you're not burying your feelings. You're very good at doing that. You think I don't notice these things, but I do."

When I was a kid, we lived three blocks away from the ocean, about an hour north of Miami. My mom and my dad used to fight every day, sometimes for hours, and a lump of cement would start growing in my stomach, getting heavier and sharper with each angry word that flew from their mouths. When the cement got too heavy to bear, I'd change into my bathing suit and walk down to the sliver of sand at the end of our road. It was more of a boat launch than a beach, always deserted because there were a million other beautiful spots nearby. The shallows were full of seaweed and beach grass, but it didn't matter. As soon as I could submerge my body, my feet never touched down.

Out I'd swim, wishing I could keep going, all the way to Bermuda or maybe even Portugal. Once the land was a far-away sliver of green, I'd take long, slow breaths, stretching and filling my lungs like my grandfather taught me when we used to go spearfishing. The water shimmered clear and blue, and as soon as I dove, the cement in my stomach dissolved.

The light would grow murkier. I'd equalize the pressure in my ears, and even though it still hurt the farther down I went, I didn't mind. It was the price of letting go, of disappearing. Lower I'd sink into the darkness, growing tinier and tinier inside myself, and by the time I reached the bottom, every-thing was gone. I'd lie there on the sand, in the perfect calm, and I'd feel absolutely nothing.

I don't know how to face the world without that escape. Everything feels impossible. I can't stop screwing up, making bad choices, hurting other people, hurting myself, and I've got nowhere to hide anymore.

"You're not going to let David make me quit diving, are you?" I say.

"Of course not!" My mom pulls me close, and I realize

there are tears on my cheeks. "Sweetie, this isn't permanent. You're going to get better, and I trust you to make your own choices. David doesn't get to make them for you."

"What if I don't get better, though?" I hate the wobble in my voice.

"You will," she says, but of course she doesn't know that for sure.

I hope Jonah isn't out there in the woods watching us. Rolling off the noodles, I drop underwater, but my lungs are too tight when I'm not in the cenote, and I can't hold my breath for more than thirty seconds. Nothing is getting better. I'm just making it all worse.

When I surface, red flower petals are floating out of the forest. Like bloodstained snowflakes, they drift on the breeze, swirling over the beach and landing in the sea.

"You're too hard on yourself," says my mother, and I know it's true, but I don't know how not to be this hard on myself. I wish I could let go of all this anger and let it fly away like those plants with their petals. Mine wouldn't be so pretty, though. It'd be black and ragged and full of bone shards and fingernails. And it would sound like a scream.

"If that accident had happened to Mia or Evie, you'd never blame them like this," she says.

She's right. But if I stop blaming myself, that means what happened to me was just a random, tragic accident. It means the world is unpredictable and nonsensical, and no matter how many ways I plan and strategize and train, I can't control

NICOLE LESPERANCE

everything. It means that a terrible thing happened to me, and I was powerless to stop it. It means more terrible things could happen.

Jack and Jill went down a hill . . .

My hands curl into fists. I may need to work on forgiving myself, but I'm not letting my guard down anytime soon. Not on this island.

"Yikes, I'm turning into a raisin," says my mom, holding up her wrinkly fingers. "Want to head back to the house? We can turn on all the fans and make smoothies and play cribbage."

"Okay," I say. Anything is better than sitting here festering in my feelings.

As soon as we emerge from the ocean, the heat wraps around me, filling my lungs with a stuffy ache.

"What's that on your towel?" says my mom, and I peer into the shade where we left our things. In the center of my towel is a sheet of yellowed paper; I snatch it up, smearing water all over it, and turn it over. My scalp begins to crawl.

"That's so sweet," says my mom, looking over my shoulder. "I didn't know Billy was an artist."

It's a drawing of me floating on pool noodles in the ocean. With just a few quick lines, my thunderous expression is perfectly captured. My mother isn't in the picture. Underneath the drawing are two words:

I'm sorry.

Chapter

29

THE FRENCH DOORS to my room are cracked open, even though I'm sure I shut them on my way out. A vine stretches down from the thatched roof and inside the room, its flowers the deep red color of a wound. Pushing the door open wide, I edge around the trailing plant, which has made it halfway across the room. Its flowers all swivel in my direction, opening wide like baby bird mouths.

"Go away," I whisper, dropping Jonah's drawing on my bed. There's a broom inside the bathroom's linen closet, and I use it to shove the vine back out the door, but green tendrils keep curling around the bristles. The mouth-blossoms open again, and puffs of pollen waft out, making the room spin. A wave of exhaustion hits me—I'm so bone-deep weary, all I want to do is lie down and sleep for days.

Finally, I throw the entire plant-wrapped broom onto the patio and slam the doors shut. Then I break down coughing in the stuffy, sickening heat of my bedroom. Once the oxygen returns to my brain, I gather up all the lilies in their vases and set them out on the patio too. I turn the ceiling fan as high as it will go, but the rotten flower scent still clings to everything, and nausea wells up my throat.

I can't keep going like this. I need to tell my mother at

least some of what's going on. If she sees what the flowers are doing, she'll understand that something is wrong. But then what? Do I force her to cancel the rest of her honeymoon over clingy plants? Do I ruin this trip she's been planning for the better part of a year because I didn't make sure the boy I was hanging out with wasn't a ghost?

After a long shower that does nothing to clear my head, I wrap myself in a towel and flop onto the bed beside Jonah's drawing. *I'm sorry*. As if that's remotely adequate to make up for what he did. Like I'm just going to forgive him and meet him at the cenote tonight because he drew me a pretty picture. The fact that he was creeping around in the bushes, watching me while I swam, makes it even worse. Everything about our relationship has been gross and manipulative, and I wonder if this is what happened with him and Lenora too.

"Your smoothie's ready!" calls my mom.

I tug all the curtains shut before pulling on clean clothes, in case he's still spying, and I'm about to head over to the main bungalow when I double back to the bed.

"You're not actually sorry," I mutter as I snatch up the drawing. "You're just sorry you got caught."

On my way across the patio, I rip the drawing into tiny scraps and drop them into a trash barrel. I hope he's watching.

Two hours later, I'm slumped in a lounger with the Eulalie Island book, staring at Jonah's drawing and wondering if he kissed Eulalie *and* Lenora in the caves. My mom and David are eating slices of the cloudlike key lime pie that Melinda brought over earlier.

"Sweetie, why don't you go to bed?" says my mom after I drift off and drop the book for the third time.

"It's too hot in my room," I say, which is half the truth. The other half is that I still feel like I'm being watched, and I don't love the idea of being alone.

"We've got some extra fans in our closet. I'll grab one for you." David gathers up the dessert plates and brings them to the kitchen. My dad never cleared the dishes, even after my mom spent hours cooking meals for us. He said it was my job, which would have been fair if he ever helped with a single one of the other chores.

While David rummages in his closet, I clean up the kitchen, and once I'm done, I discover that my room has been transformed into a breezy oasis with the help of three new fans in strategic locations.

"Thank you!" I call, poking my head outside. David gives me a thumbs-up while pouring my mom a glass of wine. While he was in my room, he opened the french doors, and I'm tempted to leave them like that because the ocean breeze is so lovely, but I don't know what might come crawling in while I sleep.

Tonight I will not set an alarm, and I will not go to the cenote. As much as it kills me not to swim in that glowing water, giving in is a weakness I can't afford. Tomorrow I start fresh. No more bad choices. No more diving in beautiful places that bend reality, that make me forget what I should be focusing on. No more sinister boys with lies on their lips.

Tomorrow I owe Billy and Violet a massive apology. I'll make her an even better bracelet, I'll bring her all the spicy snacks we've got, and hopefully she'll tell us more about her sister and what exactly happened. I've still got time to fix things, to help her. To stop her from starting more fires. To set everything back on the right path.

After cycling through two rounds of breathing exercises, I lock my back door and shut the french doors, bracing the handles with a chair and closing the curtains around them. It's as much to stop myself from sleepwalking out as it is to keep things from getting in.

The heat is just about bearable with all of David's fans, and I'm so exhausted I don't think it will matter. I still can't shake the prickly feeling of being watched, but the doors, windows, and drapes are all firmly closed.

As I brush my teeth, I keep thinking I hear harp music, but every time I stop brushing, it disappears. With shivers on my skin, I leap across the room and land on my bed, like the imaginary monsters under there might have returned from my childhood. As it turns out, there are just different monsters now. Before shutting off the light, I check under the bed, just in case, but there's only the little flower nosegay, slowly turning black.

As much as I still want to help Violet, I'm counting the days until we leave this place.

Chapter
30

I DREAM I'M swimming through the narrow underground tunnel and everything is cloudy and dark. It's only nine meters, I keep telling myself, but I'm certain I've swum at least twice that distance by now. An amber light gleams somewhere ahead, and I kick toward it, but then the tunnel bends to the right, narrowing and narrowing until the walls scrape my shoulders and stomach.

This isn't the right way. I need to go back, but there's no room to turn around. I try pushing myself backward, but my hands slide uselessly along the bottom of the tunnel. Bubbles stream out of my nose, and I shouldn't let go of what little oxygen is left in my lungs, but I can't make it stop. I need to get out.

Don't panic, Addie, just swim.

My legs propel me forward, but my movements are growing frantic despite every calming thought I'm trying to force into my brain. The tunnel bends downward, and this cannot be the right direction, but I can't turn around. I have no choice. Down into the darkening water I descend, and the island's throbbing heartbeat becomes my own panicked pulse.

Boom, boom, boom.

The tunnel ends in blackness. I fumble around, searching

for an exit, clawing at the stone with my fingernails like I can somehow rip open a crack and slip through. More bubbles pour out of my nose, and a crushing roar filles my head as I suck in a breath, not caring anymore if I inhale the water.

Something grabs my ankle and tugs, and I'm swirling backward, breathing in thick mouthfuls of water as I cough. Suddenly, I'm out of the tunnel, out of the water. I'm lying on flat stone, gasping, and then someone is pulling me up to sit. It's Jonah, but his eyes are blood-red flowers. I can't move as he leans in closer, the sweet rot scent of his breath filling my sinuses and coating my tongue. The flowers shut and then open as he blinks, and I scream.

I wake on the dirt path in the middle of the woods.

A filthy hand clamps over my mouth; a bony finger slips between my lips, and I gag, shoving away.

"Don't scream again," hisses a girl's voice. "Or he'll hear. *It* will hear."

"Lenora?" I whisper. There's no moon, and I can barely see my own hand in front of my face.

"This isn't the place for chitchatting," she says. "Come with me. Quickly."

"How do I know you're not trying to lure me into another sinkhole?" I say.

Her laughter is sandpaper and skittering insects. "If I wanted to kill you, I'd have strangled you in your sleep."

I resist the impulse to run my fingers over my tingling throat. In the trees to my left, there's a flash of blue.

"Don't you want to know the truth?" she hisses with rotten breath.

More blue flashes, coming closer.

"Yes," I say.

"Then come. Right now. Or it will be too late."

Before I can answer, she grabs my hand and dashes away. Lenora is startlingly fast, and I keep stumbling over roots and branches as we veer off the path and tear through the undergrowth. From high overhead comes another blue flash.

"Don't stop," she whispers, tugging me up like a toddler as I fall to my knees. "You almost went to him again. He's waiting for you. We haven't much time."

With a jolt, I realize that all these nights I've been sleepwalking, I've been going to the same place. I've been heading to a destination. To Jonah. It's like he's been pulling me to him. My sour stomach churns, and I almost fall again.

The starlight brightens, and the floral scent begins to fade, replaced by the reek of decaying seaweed. We shove through another cluster of bushes and step onto a narrow strip of beach covered in driftwood and detritus. This must be the other side of the island, the outer edge of the crescent moon shape. To one side, a nest of mangroves stretches into the sea, long roots tangling underwater. Lenora pulls a pile of palm fronds off an overturned rowboat and struggles to flip it over. She swears as something flies out of her hand, and as she bends down to retrieve it, I realize it *is* her hand. With a shudder that makes her bones clack, Lenora jams it back onto her wrist.

"Stop staring," she hisses. "It's worse for me than it is for you."

"I'm—I'm sorry," I say. "And you're right. God, that must have hurt."

"Why don't you help instead of standing around feeling sorry for me," she says, flexing and clenching her bony fingers.

I eye the boat's cracked hull and rotting wood. "Are you sure this thing is seaworthy?"

"It's seaworthy enough. We only need to get past where it can hear."

A chill slithers up the back of my neck. "What's *it*? Jonah?"

She leans in close, and my eyes water at the death stench of her. "The island," she whispers. "And Jonah. There's no difference."

Lenora tries to flip the rowboat again, and this time I help her. It lands with a splintery crunch, revealing two oars in slightly better condition than the boat. I really should go back to the house and lock my doors. This is another one of those choices I may live to regret . . . or not live to regret. But if Jonah can make me sleepwalk, then not stopping him—and whatever horrible plan he's working on—could end up being a worse choice.

"Do you promise you won't hurt me if we go out?" I say.

"You have . . . my word. Just . . . hurry." She's tugging again, trying to pull the boat into the water, and I don't want her hand to come off again, so I move to the stern and push.

Together, we shove the boat into the lapping black water, and Lenora jumps inside.

"Hurry!" She picks up the oars.

Every instinct I have is screaming not to do this, but I climb into the boat, instantly flashing to my dream of her, to the bodies in the water.

"Not too far, right?" I glance back at the shoreline, which is receding at a much faster rate than it should be. Lost in her rowing, Lenora doesn't answer. Night air whistles in my ears as we rush faster, faster, and my heartbeat speeds with the slap of the oars. If she doesn't stop soon, I'll jump out and swim back to shore.

"Did you take the bracelet off your statue?" I ask.

Lenora cocks her head. "What statue?"

"The one in the cathedral cavern," I say. "I left Violet's bracelet on its wrist, and when I came back, it was gone. I thought you might have taken it."

"No." Lenora grunts as she leans forward, digging the oars into the sea. "I stay out of Jonah's caves."

Something darts overhead, then wheels around and dives at her head. It's a bat, its wingspan as long as my forearm. Lenora lifts an oar and smacks it into the sea, and there's no time to see where it fell, because in seconds we're far past the point where it splashed in. She bends low and swings back, and as her weedy curls tumble forward, she blows them off her face. The simple, human gesture is made uncanny by her skeletal face. She peers at something over my shoulder, and I turn to look too.

The island is gone.

Terror surges up through my chest, and I shove it back down. Panicking won't help me now, and neither will coughing. Taking a slow breath, I memorize the pattern of stars directly above where the island used to be. I can still find my way. I'll swim until I'm tired and then I'll float, and I'll keep doing that until I'm back. I'm not afraid of the water, but it's so black tonight and I can't stop thinking of those bodies from my dream.

Lenora tips the oars up into the boat, and we slow to a drift.

"You said we wouldn't go far." I speak through clenched teeth so they won't chatter.

She grins, her broken-glass teeth flashing in the starlight. "We didn't. I gave you my word, and I intend to keep it. Unlike some people." She twitches and shivers, rattling something deep inside her chest. "Is there really a statue of me down there?"

"Yes. It's beautiful, actually." I neglect to mention its head is no longer attached to its body.

Lenora snorts, but pain flickers in her sunken eyes.

Gulping down the sour blend of revulsion and terror in my throat, I dig my fingernails into the splintery wooden bench under my legs. "What did you mean when you said there's no difference between Jonah and the island?"

"It can hear us," she says. "It creeps and it slithers and grows. It sends its earthy roots far out into the sea, and it listens to every word."

"The island, or Jonah?"

"They are the same thing."

"But how?" I'm starting to wonder if she's incapable of making sense, if I've let a ghost row me out into the middle of the ocean for no reason whatsoever. Maybe I've made the wrong choice after all.

"He's part of the island. Or the island is part of him. It's hard to say which." Lenora gives a hissing laugh as she leans back and stretches out her bare legs. Her toenails look like they might be shells. "But they can't hear us now, so we can speak plainly."

Can we, though? I try again. "Did Jonah do something to you?"

Her laugh curdles, rattling in her throat. "Something like kissing me in ethereal caves and making me think he loved me? Something like he's done to you?"

Despite all my anger, the confirmation that he did the same thing to her stings. "I guess so, yes."

"I did warn you." Lenora's sunken eyes gleam.

"Your note wasn't exactly clear," I say.

"*You* try writing with these fingers," she snarls, holding up her hand. "*You* try clawing your way back from death and pulling the pieces of yourself back together, night after night, so you can find your only sister. Then we'll talk about the subtleties of persuasive writing."

"Why can't you find Violet?" I say. "She's still on the island too."

A black tear slides down the hollow of her cheek. It smears like ink as she wipes it away. "I only wake at night, and all I find is traces of her. Strands of her hair caught on branches.

Flower stems tied in braids. The letter V scratched in the sand. I don't know what he did to separate us by day and night, but he'll never win. I may have forgotten what sunlight looks like, but I'll never give up."

She tucks her bony arms around her middle, curling in on herself, and I'm struck by how small she is, how young she must have been when she died. She can't have been much older than sixteen.

"What does Violet look like?" she asks. "Is she all right?"

"She looks"—*dead, bloated, horrible*—"about how you'd expect. She's a really sweet kid." *When she's not setting things on fire.* "She has this amazing sense of humor."

Something like a smile crosses Lenora's skull face. "She always made me laugh. Even when she didn't mean to."

"Yeah, she's still like that," I say. "But she's so lost, and she needs someone to take care of her. I . . . I want to help you find her, but I'm not sure how."

A wave smacks the boat's stern, but Lenora is lost in her thoughts, staring at the empty horizon.

"I don't see how you possibly could," she says finally.

My teeth are chattering now, and I don't bother to hide it. "Can you tell me how it all happened? I don't know if it will help, but maybe there's some detail that I'm missing, some way to figure this out." As much as I want to help Lenora and Violet, I also want to know what's going on with Jonah, how it might affect me too.

A centipede slips out of the collar of Lenora's ragged dress and crawls up her neck, and I can't believe I've just offered to help this . . . creature. But looks are deceiving, and I can't help but feel that Lenora, Violet, and I share a strange and inexplicable bond. Our deaths got disrupted. I was lucky enough to come back, but they got stuck somewhere in between.

"Jonah found us about a week after our house was built and the ship had left," she says. "Violet and I were bored half to death." She laughs bitterly, and the centipede scuttles under her hair. "Father spent all his time cataloging plants, and Mother was so ill from the heat that she scarcely left her bed. We had nothing to do but wander the island. Ironically, we still have nothing to do but wander the island."

Another wave smacks the boat, and I grab the bench tighter, but Lenora continues, unconcerned.

"When Jonah first climbed down out of a tree, Violet and I were too afraid to scream. But he promised he wouldn't hurt us, and he begged us not to tell our parents he was on the island. It was just the beginning of a long and twisted series of lies. He told us he'd jumped off his Royal Navy ship in the middle of a voyage back to England, swum to the island, and made it his home. He said if we reported him, he'd be flogged as a deserter and forced back onto his ship. Of course, we didn't wish that on him." Lenora reaches into her hair and pulls out the wriggling centipede. "Since then I've wished far worse fates on him."

"I can't blame you," I say, and she inclines her head in a gesture of thanks. Another wave hits the side of the boat, tipping us at an unsettling angle.

"The flowers started changing right after we met Jonah."

Lenora rolls the insect between her bony fingers. "At first, they'd been white, but then there were colors. Pink, purple, red."

"That's happening now too," I say, leaning forward but staying clear of the centipede.

"I thought that might be the case," she muses, letting the insect crawl onto her open palm. "I can't see the colors at night, but I knew they were no longer white."

She snaps her hand suddenly shut. The squelch makes me gag.

"Can't hear us now, can you?" she shrieks, wiping the squashed remains of the centipede on the side of the boat.

"Can he hear things . . . through bugs?" I stammer.

"I wouldn't put anything past *them*." Her voice is ice. "You'd do well not to, either."

The boat lists sideways as another wave hits it, and I hang on tight, biting my lips to keep from screaming. Lenora dips the oars back into the water and turns us so that the bow faces into the waves.

"I thought you said he couldn't hear us if we went out this far?" Now that she's turned the boat, I've lost my sense of the exact direction that we came from. Lenora begins to row at that inhuman speed again, but the waves keep coming, splashing over the bow and dousing us both.

"Where are we going now?" I yell as the hull slams down in the hollow between two waves.

"Back."

My relief dies as I spot the enormous wave barreling toward us. It's twice as high as the boat, frothing at its crest.

"I watched you two swimming in the pool," yells Lenora over the roar. "It took me far too long to realize where you were going, because that's not the way we went in." She tips the oars up and braces as the wave makes contact and launches us skyward. I bite back a sob as we hang, suspended in the starry night, then drop. With a splintering crack, we slam down, and my teeth clack together.

In the eerie lull, Lenora's black eyes gleam. "He used ropes to lower me and Violet through sinkholes and into those pretty, pretty caves. We can't swim, you see, so he had to find other ways."

"Did he kill you in the caves?" I ask.

The boat lurches as the water swells into a wall, and my body goes rigid. Up, up, up we float, like we're riding some nightmare rollercoaster with no sense of where the top is. Lenora bares her glass teeth in a grimace.

"I went into the hole in the island's heart. But it wasn't me the island wanted."

The wave breaks.

The boat careens down its back, nearly vertical, then vertical, and then we're tumbling and the night fills with the hideous sound of splintering timber and rushing water. I throw my hands up to protect my face and roll away from the flying fragments of boat and oar. Gasping in a quick breath, I dive into the black sea, pulling myself down and away from the carnage. Everything goes still and silent as the ocean welcomes me home. A long white bone floats past me and falls into the inky depths.

Already my lungs are screaming because this isn't the cenote. It's real life, and I'm about to drown if I don't pull myself together. Tucking and turning, I kick upward. As soon as my head breaks the surface, I thrash toward a floating chunk of boat and cling to it, coughing.

Starlight gleams on the perfectly calm water.

The island lies flat and black on the horizon.

Chapter

31

THE WATER CURLS as it takes hold of the rotten timber, pulling me back toward the island. Lenora is nowhere to be seen, and I can only imagine she's gone back to wherever it is she goes in the day, because the sky is starting to lighten. I hope when she comes back, she won't have to search for her bones at the bottom of the sea.

The current picks up speed, rushing me along, and I should be grateful that I'm not going to drown in the middle of the ocean, but I don't understand how Jonah—or the island—is doing this. The book mentioned strange currents and magnetic fields, but still, it seems impossible that the boy I thought was Billy's brother is capable of this.

"I'm not your puppet!" I yell at the rushing water. "You can't just make me go wherever you want."

But maybe he can. After all, I've been sleepwalking to him every night since I got here. This entire situation has gone so far beyond dangerous. But as terrified as I am of what he can do, I want justice. Not just for myself, but for Lenora and Violet too. I want closure for them. I want Lenora to stop having to put her bones back together every night, and I want Violet to find someone who loves her, who can take care of her. I don't know what moving on means for them, where they'll go or what will happen, but they can't stay in this island prison forever.

The cliff with the house at the top comes into view. As my toes brush the sandy bottom, I let go of the timber, which beaches itself in front of the wooden stairs. I guess I should be grateful that I didn't have to trek back through the woods from the other side of the island, but it's just another reminder that I am a puppet.

My arms and legs ache, and all I want to do is sleep for a few hours, but I'm afraid I'll sleepwalk again if I do. As I climb the stairs, I muffle my coughs in my elbow. No one else is awake, so I change out of my wet clothes, slip into the kitchen, and pull a bag of coffee from the fridge. Caffeine is exactly the wrong thing for my nerves, but I won't make it through this day without it. Once it's done brewing, I take the entire pot back to my room along with a mug and a few pieces of toast, and I sit on the bed with my anxiety picnic, watching an impossibly lovely sunrise paint the sky.

At seven thirty, I tuck Lenora's folding knife into my shorts pocket. I leave a note for my mom saying I'm going out for the morning with Billy, and I head down the beach to the lighthouse. Sitting in the palm tree shadows near the jetty, I wait for Billy to emerge. I bet Jonah doesn't feel like a creep when he does this, but I do.

Luckily Billy's the first one out of the lighthouse. He jumps into the sand at the side of the jetty and starts gathering up an armload of humane animal traps. As I step out of the shadows, he startles and drops one on his foot.

"Jesus, you scared me," he wheezes, pulling out his inhaler.

"Sorry," I say. "And I'm sorry again about everything else."

Billy says nothing as we collect the traps. He holds out his arms for me to pile the last two on top of the others, but I keep them.

"I'll help you," I say.

He wrinkles his nose. "You don't want to do that."

"You're right, I don't," I say. "But I'm going to anyway. Where do these go? In the woods? Near the garbage cans?"

"In the woods. And we have to check the other ones for rats." His tone is still frosty, but he did use the word "we" in his plans, which seems like progress.

"Great," I say. "Let's go."

As we step under the leafy canopy, the temperature sky-rockets and the air grows sticky. The flowers have faded to a mottled pink—the color of raw meat—and I'm careful not to let them touch my skin as we head down the path.

"So you don't kill the rats?" I say.

"Nope," says Billy. "My dad puts them all in a big cage, and when it gets full, he brings it over to Tortola and sells them to a guy who owns a python."

"Gross," I say. "I'm not sure that's any better than them getting instantly killed in a regular trap."

Billy shrugs. "Snakes have to eat too. Is it really any worse than the chickens you buy at the store? At least the rats got to be free for most of their lives."

I think back to the roast chicken we ate a few nights ago. He's right that the rats probably had a better life than those chickens. Still, it doesn't make me feel great about what we're doing.

"Anyway," continues Billy. "I usually let at least half of them go. The snake doesn't need *that* many. Don't tell my dad. He says they're an invasive species, but they've been here longer than we have."

"Some of their ancestors probably came over on the boat with the Wells family," I say. And Jonah's ship too. I'm dying to tell Billy everything I learned last night, but I'm wary of what Lenora said about the island hearing.

"Sean's still lying about you guys," mutters Billy as he shoves through a wall of ferns, not bothering to hold them for me. "He swears he never saw you before yesterday. I almost punched him."

"He wasn't lying," I say.

The forest goes silent, and we both pause. Then Billy scoffs. "Okay, well, one of you was."

Before I can answer, he drops to his knees and crawls under a bush with a red strip of plastic tied around one of its dripping branches. When he comes back out, dragging a trap, his T-shirt is spattered with water and his damp hair sticks up like porcupine quills.

"Something's in here, but it's not moving," he says.

In the back corner of the trap is a rat-sized lump, and my stomach flutters as I crouch to get a better look. A whiff of decay wafts out. I muffle a cough in my elbow, fighting the urge to tell Billy to just throw the trap back under the bush.

He opens the wire door and pulls out a leaf-wrapped bundle.

"Don't," I say as he starts to peel it open.

His blond eyebrows lift. "What are you afraid of?"

What am I not afraid of at this point? But now that he's started opening it, I need to know what's inside. The leaf falls open, releasing a wave of rotten stench and revealing a blood-stained paper package. My mind races to a million dark and gruesome places. Dead rodents, bugs, body parts. Billy leans away, gagging, but I can't stop myself—I snatch the parcel up and tear it open.

Inside, a white flower bud sits in a pool of crimson sap. Slowly the petals unfurl, and with a small puff of putrid air, the flower whispers my name.

"What. The. Fuck." Billy is on his feet, backing away.

The warm sap drips onto my hands, onto my legs, but I can't move.

Chapter

32

"COME ON, ADDIE. Get up." Billy is tugging on my arm, but my legs don't want to straighten, and there's blood all over my hands and legs and staining my clothes, and black spots are dancing in my vision.

Not blood. Sap. It's sap, and I am okay. I just need to stand up and walk away from this. But every breath I take reeks of flowers and rot, and there's no oxygen getting to my lungs. I'm afraid if I try to stand, I'll pass out.

Breathe, Addie, breathe.

The video begins to play in my mind: the glittering sea and the boat full of screaming people. My dead eyes, the trail of pink foam. Someone is shaking me, pressing something to my mouth, and maybe it's a safety diver giving me CPR.

"Addie, hey. *Hey.* Come on."

My eyes blink open, and there's Billy's worried face and his water bottle pressed to my mouth. I take a long gulp and cough it back out, spattering red liquid onto the ground.

"That's not water," I gasp, scrabbling backward before the vines start to grow.

"It's Kool-Aid." Billy pauses. "Okay, it's my mom's organic version of Kool-Aid. I think it has beets or something in it."

Who carries Kool-Aid around in a water bottle? is what I

want to say, but I don't have enough breath. I wipe my mouth with the back of my hand, smearing sap and fruit-flavored liquid across my cheek. "Help me up. Please."

"Drink some more of this first," he says, holding out the bottle again. "Your mom and David will kill me if you faint and hit your head."

For some reason, this is hilarious. The harder I laugh, the more nervous Billy looks.

"If that's the worst thing that happens to me, I will be very lucky," I say, gulping down the rest of my laughter before I start to cough. More sap smears as I wipe my streaming eyes.

"You look like a murder victim," says Billy, rummaging in his backpack and pulling out a crumpled beach towel. I do my best to clean off my face, but everything is so impossibly sticky. Already, flies and mosquitos are swarming.

"Just leave the traps," says Billy. "I'll come back for them later."

He hovers close as we walk back through the woods, like I'm about to keel over at any moment, but I'm better now. Physically, anyway.

"Can we take the kayaks out?" I ask as we step onto the beach.

Billy gawps. "You're kidding, right?"

I cross the beach and crouch at the tideline, splashing water onto my sticky face and using sand to scrub my hands and legs. There's not much I can do about my shirt, so I peel it off. Thankfully, I wore my swimsuit underneath.

"Nope, not kidding." I drop my voice. "Please, just trust me."

It might be foolish to get back into a boat, but I'm hoping that if we don't go too far out, we'll at least be able to talk without the unsettling sensation of someone listening. Even if they are technically still listening.

The bright yellow kayaks lie upside-down on the beach to our left, and Billy ducks into the lighthouse to tell his parents we're taking them out. By the time he returns, I've got both boats in the water.

"Why are we doing this?" he asks as we clamber inside and begin to paddle.

"I'll tell you in a minute." The irony isn't lost on me that I'm behaving like Lenora right now. I just hope I don't end up like her.

Sunlight streams down on the gentle turquoise waves, and even out on the ocean, there's almost no breeze. It's even more humid than yesterday. We paddle out until the sandy ocean floor drops away, and I glance down into the gorgeous deep water with a sigh.

The water gets choppier as we round the northern tip of the island, but then it flattens again. This part of the island has no beach, just a rocky incline that connects the forest to the sea. In one spot, a small waterfall tumbles into a rock pool, then down into the sea. A perfect, hidden gem of a spot, if you don't know what lurks underneath. I pull up close enough to grab the side of Billy's kayak and motion for him to lean in.

"I wasn't lying about Sean, and neither was he," I whisper.

Billy rolls his eyes, but I cut him off before he can speak. "It wasn't Sean I was meeting. It was . . . someone else."

Billy's eyes narrow. "Then why did you tell me it was him?"

"Because I thought it *was* him," I say. "Look, I know I'm the biggest fool ever for not realizing it wasn't your brother, but he told me that's who he was, and I'd never met Sean until the fire, so I believed him."

Billy's silent for a moment. "Okay, but who else could non-Sean be?"

"Jonah Burke," I say. Back on the island, a wave of movement rushes through the bushes, even though there's no wind, and shivers race across my damp skin.

"Who?" Billy stares at me like I've just spoken a foreign language.

"He's one of the crew members of the *Fortuna*," I say. "The sailors who found Eulalie. I'm pretty sure he's been on the island ever since then. Have you ever seen a guy who looks a few years older than me? Ashy blond hair, tall, good-looking if you ignore the fact that he's kind of a sociopath?"

The bushes rustle again, and I swear I hear laughter.

"I have absolutely no idea who that is," says Billy.

Pushing away from his kayak, I dip my paddle into the water again and motion for him to follow me out deeper. A wave gushes up from out of nowhere, tipping me sideways and almost capsizing my boat. That was a warning.

"I wonder why you've never seen him in all the time you've been here," I say.

"I've never seen Lenora either," says Billy. "Is he only around at night like her?"

"Mostly," I say. "But the last time I saw him, we watched

the sun rise and he didn't shrivel up or turn into dust or anything. And he doesn't look all ghosty like Violet and Lenora. There's something different about him."

"So he stays hidden away—unless there are hot girls on the island," muses Billy, and I jab him with my paddle.

"I think he's preying on girls," I whisper. "I met Lenora last night, and she told me he lied to her and tricked her, and now she and Violet are stuck here."

"Jesus, do you ever sleep?" says Billy. "I swear you've done way more stuff here in a couple of days than I have in years."

"You should consider yourself lucky," I say. "We went out in a rowboat in the middle of the night and he—or the island, I don't know which—didn't want us talking, so he—it—sent a bunch of huge waves that smashed the boat and almost drowned me."

Billy opens his mouth, then shuts it. He tries again, then stops. "Are you sure you weren't dreaming?"

"Positive," I say. "Listen, I know how ridiculous it all sounds. It's what Lenora told me, and she's a ghost, so who knows how much of a grasp she even has on reality." My words are spilling out at a frantic pace, and I force myself to slow down. "But I'm sure there's some truth in what she said. Jonah did something to her and her sister, and I need to figure out what it is, because I'm afraid I might be next."

Billy drums his fingers on the side of his kayak, and I wait for him to tell me I'm hallucinating.

"Do you think that flower was from him?" he says.

"It was definitely from him." I glance at the swaying

bushes and shudder. How could I possibly have kissed a boy who thinks that's a romantic gesture? Then again, maybe he didn't mean for it to be a romantic gesture.

"I guess you probably want to leave now," says Billy. "I mean, I wouldn't blame you. That's creepy as hell."

"I do want to leave." Deep in the forest, a bird shrieks, and I drop my voice to a whisper. "But I'm not going to. I can't. Not until I help Lenora and Violet. Or until it's time for us to go home. But I'm going to figure this out before then."

Billy laughs, incredulous. "You're kidding, right?"

"I'm really not," I say. "When I make a plan, I make it happen." Except when my plan is to force my body to recover from a near-fatal injury in record time. "Anyway, if I don't do something, what's to stop him from doing this to the next girl who comes here?"

A wave rolls in from the island, tipping us a little harder than the last time.

Billy rubs the back of his neck. "Maybe I could hack into my dad's reservation system and cancel anybody who's planning to come here with their daughters?"

"And anybody who swims in that cenote or dives without permission?" I whisper, turning my kayak to face the waves and gesturing for him to do the same. "I don't think Roland's death was an accident either. But how could we explain any of this to your parents?"

"Considering I tried for months to get them to believe me about Violet and they made me see a psychiatrist who put me on meds?" Billy makes a long, wet fart sound.

"So we need to do this on our own," I say. "If you're willing to help, I mean."

"Of course I am," says Billy. "You really thought I was going to leave you all on your own with some undead stalker-slash-murderer?"

I can't help but laugh even as I shush him.

"Do you have an actual plan?" he asks.

Another wave rushes toward us, this one wild and foaming.

"I'm working on something," I say quietly. "Do you think you can create a distraction later this afternoon so I can talk to Violet?"

"Sure, what did you have in mind?"

"Whatever you want." I pick up my paddle and gesture for him to follow me. "The world . . . well, the island is your oyster."

Billy laughs, and as we slosh over another wave, heading back toward the northern point, he mutters something I can't quite hear.

"What?" I say over my shoulder.

"I'm so glad you didn't hook up with my brother!" he yells.

Chapter

33

We're out snorkeling for the afternoon. Sandwiches are in the fridge. Love you.

Mom xoxo

BILLY'S ON THE other side of the island, setting up his distraction, and I'm absentmindedly eating a tomato-basil-mozzarella sandwich while drinking my way through another pot of coffee and assembling Violet's new bracelet. I've collected a handful of pretty trinkets: a pink shell with a hole in its center, a triangular piece of sea glass wound up in wire to create a pendant, a silver bell from one of my mother's anklets, a handful of purple plastic beads from a Mardi Gras necklace that Billy stole from the real Sean, and orange, green, and yellow ribbons from Melinda's crafting supplies.

It's too much for a little girl's wrist, but nothing feels special enough to stand on its own. I sip my scalding coffee and stare at the gaudy bracelet, zipping my medallion back and forth on its chain.

Wait.

My fingers close around the medallion. Even though this is the last possession I'd ever choose to give up, it's the only thing that means enough to replace a bracelet made by Violet's sister. I'm not sure I can let it go, though. I've had it since I was ten, and when I started competing, I tucked it inside my wet suit and wore it on every single dive. After my accident happened, I wondered if it stopped protecting me or if it saved my life.

Maybe it's time to let it save someone else.

I pick up the walkie-talkie Billy gave me. "Are you almost ready?"

The line chirps, and his crackling voice blares out. "Give me two more minutes and then go for it."

Unclasping the safety pin from my neck, I head outside and sit on the patio beside Violet's favorite bush. It's not too late to go back into the house and get that handmade bracelet. A regular three-year-old would love all the bright baubles, but I know it won't mean anything to Violet. This gift has to mean something.

I let the medallion swing back and forth like a pendulum, ticking off the seconds until Billy is ready. It's time to start letting go of the things that make me feel safe and trust myself.

From the distance comes a crackle, then a loud whistling hiss. Billy's distraction is moving forward.

"Violet?" I call.

Another shrill whine and then a loud bang as Billy sets off another firework.

"Violet, are you there?"

The bush shivers and a dirty, gray face pokes out.

"Is there thunder?" asks Violet, peering up at the blue sky.

"No, that's just Billy doing some stuff on the other side of the island," I say. "Can we talk for a minute?"

"Are you going to lie to me some more?" Her lip juts out in a pout, and I scoot closer.

"No more lying," I say. "And because I'm not lying anymore, I need to tell you that I can't find your sister's bracelet."

Violet's lip trembles, but as she opens her mouth to wail, a crackling crash cuts her off. "Is Billy *esploding* things over there?" she asks.

"No, he's getting rid of some old . . . stuff," I say, thinking it's better not to distract her with a fireworks show. "But listen, I wanted to give you something of mine to make up for losing that bracelet. Something really special to me."

The medallion glints in the sunlight as I hold it up, and Violet's sunken eyes snap to it.

"My grandfather gave this to me," I say. "He died too, and I miss him, but probably not as much as you miss Lenora."

She grabs the medallion, and my heart snags as the talisman leaves my fingers.

"What's on it?" A spider dangles from the hem of Violet's dress, and another crouches on the bodice like some creepy, living brooch.

"That's Saint Brendan, the patron saint of sailors and divers and stuff that has to do with the ocean," I say. "When I was ten years old, my grandpa taught me how to spearfish and dive, and he said this would keep me safe."

"Mama used to pray to the saints sometimes." Violet holds

the medallion about an inch away from her eye. "Is it real silver?"

"Yes," I say. "So you have to be really careful with it, okay?"

"*You* are the one who's always losing things, Addie-dee." Violet gives me a weary look.

"You're right," I say. "It's just that it means a lot to me, and I'll miss it. But I think it should belong to you."

She nods solemnly and then turns around so I can put it around her neck. It hangs all the way down to her stomach.

"Thank you," she says. "I almost forgive you now."

"That's fair." Seeing my protective medallion on this tiny, lost girl makes me feel better than wearing it ever did.

Another boom thunders through the trees, shivering their leaves, and I hope Billy knows what he's doing.

"I want to keep helping you," I say. "But I need to know what happened if I'm going to fix everything. Do you think you could tell me more about Lenora and . . ." I trail off, not wanting to draw his attention.

"Jonah?" she says, and I clamp my hand over her mouth, instantly wishing I hadn't. Violet's lips are coated in a film of slime and dust, and they're unbearably cold. Her sandpaper tongue flicks across my finger, and I bite back a scream as she dissolves into hitching giggles. The spider on her dress leaps into her pocket.

"Yes, him," I say as another boom reverberates across the island.

"She was always writing about him in her diary," says Violet. "I tried to read it, but I don't know all of my letters yet."

"Do you still have her diary?" I ask.

Violet twists the chain tighter and tighter around her neck, and I want to tell her to stop because it will break, but it's not my necklace anymore. Then she stands up, bends forward, and lets go, watching as the chain unwinds and the medallion spins.

"Violet, do you have your sister's diary?" I ask.

She starts to hum, swaying back and forth, and I decide to try a different line of questioning.

"What happened to Lenora the night she disappeared?"

Violet begins to twirl, her ragged dress whirling around her. "Jack and Jill went down a rope into a cave of water," she sings, throwing her head back as she spins. "Violet fell down and broke her crown."

"Did you try to lower yourself into the caves too?" I say.

"I *did* lower myself." Violet staggers out of her turn, trying to aim her dizzy gaze at me. "I fell into the water, but it still hurt and then I was bleeding. Look."

She lifts up her hair. Behind her ear, there's a black gash, ragged and crusty at the edges.

I hiss in my breath. "That must have hurt a lot."

Violet nods solemnly. "I cried, but nobody heared me."

My heart aches for this child, trapped and crying, all alone in a cave. "Was that how you . . . died?"

She starts to twirl again. "I'm not dead, though."

I start to answer, then gulp down my words. Today is not the day I explain mortality to a ghost.

"Spin with me, Addie-dee!" she yells, throwing her arms out and whirling faster. "It's so much fun!"

Another crackling boom shakes the forest, and I hope Billy isn't going to set anything on fire.

"Can you tell me what happened after that?" I say, getting up and turning in a slow circle.

"I went to the big cave that's like a church, and I saw them running away," says Violet. "I yelled for them to wait but they didn't. Not even Nora. Jonah was whispering in her ear, telling her more of his lies, and she was laughing. I ran to catch them, but my head was bleeding and I fell down again, and when I got up, they were gone. But I knew where they were going."

Bile wells up my throat as I spin faster, the leafy branches overhead turning to a green blur.

"I came to the tunnel under the water, and I was afraid, but the whispers told me not to be scared," says Violet. "Jonah always makes us grab on to a rope and hold our breath and then he pulls us through. But the rope wasn't there, and neither was Nora."

I swallow a cough, unable to comprehend what kind of monster lets a three-year-old child hold a rope while he pulls her through a thirty-foot-long underwater tunnel.

"I was crying for Nora to come back, but she didn't hear me," says Violet. "I waited and waited and waited, and then the whispers told me swimming wasn't that hard, so I decided to try."

"Oh God, please tell me you didn't swim through that tunnel," I say, nausea filling my mouth.

"Mama says we mustn't take the Lord's name in vain," says Violet.

"I'm sorry," I say as another boom thunders across the island. "Did you try to swim?"

"Yes, but it was too hard," says Violet. "So I decided to crawl on my belly through the tunnel."

I stagger to a stop, and the green keeps whirling around me.

"I crawled as fast as I could, but it was more like floating and it was much slower than when Jonah pulled us on the rope," says Violet. "The rocks were cutting my hands and I kept bumping my head even more, and then I decided to go back but I couldn't turn around, and I only just wanted Nora, but she was gone and then . . . and then . . ."

She collapses in a gasping heap, and I rush over to her.

"It's okay, you don't have to say it," I whisper, smoothing her dusty hair. "You poor, poor thing, I'm so sorry."

"I should have listened to Mama and stayed at home," she sobs. "I didn't listen to Mama, and now everyone is gone."

"Shh, it's okay. Everybody makes mistakes, and none of this was your fault." I try to pull her onto my lap, but she won't let me. "I know I'm not Nora or your mom, but I still care about you."

"You're going to leave too," she says, and it's true. If I don't figure something out soon, I'm going to be just like everyone else who left her. Violet's eyes snap to something in the woods behind me; she gasps and jumps to her feet. I'm not fast enough to grab her before she dashes away into the bushes.

Aa-dee-dee-dee, call the birds.

Dread makes every part of me heavy as I turn slowly around, but there's nothing there. The walkie-talkie chirps, startling me.

Billy's voice blares out. "Addie? You there?"

"Hey, I'm here."

"All good with Violet?"

"Yeah, we talked for a little while, but she just disappeared." A chill washes over me as I scan the bushes and trees.

"Good. My mom heard the fireworks and went ballistic. I have to clean it all up and then go straight home."

"Thanks for doing that," I say. "Sorry you got in trouble."

"Eh, she'll get over it," he says. "You should have seen the fireworks, though! It was awesome. Are you okay by yourself? You can come hang out at the lighthouse until your mom gets back."

"Thanks for the offer," I say. "Violet mentioned Lenora had a diary, and I want to see if I can find it at their house."

"Are you sure you want to do that alone?"

I'm not sure. Not at all. But I also don't want to wait any longer.

"Yeah, it's fine," I say. "I'll check in with you in a half hour, okay?"

"Be careful," he says. "Don't cough on the ground."

"I won't, I promise."

A breeze sweeps through the trees, bringing the sweet scent

of rot and flowers, and my stomach fills with the same nerves I always get before a competition dive. Before I start down the stone stairs and into the woods, I check to make sure Lenora's knife is still in my pocket.

Chapter
34

THE FOREST BREATHES in as I step onto the path. Then it exhales, branches and leaves and blossoms rustling and bending in my direction, and Lenora's words echo in my head.

He's part of the island. Or the island is part of him. It's hard to say which.

I trail my fingers through the plants as I make my way down the path, and the mottled pink flowers darken to fuchsia and magenta. There's something both alluring and hideous about the way they—the island, Jonah, maybe both—respond to me.

Aa-dee-dee-dee, warbles a bird, then another and another, a chorus of inhuman cries all calling my name. I should run home and lock myself in my room. I should wait at the lighthouse until my mother and David get back. I should get on a plane and never come back to this strange, sinister place that inexplicably seems to love me. Or that wants something from me. I need to remember those aren't the same thing.

The walls of the Wells house are covered in trailing vines and crimson flowers today. It's almost unrecognizable from the first time I came here—it looks more like a living, breathing thing than an old pile of ruins. I pause in the doorway and pull Lenora's knife out, my heart rocketing as I unfold the sharp blade from its ivory handle.

Breathe, Addie, just breathe. It's only a house.

My arm brushes the threshold, and a vine wraps around my wrist. With a quick flick, I slice it off with the knife, and it falls, shriveling and blackening, to the dirt. Another vine crawls toward my ankle, and I hop away, hurrying for Lenora's room. I should have waited for Billy to come with me after all. But I'm here now, and I can't let myself be afraid of a bunch of plants. I can hear them crawling the walls, their leaves slithering over the mossy stone.

"Leave me alone or I'll come back with fire," I whisper, and the rustling pauses.

There's nothing around or under Lenora's harp. I use the knife to hack the vines away from the wall where I found it, but there aren't any cracks big enough to hold anything resembling a diary. Sweating and dizzy, I rip the plants from the other walls, but there are no more breaks or cracks, and the greenery grows back as fast as I can clear it.

"Where did you put it, Lenora?" I mutter, but the only answer is a bird repeating my name. I rack my brain, trying to remember what Violet said: that she tried to read it but couldn't.

Kicking vines out of my way, I hurry to the kitchen, to the nest on the floor beside the fireplace, and start pulling things out. Shredded palm fronds, wet banana leaves, sticky white feathers, and rotting clumps of seaweed. The remains of the flower crown I made for Violet, now brown and shriveled. Tufts of unrecognizable fur, stringy strands of hair. The stench is unbearable, and I pull the neck of my shirt up over my nose as I sift through the decaying debris, but it doesn't help.

My fingers find dirt at the bottom of the nest, and I'm about to give up when the papery edge of something slices my thumb. Eyes watering, I reach once more into the festering pile and pull out half of a small book, snapped down the center of its spine. The back cover is made of rotten gray cloth, and the yellow pages are soaked through, the faint handwriting on them nearly washed away.

Vines slither around my feet, winding around my ankles; I slice them off with the knife and dash outside, not stopping until the crumbling, writhing old house is far behind me. Then I drop the half-book, cover my mouth tight with both hands, and cough until my lungs are empty and my stomach cramps.

Still gasping, I slide down to sit against the wide trunk of a tree, holding the diary in a beam of sunlight that's managed to slip through the dense canopy. The writing is tiny and cramped, and the old-fashioned cursive letters are hard to decipher, but my brain slowly makes sense of the words.

> *I am coming to the inevitable and devastating conclusion that the flowers aren't changing because of me. It's Violet. I should tell Jonah that it's my sister whose touch turns them from white to pink to red, not mine, but he is so enamored with the idea that it's me.*
>
> *"The island loves you," he tells me, and I think perhaps he's saying he loves me too.*
>
> *What will happen if I confess that it isn't me*

the island loves? Will I remain so fascinating to
him? Will he still find me at night and take me
to the secret places he knows? Will he still

The rest of the writing on the page has been washed away. It's all so similar—the things Jonah has been saying to me, the things we've done—it turns my stomach. But in this case, I'm certain it's me who's changing the flowers, me who the island loves. I don't know if that makes it better or worse. Nerves rattling, I reach for my medallion before remembering it's not mine anymore. I turn the page.

Tonight he's taking me to the island's heart.
He won't say what that is or what it means, but
I can tell by the way his eyes dance when he
speaks of it that it's something truly remarkable.
We must go alone, he says, and my own heart
trembles when I contemplate the reasons why
that might be.

"Your heart should be trembling," I mutter, but in truth I've been just as foolish and gullible as Lenora. If Violet hadn't set that fire in the lighthouse, I'd still be falling for Jonah's charming lies.

"Find anything interesting?"

With a gasp, I look up, and there he is, leaning against a tree.

Under the moon and the dim light of caves, Jonah was

undeniably good-looking. In daylight, he is recklessly, impossibly beautiful. His skin is bronzed to a deep tan, and his arms are lean and muscled. His wide-set eyes are just as dark as they were at night, the irises so large there's almost no white. He searches my face, just like when we met, like he's looking for the answer to a question no one asked. This boy is a liar and a murderer, but it takes a long minute to shove that reminder back into my brain.

"What do you want?" I say.

"I want to explain." His accent is different now, leaning more toward English than American. His black gaze holds mine, and it's nearly impossible to look away.

"Explain which part?" I say. "The part where you pretended to be someone else for days, or the part where you dumped me into the open ocean in the middle of the night?"

"That wasn't me," he says. "It was the island."

I scoff. "And you had nothing to do with it?"

Jonah's gaze drifts sideways. "Not really. But I wouldn't have let you get hurt."

The implication that he was keeping me safe—after my boat was literally smashed apart—fills me with rage. "Okay, then how about you explain the part where you *killed* two girls?"

He sighs. "I didn't kill them. Will you come for a walk with me? I'll explain everything."

"Why can't we talk here?" It's not like I'm any safer in these empty woods than anywhere else, but it feels better to control where I am.

"I want to show you a few things." As Jonah steps closer, a sunbeam catches the angular planes of his face.

Murderer, he's a murderer.

"I'm not going back to the cenote or the caves," I say. "And you'd better not try to take me to the island's heart."

He laughs. "You've already been to the island's heart. And nothing terrible happened to you there, other than kissing me."

My cheeks go hot at the memory.

"I pretended to be someone else, and I lied to you," he says. "But I wasn't pretending then."

I grind the heels of my hands into my eyes, trying to scrub away the mental image of his lips against mine. "Why were you pretending to be Sean in the first place?"

"Do you remember when we met, and I asked you if you were real?" he says. "You said you wished you weren't. I agreed with you, but deep down, I was wishing the opposite."

"Why?" Wrapped up in my fury is a desperate need to know why he did this, why he's still doing this. I need to make some sense of this sordid story.

"I've been trapped here for almost three hundred years," he says. "When Lenora told you I was part of the island, she was right. I've lost all sense of time, all sense of humanity. When you crawled out of the ocean and thought I was a normal person, I wanted it to be true so badly, I just . . . let it be true. It felt like reality was suspended that night, didn't it?"

I don't want to agree with him, but everything about that night still feels like a dream.

"I knew you'd find out eventually," he says. "I didn't think it'd last more than a day or two, but I decided to hang on to it as long as I could. I'd been numb for so long, I just wanted to feel something."

"How did you think *I'd* feel when I found out?" I say.

He sighs. "I figured I'd disappear until you went home, and you'd get over it. Maybe you'd think you imagined me."

"But you didn't disappear," I say. "Why?"

Jonah rubs the back of his neck and looks away. "I told you, I wasn't pretending that night when I kissed you. I'm sorry. It was manipulative and cruel, and I somehow got caught up in my own lies."

It's still manipulative, him telling me this. I absolutely do not want my pulse to be rocketing the way it is right now. But I need to know everything about that night with Lenora so I can figure out how to reverse whatever he's done. With a nervous cough, I get to my feet, tucking the diary into the back pocket of my shorts and making sure the walkie-talkie is still clipped there and I still have Lenora's knife.

"All right," I say. "What do you want to show me?"

Chapter

35

THE FIRST PLACE we stop is a massive tree at the edge of the beach. Ancient and gnarled, its limbs stretch in all directions, some weaving deep into the forest and others reaching for the blue-green sea.

"This is where I found her," says Jonah, reaching up to grab an overhanging branch.

"Lenora?" I say, remembering her story of how he climbed down out of a tree and startled her and Violet.

"Eulalie." He lifts his feet, and his forearms flex as he hangs. "The day after we came ashore, I spotted her, sitting up in this tree. She couldn't speak a word, but she made it clear that she didn't want me to tell anyone she was here." He gives a rueful laugh as he swings back and forth. "I actually felt honored that she chose me."

"You drew her in this tree," I say.

Jonah nods. "It's funny that my drawing made it back to England, but I didn't."

"Not really *that* funny, though," I say, and he gives me an unreadable look.

"In less than a day, Eulalie was speaking simple phrases and slowly putting together sentences," he says. "I wondered if she'd spoken English as a child and somehow forgotten, but all she could tell me was that she'd been on a ship with her parents, that it had sunk, and that she'd washed up alone on the island. She didn't know the name of the place she'd come from. Sometimes I wonder if any of that was even true."

"How else could she have gotten here?" I ask.

"Maybe she was always here." Jonah walks his feet up the trunk and pulls himself onto the branch. "I kept her secret for two days before she was ready to meet the rest of the *Fortuna*'s crew, who were all just as captivated with her as I was. But still, I was the one she singled out, the one she woke at night to swim with. She showed me the island's secrets, things I could hardly believe, even as I saw them happening. The flowers turned pink the day I met Eulalie, and that was just the beginning."

Goose bumps whisper across my arms. "Did you love her?"

"I was in love with the idea of her, with all of this." Jonah gestures at the trees, the white sandy shore, the glittering water. "But no, I didn't love Eulalie. I was betrothed to a green-eyed girl named Annabel who was waiting for me back in England."

Jonah leaps down from the tree, stumbling and landing on his knees. Blood seeps through the dirt that coats his skin, but when he wipes it away, there are no cuts. A vine slithers around his ankle and crawls up his calf. He ignores it.

"Eulalie kissed me one night in the pool—the cenote, as you like to call it," he says. "I never should have let it happen, but I felt like I was losing control, like I was drunk on this place. She told me she loved me, and she wanted us to be together forever."

"Clearly that didn't work out," I say, and his dark eyes snap to me.

"Clearly not." He runs his hand over his jaw. "I told her the truth, that I loved Annabel and planned to marry her as soon as I got back." Jonah blows his breath out in a gust. "She didn't take that very well."

"She trapped you here and went back to England on your ship?" I say, and he nods.

"I felt terrible for kissing her, for leading her on like that. She told me she'd forgive me if I jumped into the island's heart. She swore it was safe, that the island would catch me and wouldn't let me die." He gives a rueful laugh. "She wasn't technically lying."

"So you jumped," I say.

"I did," he says. "And when I finally woke, the landing boats were leaving. I tried to swim after them, but I was so weak I couldn't yell loud enough for anyone to hear. I couldn't make it farther than a hundred yards offshore before the island dragged me back. The ship sailed away, and I was alone. I actually had no idea what happened to Eulalie until the Wells family arrived and Lenora told me her story."

"And you never saw your fiancée again?" I ask.

Jonah shakes his head. "Annabel's been dead for two centuries. She's dust now, and here I still am."

I want to tell him I'm sorry, but the word sticks in my throat. It's truly, utterly horrible, what happened to Jonah. And yet I'm still so furious.

"I used to count the days," he says. "Then I counted the

months, then the years. I stopped counting on Annabel's hundredth birthday."

His face twists with raw emotion, and my stomach twinges, but my feelings are tangled. I want to empathize with him, but I can't quite summon up the compassion. Not after everything he's done.

"What Eulalie did to you was hideous," I say. "But how could you wish that on somebody else? How could you think Lenora would be okay with you making that choice for her?"

He flinches. "Lenora made her own choice."

I start to argue, but he turns and heads off into the woods. "Come on, there's more," he says.

It isn't a good idea to keep following him, but he hasn't done anything aggressive or taken me anywhere unsafe yet, and if I'm going to help Violet and Lenora—and possibly save myself, if things go sideways—I need the rest of the pieces to this puzzle. I need to hear the end of Jonah's story. Sweaty and slightly nauseated, I unclip the walkie-talkie.

"Billy, are you there?"

Silence.

"Billy? Hello?"

Jonah's invisible in the woods now, but the birds are still calling me.

Finally, the line crackles.

"Hey," says Billy. "What's up?"

"I'm with Jonah," I say.

"What?" he yells. "Addie, what the hell are you doing?"

"That's a very good question," I say. "I'm pretty sure I'm getting answers." I just hope they're true answers.

"Are you okay?" yells Billy. "Jonah, can you hear me, you absolute turd?"

From somewhere deep in the trees, I hear his laugh.

"Yeah, I'm fine," I say. "But I'm going to check in with you in twenty minutes, okay?"

"Fifteen minutes," says Billy.

"Fifteen," I say. "Thanks, Billy."

"Be careful!" he yells, and I tuck the walkie-talkie back into my waistband and wipe my sweaty hands on my legs.

Breathe, Addie, just breathe.

Chapter
36

THERE'S NO SIGN of where Jonah has gone, but as soon as I step into the humid forest, the bushes begin to sway and shift, and a path opens up. A hundred flowers all tip toward me, unfurling their petals, and a cloud of pink pollen wafts out, tickling my cheeks and eyelids and nose.

Aa-dee-dee-dee, call the birds.

The buzzing insect drone fills my ears, the heat drapes around me like a blanket, and everything slows until I'm moving like I'm underwater. I understand what Jonah meant when he said he felt drunk on this place. It's the same feeling I get when I'm in the cenote. The dirt under my feet is softening, slowing me down even more, and I'm not sure I mind. Pollen billows in the slanted sunbeams. It coats my face and slides, smooth and syrupy, down my throat.

More flowers turn their faces to me, following my every step, and as reality begins to bend, the pain in my body melts away. It's like diving, this narrowing, this erasing. I stretch my arms out into the plants, and sap runs down my skin, warm as a kiss.

The path rounds a bend, and there's a clearing full of feathery fronds and scarlet flowers shaped like bells. Nothing makes sense, and I wonder if I'm sleepwalking again. I don't think I care. I sink to the ground, and the tiny flower bells whisper *Addie, Addie, Addie*. It's like floating. It's better than floating. A shiver rolls over me, and the island shivers with me, petals drifting down and landing feather-light on my face.

A sudden, high-pitched chirp. Fizzing static, and then Billy's voice.

"Addie? You there?"

My eyes snap open; I'm lying in a jumble of ferns and flowers. My ears are ringing with the shrill whine of insects, and my lungs are on fire. I reach for the walkie-talkie, but there's a vine wrapped around my wrist. With a shudder that makes my jaw hurt, I rip it off. It falls to the ground, shriveling, as I grab the walkie-talkie.

"I'm here. Can you hear me?"

"Loud and clear. Everything okay?"

I bury my face in the crook of my elbow and cough. "Mostly."

"Do you want me to come find you? My mom's taking a nap. I can sneak out."

"No," I say, still wheezing a little. "I need you to get out of trouble as quickly as possible, okay?"

"Got it. Talk to you soon."

The insect whine cuts out as Jonah appears, threading his way through the plants like a cat.

"What just happened?" I say.

He crouches beside me, then reaches for my hand. I shrink back.

"I already promised I wouldn't do anything to hurt you," he says.

"You probably promised Lenora the same thing."

He flashes a wicked grin. "She didn't ask me to."

"That doesn't make it—"

Gently, he takes my hand and presses it to the center of his chest. His heart pounds under the thin fabric of his shirt, a steady, measured rhythm, and I feel my own heartbeat slowing to match it. The greenery around us throbs with the beat, the colors melt, and I should pull my hand away, but the pain is draining from my lungs again, replaced by that peaceful, floating sensation. I draw in a luxurious, clean breath and exhale. It feels like blowing bubbles.

Jonah watches me intently. "Just let go," he says, and I shouldn't but I do.

I can feel every molecule of the island. The grains of sand as the sea rushes over them, the individual petals on each flower, the whirring heartbeats of the birds. I am everywhere at once. I am the sunlight painting the dewy leaves, the pollen floating on the breeze. The centipede crawling along a branch, each leg moving in synchronicity. I am the crust of bark on the tree, I am the sap flowing up its trunk, the roots stretching down through the soil. I am the water flowing under the soil, sliding over stone and streaming through endless chambers. I am the heartbeat, I am the center, I am nothing and everything.

My eyes snap open. My ear is pressed to Jonah's chest, and my head is full of the earthy, mineral scent of him. With a gasp, I lurch backward.

He laughs, and the bell-shaped flowers echo the sound. "What did you think?"

"I didn't think ... anything." A flush washes up my neck and over my face. "It was incredible. It was beyond explanation."

Jonah's face lights up. "What if you could have that all the time? What if you could let everything else go? You were miserable and destroyed before you came here, Addie. You still are. But you don't need to be."

I laugh, incredulous. "Are you asking me to agree to be trapped here for eternity instead of you?"

"It wouldn't have to be forever," he says. "I'd come back."

"Right," I scoff. "I totally trust you to do that."

"Do you know how many people would kill for the chance to do this?" says Jonah. "I could go out into the world and set up a secret organization to spread the word and recruit them. You could stay here for a year or so—until you're healed. You could dive every day, for as long as you wanted. Think how strong you'd be, Addie. You'd be unstoppable by the time you went back and started competing again."

The fantasy is so perfect, it makes me ache. After a year of healing and diving with no limitations or obligations, I really would be unstoppable.

"How could I possibly trust that you'd come back, though?" I say.

"Because I don't actually want to trap you here." Jonah holds my gaze. "I just want to get out."

He leans in so close I think he's going to kiss me again. My head is whirling, and I want that magical, impossible fantasy so badly, but it's not that simple. And Jonah is a liar. I press my palm to his chest and push him away as the island thrums under my fingers.

"What if it didn't work and I ended up like Lenora?" I say. "Or what if it did work, but then the island didn't want any of the people you sent?"

"I'll keep sending people until it does. You have my word." The ferns behind Jonah are growing like they're in a time-lapse video, unfurling leaves and fronds and looming over us at an unsettling speed. I'm about to tell him his word doesn't hold a lot of weight, but the walkie-talkie chirps.

"Addie? You there?"

"Yeah, I'm here," I say, dragging myself away from Jonah's impossibilities. "Everything's okay."

As tempting as it is, I cannot get caught up in this beautiful boy's beautiful ruses. I have an actual life that I need to go back to and face, as much as I hate it. I can't stay on the island for a year to heal and train. I can't trust Jonah to hold up his end of any bargains. And with every captivating promise that he spins like spiderwebs, we drift further away from the one thing I need to be focusing on. I have to find out exactly what happened to Lenora and Violet.

"Is non-Sean still there?" says Billy.

"Yep," I say. "He's behaving himself."

Jonah lifts an eyebrow, and I curse myself for ever wading into the ocean that night.

"Okay, talk to you in fifteen," says Billy, and I really don't deserve him, but I'm so grateful he's there.

"If I let you . . . bind me to the island," I say to Jonah, "that means Violet and Lenora will get to leave too, right?"

Jonah's jaw goes tight. "Lenora can leave any time she wants."

"But she won't leave until her sister does," I say.

"I don't know why she bothers." The towering ferns begin to droop and shrivel. "They haven't seen each other once since they tricked me."

"But if you and the island are the same, how did they trick you?" I say.

"The island and I are *not* the same." Jonah's voice is edged with fury. "There are a lot of overlaps, and I don't always know where the boundaries are. But I'm still myself." He lets out a sardonic laugh. "Barely."

"Are you keeping Lenora and Violet apart, then?" I ask.

He shakes his head. "The island hides Violet at night so Lenora can't find her. It still hasn't forgiven them for fooling me."

"And you have no idea where she is?" I narrow my eyes.

"I don't actually know everything about this place," he says. "Even after all this time. But I know Violet fades away at night, and the island destroys Lenora every time she comes back and starts trouble."

"And you've never tried to help them," I say.

"Why would I?" he scoffs, and I'd like to wring his gorgeous neck.

"You still haven't answered my first question," I say. "Will the island let Violet go if it has me?"

Jonah plucks a bell-shaped blossom and holds it out. The flower swivels to face me, and then opens like a mouth. Blood-colored sap drools out.

"Yes," it whispers.

Chapter
37

AS WE WEAVE through the woods, I stay close to Jonah, not wanting a repeat of that pollen-induced fever dream. The plants have doubled in height since we came out here, and the racket of birds and insects is overwhelming. Jonah thinks he's winning me over, and as long as I keep pretending he has a chance, he'll keep giving me information.

"I have one more thing to show you, and then you can go back to your nanny," he says.

"Oh, come on," I say. "Billy's just looking out for me."

"He follows you around like a lovesick puppy." There's a sour note in Jonah's voice.

"At least he's honest about how he feels," I say.

Jonah whirls around, and his eyes are like a storm. "I don't know how to make it any clearer to you how I feel, Addie."

"But is it really you, or is it the island?" I say.

He pauses, his expression a mix of embarrassment and irritation. "It's probably both."

I have no idea how to respond to this strange affection from an undead boy and an actual island.

"But you probably felt the same way about Lenora," I say.

"I didn't." The flowers around us fade to pink, then bone white. Jonah's expression is unfathomable. A shiver races up the back of my neck as he lets his breath out slowly, then turns and continues down the path.

The path slopes upward, the terrain growing rockier. Sweat drips down my neck and inside my shirt. I'm getting dizzy again and I need to cough, but I'm afraid to let anything out with all these flowers crowding me. Then there are blue gaps through the trees and salty air rushes across my face, bringing cool relief as the sound of waves grows louder.

Jonah clambers onto a boulder at the edge of the vast blue, and after coughing into my arm, I climb up too. Below us, a rough slope of boulders cascades into the sloshing ocean. To our left, a waterfall pours out of a hole in the rocks, tumbling into a shallow, circular rock pool that might be a distant cousin of the cenote. Its infinity edge drops the water in a flat sheet into the sea.

"It was midnight when I went into the caves with Eulalie," says Jonah. "And I woke up in that pool at dawn."

"So the waterfall is connected to the caves." My brain races, finding connections, searching for enough pieces to start putting the puzzle together.

"I jumped into the heart," he says. "I fell into a tiny chamber and drowned, and then my body floated through the island's tunnels and eventually came out here. You wouldn't believe the bruises I found all over my skin, but they faded."

My stomach churns as I imagine Jonah's bruise-covered body falling out of that watery hole, the sound it must have made as it landed in the shallows. "Do you think you died?"

"I think I was reborn," he says. "Somewhere in those

tunnels, the island took my life and replaced it with something else."

I shudder, thinking of the time I was reborn, lying in a boat with someone pounding air into my chest. They broke two of my ribs, but at least my life wasn't replaced with . . . something else.

"With Lenora, it was different," says Jonah. "I came here, and I waited and waited for her to come out—but she didn't. I went back into the caves, trying to figure out what could have gone wrong." His jaw goes tight. "I found her body floating in the cavern behind her house. She was already starting to rot."

No wonder that cave fills me with dread every time I set foot in it.

"I heard their mother wailing for Violet, and I knew everything had gone very, very wrong," says Jonah. "I kept searching the caves. Can you guess what I found stuck in the tunnel between the whispering cave and the heart?"

"Violet," I whisper.

"I didn't even think," says Jonah. "I pulled her body out. I ran to the heart and threw her in. While I waited, I buried Lenora in the woods."

"Were you even sad that Lenora died?" I ask.

"I felt a thousand things at once," says Jonah. "Confused, horrified, devastated. But once I realized what she'd done, I was furious." He shoves a rock with his foot, and it crashes down the slope, breaking into pieces as it tumbles into the ocean. "Violet came out of that waterfall a few hours later.

The island loved her. It kept her. But it wouldn't accept a dead girl in my place."

He shoves another rock at the sea, and I back away, imagining what my body would look like tumbling down that slope, the way the bones would break and crunch.

"I didn't understand what had gone wrong until I found Lenora's diary," he says. "That foolish girl killed her sister with her lies. She doesn't deserve to ever see Violet again."

"Wait a minute—" I bite back the rest of the sentence as he lifts a massive rock and hurls it with inhuman strength at the sea. It wasn't Lenora's lies that killed Violet. It was Jonah's murderous, misdirected plan.

"Do you know how many thousands of rocks I've smashed since 1762?" he says. "Can you begin to imagine what this kind of endless, soul-destroying stagnation does to a person?"

"No." I take a cautious step closer, holding my hands out by my sides like I'm calming a wounded animal. "What Eulalie did to you was beyond cruel. But there's got to be a way to break this cycle without doing the same thing to someone else."

"Do you honestly think I haven't tried?" Jonah leaps to another boulder. "The Wellses aren't the only people who've washed up on these shores over the centuries."

My mouth goes dry. "How many?"

"I've lost count," he says, jumping again, lower and lower down the incline.

"Was Roland the last one?" I say.

Jonah scoffs. "The island wanted nothing to do with Roland. *I* wanted nothing to do with Roland. He got himself stuck."

"And you didn't help."

He shrugs. "At least he got to leave the island."

As terrible as my life has been, I've never thought of death as a better option, especially now that I've experienced it. I wish I had more empathy for Jonah and his torturous situation, but he's killed more people than he can count. I need to always remember that, no matter how many beautiful webs he spins. My hand strays to my neck, the habit still present even though the medallion is gone.

"Give me a day to think about this," I say.

For a flash of a second, his face is a jumble of hope and doubt, elation and anxiety. I don't know if he suspects I'm plotting something—he'd be a fool not to. He can't possibly believe I'd trust him with my life after everything he's told me, but maybe he's still in the habit of underestimating girls. A mask of calm slides over his perfectly symmetrical face, smoothing away all the emotions. His black eyes glitter in the sunlight.

"Of course," he says. "Take whatever time you need."

Chapter
38

THE CATAMARAN BOBS in the shallows next to an inflatable Zodiac boat, which means my mom and David are back. Before I head for the lighthouse, I stop to wash the pollen from my skin, fix my ponytail, and calm my expression into something less frantic.

Melinda opens the door, and her smile falters. "Addie! Is everything all right?"

"Yes, totally fine." I cough into my elbow. "Is Billy here? I know he's in trouble, but I was hoping I could talk to him for a couple of minutes?"

"Of course." Melinda scoops up Kylo, the black cat, before he can dart outside. "Come on in."

I can't help but gasp as my eyes adjust to the dimness inside. The room is a circle with a wide white column rising up through its center. To one side is a kitchen with counters rounded to fit the curving walls, a small stove, and four stools set along a bar that hugs the curve of the inner column. The other half of the space is a living area with built-in, curved sofas and pendant lights made of clouded blue glass. Through an open doorway in the column, I spot a set of spiral stairs leading up.

"This is incredible," I say, and Melinda smiles graciously.

"Do you have any idea why Billy was setting off those fire-works?" she asks. "Ken was saving them for the last night of your visit."

"Oh, um, I have no idea." I owe Billy massively for taking the fall for this. "Sorry."

"Don't worry about it." Melinda picks a stray thread off one of the sofas. "I'm just glad nobody got hurt."

"Addie?" Billy's voice echoes inside the column, and then the metal stairs clang as he races down them. He pokes his head through the doorway, glancing from me to his mom. "What's going on?"

"I was hoping we could talk for a minute?" I widen my eyes at him, then glance upward in the direction where I assume his room is.

"Oh, yeah, sure." His entire face goes red. "Just give me two seconds to clean up."

As he dashes back upstairs, Melinda offers me a muffin from a plate on the counter. "I'm so glad you came over, Addie. I've been trying to get him to clean his room all week."

My hands are still trembling, but the sugar in the muffin helps, and the berries are just as gooey and delicious as ever. I'm about to ask Melinda for another one when Billy comes clanging downstairs again.

"Okay," he says. "Much better."

Melinda flashes me a thumbs-up as I follow him to the staircase, Kylo trailing behind us. The railing is wrapped in gold fairy lights that cast a pretty glow on the white walls. At the next landing, Billy ducks through a doorway, and I follow him into a room with a similar layout to the downstairs, with rounded couches on one side and bunk beds built into the wall on the other. In the top bunk, the real Sean lies snoring, wearing a pair of basketball shorts and huge gamer headphones.

"Don't worry, he's dead to the world," says Billy, which makes me cringe. A lot of things are dead to the world around here.

"Do you mind if I borrow your laptop?" I ask, and Billy squints at me.

"Really?"

"Yeah. Is that it over there?" I point to the very obvious laptop on the couch, and he dashes over and turns it on.

"Aren't you going to tell me what's going on?" he asks, and I shake my head as I sit beside him. The couch is surprisingly comfortable, and I fight the urge to lean back and close my eyes for a few minutes. The caffeine has long since worn off, and everything about today has been utterly draining. Kylo jumps up beside me, settles in against my leg, and begins to purr.

Once the laptop loads up, I open the notepad program and start to type.

- you know how J is trapped on the island?

Billy nods, and I continue typing.

- he's trapped here because Eulalie bound him to the island and left

Billy's typing is surprisingly fast, considering he only uses two fingers.

> - is he trying to do the same thing to you?

> - sort of

> - but why you of all people? we've been here for
>   2 years, other people have been here too

> - the island will only accept certain people. it has to

I pause, because it's wrong to say the island has to love you. Clearly this isn't love.

> - want you. and apparently it wants me. J says the only
>   way to free V and L is to bind myself to the island. then
>   it'll keep me and let them go
> - and let him go too

> - this sounds like a trap

> - i know. but i don't think he's lying

> - wtf is wrong with that guy, why would you ever
>   agree to that

A blast of wind buffets the lighthouse as I type.

> - because it's completely horrible that V and L are stuck
>   here. and if i don't do something, who will? apparently

> he's killed a bunch of people already trying to get off the
> island. it needs to stop.

Billy reaches for the keyboard, but I keep typing.

> - i'm just wondering if there's some way i can trick the
> island into letting them go but not taking me

Billy's mouth drops open, and the walls shudder as another gust of wind slams the building. Ears flat, Kylo leaps down from the couch and scurries under the bed. Billy starts typing again.

> - how are you going to do that

> - if i can figure out how to stop the process somewhere in
> the middle, maybe it'll let them go without realizing it
> doesn't have me yet

> - this is messed up addie

> - i know

> - don't do it

> - i haven't made up my mind yet, i'm just thinking

> - stop thibking. make up someexcuse to your mom
> amd get the hell out of here!1!!

Billy pounds out the words.

> **- ill miss you but id rather never see you agaim than see you stuvck here foreve r**

That is how I know Billy actually cares about me. Whatever Jonah says he or the island feels, it's not really love. It's a selfish need; it's taking. I lay my head on Billy's shoulder, and he gives a shuddery sigh.

"I'm sorry," I say, and it's for a lot of things. For dragging him into this mess, for asking so much. For pulling him so close even though I'll never return his feelings in the same way. The wind roars again, and something splats on the round window behind us. Water runs down the pane.

Sean sits up in bed and yanks off his headphones. He spots me and Billy on the couch, and his eyes narrow. "What the hell is going on?"

"The island is getting mad," I say, and Billy snorts.

"What?" Sean gawks at me like I have three heads, and Billy and I break into hysterical, nervous laughter. Another wave sloshes over the window, and I grab the laptop.

> **- do you know if those maps Roland drew of the caves are still around?**

> **- yeah i think my dad has them in his office**

> **- can i look at them sometime?**

Billy gives me a wary look, but I continue typing.

- i swear i'm not going make any decisions until i have all
the information

"Kids?" Melinda pokes her head through the doorway. "Stay away from the window, okay? There's a big squall blowing in."

"Wow, thanks for the news flash." Sean flops back on his bed and throws a pillow over his face. His mother ignores him.

"Addie, hon, you can stay here until this blows over. Ken's up at your house, fixing a broken toilet, so I'll radio him and have him tell your mom you're here."

Outside, the sky is greenish gray, and a mammoth set of waves is rolling in, sloshing up the sides of the lighthouse and the jetty. Melinda continues upstairs, and I hear her relaying the message, then a cracking static response from Ken.

"This is so not okay," I mutter, deleting the conversation and setting the laptop down.

"I'm telling you, the guy is a sociopath," says Billy. "Don't even try to negotiate with him."

A wave hits the window so hard it cracks the glass, and a line of water dribbles inside.

"You piece of shit!" yells Billy.

"Will you two shut up?" groans Sean from under his pillow.

"I'm leaving," I say, heading for the stairs.

As I pull the front door open, the heaving wind slams it against the wall, and I cringe, hoping I haven't broken it.

"I'm here!" I step out onto the slick jetty as another wave gushes over, throwing me off balance. Billy grabs my arm before the roaring water drags me off the side. "Stop it, okay? We're done."

The wind slows, though the water is still rolling and sloshing and dark clouds billow overhead.

"This isn't the way to convince somebody to help you," I say.

"You can still leave," mutters Billy.

The wind gusts again, and a flock of scarlet butterflies flit out of the woods. They spiral in a great whirling cloud, then float slowly earthward, landing in the water, on the jetty, at my feet, in my hair, but as they touch down, their wings turn to petals, and they fall to pieces.

I think Billy might be wrong about that.

Chapter
39

I'M HALFWAY DOWN the drenched beach, skirting around leaves and branches and withering red flowers, when I hear a sharp whistle behind me. Billy comes jogging up, holding a canvas bag with the sharp green crown of a pineapple poking out the top. He bends low and pulls out his inhaler, and my own lungs twinge in sympathy.

"My mom . . . wanted . . . to give . . . your mom . . . fruit," he wheezes, then takes a long puff.

I peer inside the bag, and among the jumble of mangoes and papayas and coconuts is a bundle of papers. "Thanks," I say. "For literally everything. I'm sorry to drag you into this mess."

Still holding his breath, he waves his hand dismissively, then exhales. "Do you even understand how boring it was before you got here?"

"I know, but still," I say. "I appreciate everything. And I hope one day soon I'll be able to stop asking you for favors and we can just hang out like normal people."

"Pretty sure neither one of us is ever going to be a normal person." Billy sticks his tongue out and somehow manages to rotate his eyes in two different directions.

I don't know whether to cringe or laugh. "We'll hang out like two weirdos then, okay?"

"It's a deal." He snaps his eyes back in sync. "And in the meantime, be careful. Stay away from non-Sean."

"I'll do my best." I smile like that's a joke, like I have a choice in the matter, but my stomach is churning.

My mom and David are in their room with the door shut, and they're laughing in a way that makes me want to vomit. Quickly, I unload the fruit onto the kitchen counter, grab another sandwich from the fridge, and flee.

The patio is littered with leaves; the pool is choked full of scarlet petals. Some of the chairs lie on their sides, and others have been shoved against the house. I wonder what it would feel like to be swept up in that wind, thrown through the sky with those leaves and flowers. I wonder where Violet goes when it storms, if she cares about getting wet, if she's afraid.

Thankfully, all of the windows in my room are shut, so everything is dry, but the hot, stagnant air reeks of flowers. I throw open the french doors and turn on the fans, then sprawl on my bed with my sandwich and poor, dead Roland's papers.

The first map looks like a professional cartographer drew it, the lines sharp and clean. I easily identify the cenote at the top, then the narrower hole at the bottom, the corridor that leads to the first cave, and the passageway to the cathedral. Two parallel lines indicate the underwater tunnel, and the island's heart is a perfect circle with a line pointing at the bottom and a question mark. Roland must have made it through that underwater tunnel at least once with his tank on, which is a disturbing thought.

The next page looks like it was drawn by a different person. The pencil marks are thick and clumsy, tearing through the paper in several places. At the center of the page is an anatomical heart. The cross-sectioned arteries and veins are labeled with clumsy arrows pointing in, arrows pointing out. Roland knew the island had a heart. The man wasn't smart enough to take his scuba tank off while swimming through a narrow tunnel, but somehow he figured that out. How did he do it? And what, exactly, did he figure out?

All around the heart, he's drawn a labyrinth of tunnels and circles that resemble the caves in the first map. Some are connected with solid slashes and others with dotted lines and question marks. In some of the caves, Roland has drawn skulls, possibly to indicate bodies he found down there. Shuddering and taking another bite of sandwich, I flip to the next page.

It's not a map at all. It's a diagram of the human circulatory system that looks like it's been copied out of a textbook, then overlaid with scribbles, question marks, and disturbingly illegible words. Arrows point down into the chest of the headless torso, leading to the heart and then to the lungs. A web of lines and circles and skulls radiates down from there.

My tired brain whirls at the connections, the significance. I know about the circulatory system from freediving: the heart pumps blood to the lungs, which fill it with oxygen, and then the blood streams through the rest of the body. Not only does the island have a heart, but it also has a circulatory system of caves and tunnels, and the water must function like its blood. Maybe it also has something like lungs that fills people with something other than oxygen as they pass through its sinister system—takes essential pieces away and changes them forever.

This feels big, like I'm on the cusp of a massive discovery. I don't fully understand the system, and I still have no idea how to stop it, but this is vital information about the island. There's an answer here somewhere, just out of reach in the slippery fog of my exhaustion. I curse myself for not making another pot of coffee, but I couldn't bear to be in that kitchen hearing . . . things for another minute.

Aa-dee-dee-dee, call the birds outside.

My chest aches. My eyes feel like they're full of sand, and I desperately need to rest, or I'll never figure any of this out. But before I drift off, I force myself out of bed. I fold Roland's papers and stuff them under the mattress. Then I shut and lock the french doors, push the dresser in front of them, and brace a chair under the knob of the locked back door. It's only a nap, but I can't take any chances.

As I curl up on top of the blankets and slowly drift into unconsciousness, my head throbs with the steady beat of a heart that isn't mine.

Chapter
40

I DREAM I'M dancing with Jonah, his arm tight around my waist as we twirl to an eerie waltz played by a single harp. We're in a ballroom surrounded by faceless people in sumptuous clothing, and the chandelier overhead is lit by candles. The women's long skirts hush across the floor, and the harp's notes reverberate through the dim, flickering space.

I can feel Jonah's heart pounding against my chest, and the ballroom warps as my heart finds the same rhythm, flowing along with the melancholy tune that gradually picks up speed. We dip and spin, spiral and whirl, faster and faster until my feet are skimming the floor. It's too much, too fast, and it's making me sick.

"Let me go," I say.

"You know I won't," he says. "And I don't think you want me to."

I open my mouth to tell him he's wrong, but blood-colored butterflies pour out, making me choke and cough. Jonah's mouth curls in a wicked smile as he twirls us faster.

"If you really wanted to leave, you would have gone as soon as you found out who I was," he whispers. "But you stayed."

It doesn't matter when I decided. It matters that I did decide. And it never meant that I chose to stay here forever. I shove him, but his arms are vines twisting around my waist, slithering up my back. As the tendrils crawl around my neck, I blink back tears, but something is wrong with my eyelashes. They're thick and heavy and coated in dust, and as I reach up to wipe it away, I realize they aren't eyelashes at all. They're petals. I draw in a breath to scream, but a blossom unfurls from my mouth, and I gag on the sap as it floods my tongue and slides down my throat.

I wake on the path, in stifling darkness, still choking on the scream. Somewhere deep in the forest, a harp is playing the same eerie waltz from my dream. The fact that I know it's Lenora doesn't make it any less unnerving. There's no moon, and even the blue flashing beetles are gone. The branches overhead are a solid mass of black, and I struggle to make out the edges of the path. Nocturnal creatures I can't see are hissing and slithering, creaking and rattling, and my skin itches with that familiar sensation of being watched.

If I'd kept on sleepwalking, I would have found my way to the cenote through this murky forest. I would have waded into that heartbeat water and let it cradle me, wash the sweat from my skin, the aches from my muscles, the pain from my lungs. I might have even dove. I might have drawn in slow breaths, turned upside down, and pulled myself into the depths, all with my eyes closed.

Panic-bitter nausea wells up my throat, and I blink hard,

trying to force my pupils to expand, to see better in this suffocating dark. I've never felt more trapped in my life. Even sixty meters below the surface with the entire weight of the ocean pressing down on me.

I'm certain that what Jonah told me in the dream is true. He's never going to let me go.

I can't let that happen.

The harp music stops as I step off the path, and I worry that I've lost it, but then it picks up again, starting back at the beginning of the waltz, the melancholy notes tripping along in sets of three. With no sense of where on the island I am, I move in the direction of the music, shoving through bushes and brambles that tear at my clothing and rip strands of my hair from my scalp.

The ground slopes down, the bushes thin, and the music grows louder, faster, a creepy, intricate melody that makes my nerves crawl. The bones of the Wells house take shape in the valley below, and my lungs crackle as the ruined building looms closer.

I slide to a stop at the entrance, and the trees all around me groan and sway. Inside, the song loops back to the beginning without stopping, and I find myself humming along. Blue flashes appear overhead, swirling lower and lower. One lands on my shoulder and I slap it away, feeling its tiny body crunch.

"Lenora?" Cold air floods over my skin as I cross the threshold. The music doesn't falter. I find her in her room, a lantern flickering in the corner. She's sitting on the ground with black tears rolling down her face and the harp on her shoulder. Her fingers fly over the stringless space, darting around the tree trunk in its center, and the music shivers and swirls in the darkness.

"Lenora," I say again, and her head snaps up.

"What are you doing here?" Her voice is brittle.

"I was sleepwalking again," I say. "I was on my way to the cenote, but I heard your harp and came here instead."

Lenora cocks her head at an unnatural angle, peering at the flashing beetles that float overhead. "Can you guess how long it took me to find my bones at the bottom of the ocean tonight?"

"I can't even imagine," I say.

"Half of my ribs are still missing." Lenora smooths the sunken front of her dress and grimaces. "Four of my fingers." She holds up her bony hands and waggles the six remaining digits. "It's not easy to play like this."

"I'm sorry," I say, and she gives a broken shrug before setting the harp down and getting to her feet.

"How may I destroy myself for your personal illumination tonight?" She drops into a low curtsy. Her sardonic offer makes me laugh, though it's a jittery, unsettled kind of laugh. Everything Jonah assumed about this girl was deeply wrong.

"Can you tell me everything you remember after Jonah pushed you into the island's heart?" I ask. "If it's not too painful to relive."

Lenora scoffs at the word *relive*. "Nothing's more painful than how I already feel. And our dear friend didn't push me. I jumped."

"Really?" My mind whirls, reframing the entire scenario of Lenora's demise.

"Don't think for a second that he wouldn't have shoved you straight in if it were possible. You have to go willingly." She curses at the flashing beetles that crawl the crumbling walls and picks up her lantern. "Follow me."

As we pass through the kitchen, Lenora stops to prod the nest beside the fireplace. "I dig through this every night to see if Violet is in there, but she never, ever is. I've dug up her grave at least a hundred times. He hides her in some secret place, but in all these years I've never managed to find it."

"He says it's the island hiding Violet, not him." I don't know why I feel compelled to make excuses for Jonah.

"And you believe that?" says Lenora.

"It probably doesn't matter what I believe," I say. "It's horrible either way."

Lenora clicks her teeth. "Jonah Burke is a horrible person."

A bat darts out of the trees and skims the top of her head, and she hisses as it flaps away with a clump of her hair. Jonah is listening. But he's not stopping us, which must mean he wants to hear what we're saying.

"Do you think he was always this awful?" I say, remembering the night when I found him crying on the beach. I wonder if all this time on the island has warped him, if it's changed entire parts of his personality or just amplified things that were already there.

"I don't particularly care," says Lenora, but she runs a

nervous hand over the top of her head as she says it. "Come this way."

The lantern casts a gruesome glow into the hollows of her cheeks as we make our way around the back of the house. My skin goes cold as she opens the rotting trapdoor in the ground, and every inch of my body protests, but I follow her down the steps.

"Close it behind you," she hisses, and I stumble back up, taking one last gulp of air before shutting us into the musty, dripping tomb of a space.

There's a sudden splash, and I dash down the rest of the stairs, my heart in my throat. The lantern sits alone on the ledge, its light glittering on the water's black surface but not powerful enough to illuminate the entire cave. At the edge of the glow, two bony feet float. Swallowing hard, I pick up the lantern and it catches the rest of Lenora, floating on her back with her ragged dress drifting like the tendrils of some underwater plant.

"How can you stand it in here?" I say, crouching by the edge. It feels like we've crawled into the belly of some nightmare beast. And Lenora looks even more like a dead body, floating like that.

Her laugh is a skittering thing, like spiders. "I can stand it because Jonah hates this cave and won't bother me here."

"I don't blame him." I rub the goose bumps on my arm, but they're not going anywhere. "He can still hear us, though, right?"

"Yes. So do mind what you say."

"I want to know everything about what happened to you when you jumped into the heart," I say. "Jonah says if I do it, the island will let Violet go."

Lenora's floating body stays motionless, but her head swivels sideways. "What did you tell him?"

"I told him I needed to think about it."

"But *why* would you do that?" Lenora's head is still sideways, her face half-submerged, and I have to keep reminding myself that it's okay because she doesn't have to breathe. I wish I could communicate everything I'm trying to do without Jonah hearing. I wish I could ask her to help me figure this out.

"He told me he'd come back for me," I say, and Lenora laughs, a gurgling sound that makes me queasy.

"And you believed him about this too?"

"Yes." I blink, cat-slow, at her, hoping she understands I don't really mean it. "I'll stay here and dive until I'm healed, and in the meantime, Jonah will find someone else that the island loves to take my place."

Lenora tips her head back to stare at the ceiling. "You'd really do that for Violet? For me?"

My stomach clenches. I can't tell if she's playing along or she really believes me. "Of course. I promised I'd help."

"I don't know what to say." Her voice breaks and guilt hits me like a sledgehammer. "Thank you."

"It's . . . all right," I say, which is the farthest thing from the truth. "But before I do it, I'd like to know what to expect. Can you tell me everything you remember?"

"We had a ceremony." A shudder goes through Lenora. "Our own little pretend wedding, where he promised to love me forever and then kissed me with lies on his lips. I was so foolish, so ecstatic. I actually laughed as I jumped."

My gut lurches as I imagine Lenora, young and beautiful like her statue, plummeting into that tight darkness.

"How far did you fall?" I ask.

"I fell for such a long time that I started to wonder if I were dreaming. I got the sense that I was slowing, the heartbeat was slowing, time was slowing, and when I finally hit the bottom, it didn't hurt." She swivels her head sideways again. "But then nothing hurts in the water, does it?"

"No." I'm sure if I went swimming in that black water with Lenora right now, all the pain would melt away from my lungs, but I can't bring myself to do it.

"I landed in a tiny chamber filled with waist-deep water," says Lenora. "The heartbeat was so loud that the walls were pulsing with it. I couldn't think. I could barely see. I didn't understand what was happening. The water kept pouring in, but it wasn't getting any deeper, and the walls kept pounding. *Boom, boom, boom*." Lenora thumps her own chest along with the words. "I couldn't hear myself screaming."

As I listen, I find myself drawing in deep breaths, picturing the claustrophobic, thundering space.

"Then the water started to drop," says Lenora. "There was this terrible sucking sensation down by my feet, and I tried to get away, but there was nothing to hold on to. Nowhere to go. It knocked me off my feet and pulled me under. I slid into a tunnel so tight I could barely fit inside. It pinned my arms over my head, and then I was rushing along so fast I lost all sense of direction. There was no air. I couldn't stop. I couldn't breathe. I *had* to breathe."

That kind of panic is exactly what I've trained myself to avoid when I dive, but it washes over me, frantic and jagged. Pieces of my accident, ones I must have blocked out, are flickering back. The convulsions. The agony in my head and lungs. The overpowering, irrational urge to breathe.

"And that was it," says Lenora. "That was the end. I remember being so disappointed when I gave up and breathed in that water and everything went away."

"I drowned too." Tears flood my eyes, and I swipe them away. "But I'm not disappointed I let it happen. I'm *furious*."

Lenora rolls over and swims to the ledge, and there are tears on her face too, though hers are black. "You can't blame your body for trying to save you."

But I can. I've been training this body like an instrument, like a machine, for so long, there's been no option for stupid mistakes like breathing water. I should have been stronger. I should have made better choices, even with no oxygen left in my brain.

"I forgave myself a long time ago," says Lenora. "But I am never going to forgive Jonah. And I'm not going to let go of Violet until I know she's safe."

"That's how you've managed to stay here all this time," I say.

She grins, her gruesome teeth flashing. "A combination of spite and ferocious, stubborn love for my sister."

I swallow, tears salty on the back of my tongue. "Do you have any sense of what might happen to you if you didn't fight so hard to stay?"

"Not exactly," she says. "There's some sort of void between here and . . . there. If there even is a *there*. In the daytime, when I fade and sleep, I'm dangling precariously close to it. But I never fully let go."

"See, that's the terrifying part," I say. "How could you ever just let go without knowing what comes next? Give up that control, your body, your entire self?"

Lenora shrugs her crooked shoulders. "I've had a bit of time to get used to the idea. Once Violet is free of this hideous place, I'll do it. I'll let it all go." She inspects her three-fingered hand, the bones worn and blackening. "Holding on wears you down, little by little. It'll break you eventually."

I don't think she's talking about just herself anymore. There's no magical cure for my lungs, but there are a lot of things I need to let go of before I can move on from my accident. It's like that anchor tied around Lenora's waist in my dream. I've got an anchor too. Clinging to it makes me feel safe, as unhealthy as that safety is. Once I let go, anything could happen.

Lenora climbs out of the water and sits beside me, leaning her bony shoulder against mine. "It's a frightening prospect," she says. "And just look at me. It's very hard to frighten someone who looks like this." She stretches out her crooked bone legs, one longer than the other, and waggles her feet.

With a broken laugh, I wipe my eyes. "I'm sorry you lost even more bones because of me."

"Soon I won't need them anymore," she says, and fear clenches my throat, not just at the prospect of death, but because there's still so much I need to figure out if I'm going to help her and Violet. I can't let them down. Lenora's spite and rage might be holding her here, but she's falling apart piece by piece. If I could just manage to get some sleep, maybe my brain would start working again and I could come up with a plan.

"I'm afraid to go back to my room," I say. "I'm scared that if I fall asleep, I'll sleepwalk again, and God knows where I'll end up. But I'm so exhausted, and I can't keep drinking coffee forever."

"I'll come with you." Lenora stands and brushes the water off her filthy skirt. "I'll wait outside your room until morning, and I'll catch you if you try to go anywhere."

The thought of her bony fingers grabbing me as I sleep is both disturbing and comforting. "Thank you," I say.

"It's the least I can do after what you're doing for us," she says, and guilt gnaws at my insides, because she doesn't know what I'm really planning to do. I don't even know myself.

As we steal back through the slithering woods, a few beetles flicker overhead, but there's no sign of Jonah. He seems to be leaving me alone, which should be a relief, but instead is unnerving. My tired mind whirls as I try to fit the pieces from Lenora's story into the larger puzzle of the island and how it works. A heart with a heartbeat and tunnels like veins. A circulatory system that keeps the island running, that somehow changes people as it binds them to itself. A tiny chamber where she was trapped. A hole barely wide enough to fit through.

A cough crackles out of my lungs, and I gesture for Lenora to stop. As I double over, hacking and spitting, I hear the vines sprout and slide on the ground, but I no longer care, because all of a sudden, the pieces are sliding into place. I'm thinking of my own circulatory system and how it got disrupted when I drowned. How the water blocked my lungs and then my heart stopped, my circulation stopped, everything stopped.

It's all clicking together.

I can't drown the island, but maybe I can stop its heart.

Chapter

41

I SLEEP LIKE the dead with Lenora sitting on the patio out-side my room, and I wake feeling rested for the first time in a while. The clock reads eight thirty-five, which is still late for me but earlier than I've woken all week. Even though there still are a million things to figure out and worry about, I feel lighter. Clearer.

My plan is coming together. Today I'm going to dive into the cenote, explore the tunnels, and find the best place to block the flow of water through them. If Jonah shows up, it won't matter because he won't know what I'm looking for. He has no idea what my plan is. Not a single soul does.

After a quick shower, I pull on a bathing suit and shorts, slipping Lenora's knife into the pocket and clipping the walkie-talkie to my waistband. Then I open the french doors and step out into the sunny salt air. The flowers are mostly still red today, but woven through the bloody hues are shades of magenta and plum, fuchsia and orchid, orangey pink and flame. Their smell isn't overwhelming yet, but I'm sure that will change as the day goes on.

"Thank you, Lenora," I whisper, but she's long gone. The only traces of her are a few dry spots of black on the patio be-side my door. My mother and David have left already, but in the kitchen there's a plate of coconut mango scones and a pot of coffee. After cycling through my breathing exercises and a few gentle yoga poses on the patio, I grab a pastry, my towel, and the walkie-talkie, just in case.

I'm halfway down the stairs to the woods when I hear it: a low hum that becomes a whir and then a choppy roar. It's coming from the beach side of the island. Heart rocketing, I dash back toward the house and skirt around to the cliff's edge.

On the beach by the lighthouse, an orange helicopter is landing. Its side door slides open and two people jump out. Someone is lying on the ground, and everyone else is rushing around—I can just make out Melinda's caftan and my mother's wide-brimmed hat, which she's clutching to her head, but I can't tell who the person on the ground is. I pull out the walkie-talkie.

"Billy? Are you there?"

No answer.

"Billy, what's going on with the helicopter? Is everybody okay?"

Still no answer, and I desperately hope that's not because it's him lying in the sand. Dropping my towel, I race down the steps, stumbling when I hit the bottom. The sand is strangely deep and shifting, and I keep sinking up to my ankles.

The person on the ground is being loaded onto a backboard now, then maneuvered into the helicopter, and I'm still only a quarter of the way down the beach. I'll never make it there in time.

"Mom!" I yell, but everybody's busy watching the people on the helicopter. The sand slides under me and I fall again.

Aa-dee-dee-dee, screams a bird, echoing my tone in a way that makes me want to be sick. Now my mother is climbing onto the helicopter too, which means the injured person has to be David. I watch, horror-struck, as the door slides shut and Ken and Melinda back away from the aircraft. Hopefully it's something simple like a broken bone, but I can't stop thinking about David's heart pills.

"Jonah!" I yell at the trees. "What did you do?"

The woods are silent. The helicopter rises and swivels toward the sea. A sickening wave of panic washes through my chest, sending a burst of speed into my legs, but the sand keeps shifting, tripping me over and over like some horrible game I never agreed to play. Finally I stagger into the ocean, where the ground is firmer and flatter. It's incredibly slow, slogging through this water, and my lungs feel like they might actually be on fire, but at least I can move forward.

"Melinda!" I scream, but she and Ken are busy rushing around between the lighthouse and the dock, loading things onto the motorboat.

The ocean swirls around my legs, sucking suddenly out and throwing me off balance.

"Wait!" I barely get the word out before a coughing fit sends me to my knees. The sea rushes back in, soaking my shorts and curling around my waist. By the time I remember the walkie-talkie is still clipped to my waistband, it's too late to save it. The boat's engine roars. A blond head pokes out of the lighthouse door, and I think with a rush of hope that it might be Billy, but it's his brother.

"Sean!" I manage to choke out as the boat pulls away from the dock.

He turns and gawks at me sitting in the waves.

"Make them stop," I croak. "Tell them not to go." But my voice isn't loud enough, and he just stands there like a useless lump as I lurch to my feet and stagger closer.

"Yikes," he says as I finally make it to the jetty, hacking and spitting and about to vomit. "Do you want some water?"

I try to tell him not to bother, but I can't get any words out. As he ducks back inside, I collapse onto the rocks. I am incandescent with rage that I couldn't make it down the beach in time. Furious with myself, with the island, with Jonah. It wasn't that far. It wasn't fair.

"Here." Sean startles me out of my livid state by handing me a mug full of water.

"Thanks," I croak. "What happened?"

"They were loading up the catamaran when David collapsed," he says. "Everybody thought he was having a heart attack, so my dad called for help on the satellite phone."

"Oh God," I say. It will absolutely devastate my mother if something happens to David. It would devastate me too, I realize. Even if he is helpfully trying to ruin everything I've worked for.

"My parents are taking the boat over to meet them at the hospital," says Sean. "I'm sure David's fine, though. He was talking when they loaded him onto the helicopter."

"That sounds promising." I take a sip of water and immediately cough it out.

"If you're going to puke, can you, like, do it in the water?" says Sean. "I don't want to clean it off the jetty."

"I'm not going to puke," I say, but he doesn't look like he believes me. I wonder if Jonah suspects my plan to stop the island's heart. Did he just exact the same punishment on David as a warning? Or was that just a coincidence? I take another shaky sip of water, and this time it stays down. "Where's Billy?"

Sean shrugs. "He's been gone since I woke up. I can't believe he didn't come back when the helicopter showed up."

I can't believe it either. The roar of that helicopter would have been audible from everywhere on this island. Billy would have come running. But he didn't. I pull my walkie-talkie out to see if it still works after the unexpected dousing in the waves. It doesn't.

"Do you know if Billy has his walkie-talkie?" My voice shakes.

"Like I already said, I wasn't awake when he left." Sean slows down his words like I'm four years old.

"Can I borrow another one?" I say, equally slowly. "Mine's broken."

Sean makes a face like this is asking too much, but I jab the walkie-talkie in his direction. "I'd like to know what's happening with David," I say. "Unless you'd rather I stay here and hang out with you all day while we wait for them to call?"

He snatches the walkie-talkie and disappears into the lighthouse, muttering something about not getting paid to work here, and it's a wonder nobody has punched this guy in the face. When he returns, I exchange my empty mug for a new walkie-talkie.

"Billy, can you hear me?" I try. "Billy, come in. Hey, Billy."

No answer. I gulp down another wave of panic. Sean yawns.

"I'm going back to bed," he says. "I'll let you know if I hear anything. But like I said, I'm pretty sure your dad isn't going to die or anything."

I don't even bother to correct him. David is just the beginning of my worries right now. Billy didn't come when the helicopter landed, and now he's not responding to his walkie-talkie. Either he can't hear it or he isn't being allowed to respond. Unbidden, an image springs to my mind of him trapped underwater, hair swirling, eyes wide, fists beating against unyielding stone.

Breathe, Addie. You don't know what happened to him yet.

As I draw in a slow, shaky breath, I wonder if I should tell Sean what's going on. That I'm almost certain Jonah has done something to his brother, in addition to getting every responsible adult off the island. But for starters, I can't imagine Sean believing any part of that story. And second, I don't think he'd be remotely helpful, even if he did. He'd just get in the way.

I clip the new walkie-talkie to my shorts and head for the woods.

Chapter

42

BILLY ISN'T ON the beach or at the cenote or any of the spots where he laid the rat traps. There's no sign of Jonah anywhere either. I'm trying not to hyperventilate as I head for the Wells house. It's the last place Billy would go on purpose. If he's not there, I'm going to start searching the caves. I don't want to think about what it means if he's down in the caves.

The sky has turned an unsettling shade of green-gray, and mist dampens my hair and skin. Humid air wafts through the trees, hot and fetid, and all I want to do is run back to the lighthouse and tell Sean to call the police, but there's no reasonable or rational way to explain any of this.

I'm still afraid for David too, but if he was conscious and talking when the helicopter took off, that seems like a good sign. Part of me is glad he and my mother are off the island, away from whatever is about to happen. I can feel it building. The island can feel it too. The hot wind keeps coming in ominous, gusting breaths. The flowers are bruised shades of purple and black and scarlet.

Over my head, branches rustle, and I bite back a shriek as a figure leaps down and crash-lands on the path. Violet sprawls onto her hands and knees, then jumps up with a triumphant smile on her little gray face.

"Surprise!" she yells, and I have to bend low to gather my breath. At this rate I'll be the next one having a heart attack.

"Holy sh . . . eep," I gasp. "That was a really big surprise, Violet."

"What's a holy sheep?" she says. "Do they have those at your church? We can't go to church here, but Mama used to read her Bible on Sundays." A frown creases her brow, and even in the midst of all the anxiety, my heart twinges for this poor kid who hasn't seen her mother in almost two hundred years.

"It's just an expression," I say. "Have you seen Billy anywhere? I'm looking for him."

"Are you playing hide-and-seek?" Violet wiggles excitedly.

"Sort of," I say. "But he's very good at hiding today. I've looked all over the island and I can't find him."

"I can always find him." Violet puffs her bony chest out, and three brown spiders squirm out of the neckline of her dress. "Did you look under the trapdoor?"

"He never hides there, does he?" I ask.

Violet pauses. "Not usually, but maybe he did today?"

Before I can answer, she dashes away down the path. By the time I arrive, sweating and panting, at the open trapdoor, she's already deep underground. Rain patters down through the canopy, getting heavier by the second and so warm it could be blood.

"Is Billy down there?" I call from the top of the stairs.

"No!" she calls.

I try the walkie-talkie again. "Billy? Hey, Billy, are you there?"

No answer. Holding my breath, I step down through the trapdoor and descend just far enough to make sure Violet is telling the truth. The ledge is empty aside from her. Not a single ripple in the black water. Before the cave's seeping dread has time to sink into my bones, I climb back up into the slightly less dreadful rain, beckoning for Violet to follow.

"We'll keep looking in other places," I say. "Have you seen Jonah today?"

Her little face darkens. "Jonah is *not* allowed to play with us."

"Of course not," I say. "I'm just wondering if he's with Billy."

"Billy and Jonah is not friends," mutters Violet. "Jonah made me promise never to tell Billy about him. He said my mama might fall down out of heaven if I did."

"That is completely horrible and also a lie." I pull her into a hug, trying not to shudder at the touch of her bloated skin and hoping the spiders keep to themselves. "Nobody falls out of heaven." Violet wipes her nose on my shirt and I extricate myself from her clinging arms. "Do you know where Jonah might be, though?"

She taps her crusty lips with one finger as she ponders. "Did you look at his house?"

"I didn't even know he had a house," I say.

Violet makes a sound like a screeching rat. It takes me a minute to realize it's laughter. "Where would he live if he didn't have a house?" she says.

"I don't know." I'm embarrassed to admit I never considered this. "I guess I assumed he slept in the caves or something?"

She snorts. "That sounds uncomfor-ble and very drippy."

"You're so right," I say. "Will you show me where his house is?"

She takes my hand in her dusty little paw, and we race through the woods, leaves slapping my face, water dripping into my hair, flowers drooling sap across my skin. The plants bend and wave and sway, and I swear the bruise-colored blossoms are growing bigger by the second, their petals unfurling and their hues darkening.

Violet stops at the edge of the trees about halfway down the beach. "Here we are!"

"Are you sure?" I peer into the damp undergrowth. I've been past this spot several times and never seen a house.

"Yes." Violet leads me through a tangle of bushes and around the back of a towering tree, then points to its vine-covered trunk. Nearly buried under the leaves are horizontal pieces of driftwood that form a ladder.

"It's a tree house!" says Violet.

I can't see a house up in the tree's boughs, but the canopy is so thick, it could easily hide one. "Do you think he's home?"

"Maybe," says Violet. "I don't want to go up there if he is."

I don't either. A few yards away from the tree, a giant iguana sits, chewing on a blood-red flower. Wiping my clammy hands on my shorts, I test the first rung. It's solid and holds my weight.

"Do you want to wait down here?" I say.

"Yes." Violet trots over to the iguana, and I'm about to tell her not to touch it when she crouches down and pats its head.

The iguana nuzzles her bloated leg, and she picks another flower for it to eat.

"Okay," I say, hoisting myself up and hoping I'm not making a terrible mistake. "Wish me luck."

"I wish for you to be very lucky, Addie-dee." Violet scratches the iguana's chin, her fingers inches from its chomping teeth. "And 'specially to not fall down."

I swallow hard. "Thanks."

Part of me wonders if I should get Lenora's knife out before I climb up, but it'll just make it harder to hold on, and I don't think a blade is much good against a guy who can't be killed. The tree creaks and sways as I climb, and as the vines start to slither around my hands, I pray I won't cough.

Aa-dee-dee-dee, call the birds, still invisible as I ascend into their territory.

"Make sure you are holding on very tight!" calls Violet from far below, and I resist looking down at her.

The branches are closer together up here, their leaves denser and broader and soaked with rain. I shove my way through, digging my nails into the driftwood to keep from slipping. If I fell from this height, it's unlikely I'd survive. Jonah would probably throw my body into the heart just to spite me.

As I hoist myself higher, swearing and sweating and nauseous, I wonder if the helicopter has landed at the hospital yet. Hopefully they'll just need to keep an eye on David for a few hours before sending him back on the boat with Ken and Melinda. Hopefully I'll have found Billy and executed my plan by then. I wish I had a time machine or a remote control to fast-forward to the part where all of this is over, but it's only just beginning, and the enormity of it all makes me want to cry.

Holding my breath, I shove through another cluster of wet leaves, and then everything opens up. Above my head stretch the floorboards of a small house braced against the tree's trunk and cradled in its branches. In the center is a trapdoor with a metal handle. My pulse beats a wild, racing rhythm as I climb a few more rungs and nudge it open a crack.

Bare floor stretches in all directions. I push the trapdoor open a little farther.

"Hello?"

Aa-dee-dee-dee is the only response.

With my stomach roiling and my heart about to crash out of my chest, I climb the last rung and hoist myself into the tree house, shutting the trapdoor behind me.

The dwelling is more of a porch than a house, with waist-high, open windows on all sides and a steeply sloping thatched roof. Outside, a handmade system of pulleys is attached to a branch, with the ropes tucked up inside the house. A hammock dangles at one end of the room, and a sheet on a rope forms a curtain that hides the other half of the space. The walls under the windows are lined with handmade shelves full of books and papers and all sorts of random objects. A diving fin, more pens and pencils than I can count, a pair of wire-framed glasses, an architecture magazine, a clunky black digital watch.

"You're a magpie," I whisper, trailing my fingers over

Jonah's stolen treasures. A pile of papers catches my eye. The sheet on top is a charcoal drawing of a girl with flowers for eyes, and I shudder at this real-life echo of my nightmares. Clammy sweat breaks out on the back of my neck as I shuffle through the drawings, some in charcoal and others in ink. They're all of me, every single one:

Me, walking alone on the path, surrounded by scrawls of charcoal night.

Me, floating on my back in the cenote, as seen from above, radiating pure bliss.

Me, sitting on a patio lounger with my knees tucked up and a look of pure fury in my eyes.

Me, crawling out of the ocean at night with long limbs and dripping hair.

Me, sitting in the ferns with Jonah, my hand pressed to his chest and a gasp on my lips.

Involuntarily, my hand lets go and the papers flutter to the floor. There's something so intimate, so deeply invasive about the way he's drawn me, both in moments where I knew he was there and ones where I didn't. I cannot believe I kissed this person who's been stalking me since the night I got here. I could cry at all that time I spent wondering if he liked me back, all those hours I spent daydreaming about him. A hot flush of shame washes over me. How could I not have realized?

My walkie-talkie crackles with static, and I yank it off my waistband.

"Hello? Billy, are you there?"

The static cuts out. I crank the volume up as high as it

will go. "Billy? Hello? Come in!" But there's no answer.

A gust of flower-scented air ripples the curtain hanging across the middle of the room, and I catch sight of a canvas tarp on the floor behind it. I can't bear to touch the drawings again, so I leave them lying there and cross the space. A wave of fear stills my hand as I reach out to slide the sheet back. Maybe Jonah's been hiding back there all this time. I can't bear the thought of him jumping out at me, or even of him just sitting there, silently listening.

Breathe, Addie. Let your fear come along for the ride.

Quickly, so I don't lose my nerve, I shove through the curtain.

A white tarp lies on the floor with something underneath. Something person-shaped. Bile swims up my throat as I edge closer. A fly buzzes and circles, then lands on the center of it.

It might be Jonah lying under there.

It might be someone else.

It might be . . .

I gag on the bile and press both hands over my mouth until the urge to vomit passes. There's no reason for Jonah to kill Billy. He knows I'd never jump into the island's heart if he did that. And yet, who else is there on the island? I watched my mom and David get into a helicopter. I watched Melinda and Ken get into a boat. Sean is back at the lighthouse. There's only Billy left.

My feet take me closer, nightmare-slow. My heartbeat is a pulsing whine in my ears. Another fly lands on the tarp, and I want to climb back down the ladder and pretend I never saw this, but the image will haunt me forever. I need to know what's under there.

"Jonah, if this is you, I will murder you, even though you're already dead." The joke rings hollow. Stinging sweat beads in the corners of my eyes. I think about nudging the figure with my foot, but I'm too afraid to touch it if it's a dead body. Slowly, slowly, I bend down and pick up the corner of the tarp.

Aa-dee-dee-dee. I can see the bird's shadow projected onto the curtain. It flaps its wings, then launches away.

Keep going. Even if you're afraid.

I yank the tarp sideways. My wobbling legs almost give out.

It's not Jonah. It's not Billy's body.

It's a life-sized statue of me.

Chapter

43

I DROP TO my knees beside the statue. It's stunningly accurate, down to the tiny scar on my chin that I got from falling off a skateboard when I was seven. Obviously I knew Jonah was an artist, but I had no idea he was capable of this. Everything is painstakingly painted except for my eyes, which are blank white. It's like looking at my own corpse.

Immediately I'm jolted back to the video of my death, to the sparkling water and the screaming, the red foam on my lips. The existential horror of looking at a body that is mine but that I'm not inside.

Gut lurching, I pull the tarp off the rest of the statue. I'm wearing a long blue dress I've never seen before. My hair is loose around my face, and my feet are bare. One of my hands touches the sculpted Saint Brendan medallion that hangs around my neck, and the other is bent at the elbow, slightly extended. Around my wrist is Violet's bracelet.

"You had it all along," I whisper, but I can't quite bring myself to touch the statue and take it back.

"So what if I did?"

I whirl around, and there is Jonah.

"Welcome." He's smiling, but there's a dangerous edge to

his voice. "I'd show you around, but it looks like you've already done that yourself."

"Why did you make a statue of me?" I say. "And where's Billy?"

"Don't you like it?" he says, stepping closer. "I've spent a lot of years perfecting my technique."

"It's the creepiest thing I've ever seen," I say, and his mouth twitches. "Why didn't you paint my eyes?"

"I'll need to see what they look like when the island is done with you," he says, and a shudder whispers down the back of my neck. "Did you know mine used to be blue?"

I swallow hard, forcing away the image of myself looking like some dead-eyed zombie. "*Where* is Billy?"

Jonah picks up a black pen and twirls it in his fingers. "I know you're up to something, Addie. You've been sneaking around with Billy, trying to hide your plans and conversations. You've been looking at poor old Roland's maps. And you had quite a lot of questions for Lenora last night."

"I'm just . . . trying to get as much information as I can before I commit to anything." My voice comes out nervous and shrill.

Jonah regards me evenly. "Exactly how stupid do you think I am?"

"I'm not lying." I grit my jaw and stare back.

"But you're not telling me the whole truth." He crosses the room in two long strides, and I shrink back, clenching my trembling hands into fists.

"Neither are you."

He tips his head, acknowledging the truth.

"What did you do to David?" I ask.

"He couldn't find his pills this morning," says Jonah slyly. "And then he had a bit of a scare on the beach. Nobody saw the snake in the sand until he stepped on it."

"You could have killed him," I say.

"But I didn't." Jonah shrugs like the entire emergency with helicopters and rescuers and boats was incidental. "It looks like you and Violet lost your game of hide-and-seek with Billy. Do you want to play another game with me?"

My blood is ice in my veins. "What kind of game?"

Vines slither in through the open windows, and Jonah's treacherous eyes glitter. "If you can find Billy in thirty minutes, I'll let him go. If you can't, then you have to jump into the island's heart."

"Why would I ever agree to that?" I say.

"Because if you don't, I'll throw him in," says Jonah. "And we both know the island doesn't want him."

"You are deeply, horribly hideous," I say, and Jonah inclines his head in a little bow.

"I am only what the island made me. And I'm only doing what I have to."

The last thing I want is to jump into the island's heart and become like him. I'd rather die. But this gives me the tiniest inkling of an idea. If all else fails.

"You'll let Billy go, no strings attached, if I can get to him in thirty minutes?" I say. It's a short window of time, but the island isn't that big.

"No strings." Jonah holds out his empty hands. "You can

leave the island once your mother comes back."

"And David," I say.

He shrugs, and my stomach clenches. Despite all the time I've spent resenting David, I want him to come back too. The vines inch across the floor and crawl over Jonah's bare feet, sprouting blossoms that open like red eyes.

"This seems too easy," I say. Billy is obviously down in the caves, probably in the island's heart, considering Jonah is threatening to throw him in if I don't find him.

A grin slides across Jonah's mouth. "Oh, I promise it won't be easy."

About a thousand furious retorts spring to my tongue, but I swallow them down. Fury doesn't help when you're trying to win. Focus does.

"All right, let's go," I say.

Jonah picks up Billy's watch from the shelf and starts pressing buttons. "I'll give you a sixty-second head start for being such a good sport."

"I don't need your sixty seconds," I scoff.

He laughs, and I want to slap him. "Give me your wrist."

The reckless energy of the island pulses out of his fingertips as they slide over my skin, and I fight to keep my face neutral.

"Thirty minutes," he says, pointing to the digital display. "Would you like to check it to make sure I'm not cheating?"

I glance at the numbers. "It looks fine."

He steps back and gestures to the open trapdoor. "Start it whenever you're ready. Top button on the right. Good luck."

His tone makes me think I'm going to need a lot more than

luck. My heartbeat has become a thundering boom, and I desperately want to cough.

Breathe, Addie. Just breathe.

I sit on the edge of the trapdoor, legs dangling, and press the button on the side of the watch. It beeps, and the numbers begin to drop. This is it.

As I slide down to the ladder, I glance back one last time.

Jonah looks like he's about to eat me alive.

Chapter

44

THE FOREST IS as still as a tomb. Not a single breath of wind ruffles the leaves. Not a chirp or buzz from the birds or the insects. Even the rain has stopped, though the sky is the same sickly greenish hue.

"Violet?" My voice breaks the silence as I hit the ground. She doesn't answer. I call to Billy on the walkie-talkie once more, but there's no response. At a brisk pace, but not quite fast enough to trigger a coughing episode, I head for the path that leads to the cenote. The color bleeds out of the flowers as I pass, the plants limply yielding as I shove through them. I don't want to check my watch to see how much of my head start has elapsed. Part of me wishes it were over already, because this ominous, silent waiting is unbearable.

A sudden whirring nearly makes me jump out of my skin. A bird soars down from the trees and lands on the path in front of me. It's about the size of a crow but much thinner, its feathers the color of blood. It clicks its long, curving beak and peers at me with pure white eyes.

"Are you the one who's been calling my name all this time?" My voice shakes, even though it's only a bird.

The creature cocks its head and ruffles its red feathers.

Run, it croaks.

A blast of hot wind hits me from behind, almost knocking me to my knees. The forest launches into motion, the tree trunks tipping and tilting, the plants rippling and swaying. The bird takes flight, and I break into a sprint. Another gust slams me, and I stagger but keep moving. A searing pain is building in my lungs, but if I can just get to the cenote, it will all fade away. I just have to make it to the water.

Run, shrieks the bird, high overhead.

Run, run, run, echo its friends.

My feet pound the dirt, and tears burn my eyes. Something snatches my ankle, and I fall, hissing as the ground scrapes the skin from my hands and knees. A sticky vine writhes up my calf, and I roll sideways, struggling to get Lenora's knife out of my pocket. The blade slices through the snaking tendrils, bloody sap spatters everywhere, and then I'm back on my feet, gasping and running.

"Addie," Jonah calls from somewhere deep in the woods, drawing out my name. My stomach turns, but I throw my middle finger up, and his laughter rings out as the bushes bend and roll like the waves in the ocean.

I'm almost to the end of the path when my left foot sinks up to the ankle. I lose my balance and pitch forward, and my right foot sticks too. It's deep, watery mud with a layer of dirt on top, and I'm sinking fast. With a furious scream, I tug on my leg, but the muddy pressure increases, sucking my foot deeper. Vaguely, I remember that you're not supposed to struggle in quicksand—if this is in fact quicksand—so I stop moving my legs, but it's still dragging me down.

Gasping, I peer over my shoulder. Jonah strides down the path, and as he opens his hands by his sides, a wash of black floods through the flowers. He lifts his arms, and the ground shakes. A dark, humming cloud billows up from the bushes. I scream and cover my head as the insects come roaring toward me, flies and beetles and dragonflies and wasps. Their wings beat my skin, their legs skim my hair, and their deafening buzz fills my skull.

If hell exists, this must be what it feels like. I can't move in the swarming mass of insects, can't form a single thought because my senses are so completely overwhelmed. I can't breathe, and this is nothing like holding my breath under-water. This is choking, both physically and mentally.

Another gust of hot wind sends the insects skittering away, and I stand frozen, shaking and gasping as my senses slowly return. When I open my eyes, the mud is up to my knees.

"If you give up now, I'll help you," calls Jonah.

"Bite me." I spit a fly off my lip and rub my stinging eyes. I will not let him see me cry. Shifting carefully in the watery mud, I pull the walkie-talkie from my shorts and then ease down onto my back. The muck trickles down the back of my shirt and seeps into my hair, but I'm no longer sinking.

"Billy, hold on. I'm coming for you," I say into the walkie-talkie, not expecting him to answer. I crane my neck to look back down the path, but it's empty. Somehow that's worse than watching Jonah storm toward me with black clouds of insects.

The timer on my watch reads 21:11.

"Let go of me," I whisper to the mud, but apparently it

only listens to Jonah. My feet are full of pins and needles from the squeezing pressure, and I can't even wiggle my toes. I force myself to stop wiggling, to hold every muscle in my body still.

Breathe, Addie, breathe. Focus on something that's not your body.

18:51

17:24

16:36

15:43

Watching the numbers drop is almost as agonizing as feeling the blood leave my extremities. I hope Billy is okay. I hope he has his inhaler. I can't bear the thought of him getting hurt—or worse—because of me.

The pressure is gradually easing, but every time I try to pull my feet out, the suction increases and I lose another inch. I need to be patient, but I don't have time for patience. I wonder if there's a faster way to get into the caves than going down through the cenote, but I don't have any rope and I don't know which sinkholes line up with which caves. If I lowered myself into a dead end, I'd never get out in time—assuming I ever got out.

13:56

Finally, the mud is loose enough around my left leg that I'm able to slide it out. It takes another precious two minutes and fifty seconds before I manage to pull the right leg out. My sandals are gone. Slow as molasses, I roll sideways until the ground is solid, and then I shake my legs and rub my numb feet, nearly screaming when the blood floods back in an agonizing wave. Coughing and filthy, I drag myself upright and wipe the mud from my face.

9:22

My legs shake, my lungs burn, and my feet are a half-numb mess as I take off again through the writhing, clawing bushes. I thought I'd be in the cenote by now. I thought I'd have more than enough time to make it through all the caves. I don't know why I thought Jonah would let it be that easy.

8:06

I reach the giant boulder, but the path that usually forks off beside it is gone. It shouldn't matter; I know the general direction, and the cenote is close enough and big enough that I won't miss it. The dive takes less than two minutes, and my lungs will stop hurting as soon as I'm in the water. In theory I'll be able to sprint through the caves once I'm there. It's going to be very tight, though.

Aa-dee-dee-dee, call the birds.

The moment I step off the path, the plants swarm me, tangling on my legs, wrapping around my waist, crawling up my torso. My mouth fills with a floral, copper tang as they slide up my neck and over my face, and I cough and spit, but that makes it worse. Buds are sprouting; petals are unfurling against my cheeks. Roots are trying to burrow into my skin. I pull out Lenora's knife, wedge the blade between the vine and my neck, and the plant falls away, shriveling.

There's a sudden, trembling crunch, and a huge chunk of ground by my feet tumbles away. Lurching backward, I let the vines grab my wrist. I start to cough, and they swarm closer, opening their greedy flower mouths to drink my blood. It's twisted and sick, but at least they're holding me tight, away from the crumbling sinkhole. I can't even see the bottom. It must be at least forty meters deep, and if Jonah opened it up on purpose, it must be a dead end.

I wait until the sinkhole's edges are done breaking and tumbling, and then I cut myself loose. The vines hiss, openly weeping sap as they writhe away from Lenora's blade.

"Thank you for not letting me fall," I whisper, though I don't want to think about what they might have done to me if it weren't for my knife. I hold the blade out in front of me as I skirt around the sinkhole, and the crawling plants cower out of the way.

The curtain of Spanish moss looms ahead, but it appears to be moving. As I get closer, I realize it's crawling with centipedes. The smallest ones are the size of my index finger. The largest ones I can't bring myself to look at.

"Jonah, you absolute bastard," I mutter, and the trees shiver and shake.

5:47

There's no time to be squeamish. I can't let myself think about how many legs there are in that writhing mess of black. Throwing one hand over my mouth and one out in front of me with Lenora's knife, I dash into the curtain, gagging as the wet, wriggling bodies hit my skin. The crawling legs are everywhere; the wet squelch of them makes vomit surge up my throat. The stench is indescribable, rot and feces and filthy earth, and as I break through the other side, there's no relief because hundreds of the crawling creatures are still stuck all over me.

Tears pour down my face as I sprint for the cenote, not stopping to remove clothes or even the walkie-talkie. I throw myself deep into the gleaming water, and as the bubbles stream up, the centipedes let go. They float off my skin, dissolving in the blue glow, and all the agony in my body dissolves too as the heartbeat fills my ears. I kick to the surface, pocket Lenora's knife, and check my watch.

4:42

I drag in a few deep breaths. There's no time to do a full warm-up, but it doesn't matter. The water will take care of me. In more ways than one, if Jonah wins this game. I hope there's enough time left to make it to the heart. I hope Billy is safe. I hope that wasn't the last time I saw my mother. I hope I'll come back, still myself, still alive, when everything is done.

With one last glance at the muddy green sky, I flip upside down and dive.

Chapter
45

THE FIRST FEW meters of the dive are clear and bright, just as they have been every other time. Even though my heart is heavy with worry and fear, my muscles sing at the release of pain, the softness of the water, the overwhelming calm of this place. But as I drop lower, as the pressure builds and the buoyancy begins to leave my body, clouds of silt billow up through the hole at the bottom. In seconds, I'm enveloped.

Just keep going, Addie. Just keep moving.

I'm far enough underwater now that all I have to do is let gravity take me down. But I can't see the hole anymore. It shouldn't be this frightening—the water always goes black when I dive far enough down in the ocean, but when I'm training or competing, I'm tethered to a line so I don't drift off course. And there are safety divers, coaches, fellow divers. Not an empty hole that leads into the circulatory system of a murderous island.

Push through it even though you're afraid. Let your fear come along.

I am terrified. I am doing this with fear. I am doing it anyway.

Down, down, down I sink until my hands brush the bottom. Nothing hurts, but I know I'm going to need to breathe soon. At this point in a dive, I'd be turning around and heading back to the surface, but this time, I need to keep going down. With a twisting kick, I propel myself sideways, trailing my fingers along the cenote's floor.

My shoulder hits a wall and I turn back, changing course slightly. Or at least I hope I'm changing course, not going back over the exact same spot. It's impossible to tell in this milky fog. I'm starting to feel giddy, which is not a good thing. Giddiness means there's too much nitrogen building up in my blood. Nitrogen narcosis is like being drunk, and it can lead to mistakes and accidents.

Keep going, just keep going.

As I kick back across the cave floor, the overwhelming urge to laugh hits me, and I bite down hard on my tongue. What if I drown down here, inches away from a hole that I just can't see? There's nothing funny about that, but my narcced brain can't seem to get the message. I bite my tongue again until I taste blood.

Then the floor under my fingers is gone. It takes me far too long to remember why that's a good thing, and then I flip and kick and shoot down inside the hole. The water brightens as the fog rolls away, and I can faintly make out the edges of the sideways tunnel that glows indigo at the other end. My muscle memory is telling me which way to go, even though my conscious brain is drunk and unhelpful. Toward that exquisite, deep blue. My nitrogen-drunk mind is certain the glowing light loves me. I love it too.

As I reach the brightest part of the indigo glow, the light

bends around me, turning my body a million shades of blue and purple, and I roll onto my back and let it filter into my eyes. The heartbeat throbs, calming and settling me like I'm a fetus in the island's womb. I could stay here forever.

But I'm not supposed to stay here forever. I'm supposed to come up for air before I drown, and then I need to keep moving. I have to find Billy before my time runs out, but I can't stop forgetting.

My head breaks the surface, and I gasp under the beautiful black dome streaked with lime green and turquoise. The heartbeat hums through the water, through my bones, and the cave radiates its same calming energy. But now that the nitrogen in my body is fading, panic is taking its place. I check my watch.

1:01

There's no time to scream or swear or think about the fact that I've just wasted three and a half minutes underwater. I throw myself at the beach, pebbles skidding under my feet, and I fall three times before I make it out of the water. Frantic, I find the hole in the wall, and as I drop to my knees, fresh blood leaks out of the scrapes that are already there.

Come on, come on, come on, I think as I crawl through the claustrophobic space. The bottom is much more slippery than the last time I came here, and my hands keep sliding out from under me. It's impossible to move as fast as I want. It's impossible to see where I'm going, but the only way is forward, and I can't give up now. My forehead slams a low-hanging rock, and tears spring to my eyes, but seconds later I'm through, ducking under the boulder and dashing into the soaring cathedral.

I should check my watch, but I can't bear to see how little time is left. The silver water shudders faintly as the island's heartbeat grows louder, louder. Tucking my chin and pumping my arms, I sprint down the aisle that cuts a line through the enormous stalagmites. I should be more careful on this wet stone, but there's no time left to worry about it. If I fall, I fall.

The altar looms closer.

But something is different. There are two statues now instead of one.

My mouth goes dry as I recognize my own face next to Eulalie's. The finality of seeing it here takes something out of me, and I stumble, skid, and almost fall into the water. Even though it's upright now, my statue still looks dead because my eyes are still blank, because Jonah is waiting to see how I'll change. I cannot let that happen.

But as I leap up onto the altar, my watch starts to beep.

Chapter

46

THE BOOMING HEARTBEAT is everywhere, vibrating through my core as I step into the white crystal cave. Jonah stands by the wall where he painted my face, back when everything was different—no, when everything was the same, and I just didn't know. He breaks into a gloating smile, and I'd like to slap it off his face, but I'm too overwhelmed with relief at seeing Billy alive, sitting at the edge of the hole with his arms wrapped around his backpack.

Jonah checks his own watch, undoubtedly stolen from some other unsuspecting guest, and cocks an eyebrow. "Five minutes and twelve seconds late? I knew you'd lose, but I thought you'd be a little faster than that."

"Shut up, you gigantic asshole." Billy takes a puff from his inhaler and glares at Jonah.

Yes, I could have been a little faster than that. But once I lost, I decided I wasn't going to play Jonah's game anymore. I was going to change the rules. So I sat down beside the statues and I came up with a new strategy. A backup plan, now that everything's fallen apart. It's a plan full of holes and maybes, but it's the best I can do under the circumstances. And the fact that Billy has his backpack has just turned one of those maybes into a yes.

"Are you all right?" I ask, and he nods.

"He said you were hurt down here, and he needed my help to get you out," says Billy. "I didn't want you to get in trouble. But holy shit, that underwater tunnel was the scariest thing I've ever been in." He shudders. "I kept wondering if he was going to let go of the rope halfway through and leave me to drown."

"He wouldn't have, because then I'd never hold up my end of the bargain," I say.

"What end of the——" Realization dawns on Billy's face. "Addie, you can't be serious."

"I am. I have to do it." Trying to convey everything that's swirling in my head, I widen my eyes at him, but he's too agitated to notice.

"You can't." His voice hitches. "I won't let you."

"She lost the game, and she *will* do it." Jonah grabs the back of Billy's T-shirt and wrenches him over the abyss. "Or you'll go in instead."

My arm shoots out to block them. Billy's gasping, his face white. "I'm going to, I swear," I say. "Just give me a second. Let go of him. *Please.*"

"I'm tired of waiting." Jonah growls, releasing Billy but staying close. His dark eyes have taken on a feverish gleam. "I thought you might make the right choice if I was honest with you, Addie. I thought you might choose to help me. I thought there was something between us, but apparently I was wrong."

I think back to the last time we were here, when my mouth

was all over his. "There was something between us. But it was never really you, was it?"

His beautiful face falls. "All of this is me. I've offered you everything you could possibly want. A perfect island paradise where you can stay and heal as long as you like, where you can make yourself stronger and faster than everyone else. I swore I'd come back for you, and I will. I *want* to see you again. I can't stop thinking about you, Addie. Why isn't that enough?"

"Because it's not my choice," I say. "You never once asked me what *I* wanted."

Jonah shakes his head. "I gave you so many choices, and look where it led you."

"Exactly to the place where you wanted me," I say.

He sighs. "You have ten seconds."

I stare into the black hole, the silver water endlessly tumbling. In a few seconds I'm going to plunge into that darkness. I can't begin to consider how it will destroy everyone I love if I fail. Especially my mother. I can't do this to her. But I have to try.

"Trust me," I say, sitting beside Billy and leaning against his shoulder.

A tear slips down his cheek, and I hate that I can't reassure him. I can't even reassure myself. I needed more time to figure out a better plan, and I never should have assumed Jonah was oblivious. I got outplayed in this awful game of his, but it isn't quite over yet. Every inch of me is covered in cold sweat.

The island's heartbeat booms up through the hole, shaking my bones as I swing my legs over the edge.

"Don't do it." The brokenness in Billy's voice nearly undoes me. "I love you, Addie."

I squeeze his trembling hand. "I love you too. I'll see you soon."

Before he can answer, I snatch his backpack and jump.

Chapter
47

I WRAP MY arms tight around the backpack as I plummet into the darkness, wind roaring in my ears and pulling tears from my eyes. It's sickening and disorienting to fall like this, with no sense of where the ground is, where I'll land, how far the walls are from my body. There's nothing but gravity and rushing mass and the screaming, animal panic inside my brain. I fall and fall and fall until I can't feel my body anymore, can't make sense of up or down.

Boom, boom, boom, beats the heart, blocking out every thought in my brain. I'm losing consciousness again, just like I did when I put my hand in this silvery water, except this time the water is all over me and I'm falling, falling right out of myself. That pure, overwhelming sense of love floods through me, but this time I know it's not right. It's not love. This time I fight it, though I'm certain it's a losing battle.

My back brushes a smooth, wet surface, and I'm sliding more than falling, though still at an incomprehensible speed. I'm airborne, then crashing down into shallow water with an enormous splash and a sickening crunch in one ankle. The backpack lands beside me.

It's as black as death down here. Maybe I'm already dead. Whatever just happened to my ankle cannot be good, but I can't feel a thing. The heartbeat's booming roar fills my ears, my skull, my chest, my stomach as I wade in a slow circle, touching the walls all around me. The space is the size of a closet, and the water keeps pouring in from above, but just as Lenora said, it's not getting any deeper.

I make another circle, this time feeling with my uninjured foot along the bottom edge of the walls. Halfway around, I find the hole Lenora got sucked down into, the one she drowned inside of, and I sink down to feel the size of it. It's just barely wide enough for a body to fit through, even narrower than the underwater tunnel where Roland died.

I think I can block it. This wasn't my first choice when I thought of stopping the island's heart, but maybe it's the best one. If Roland's unfinished maps are correct, I'm somewhere between the heart and the lungs, which I hope to never see. Ripping open Billy's backpack, I rummage through blindly, hoping to find something that might keep me from getting sucked through that hole.

Granola bars, water bottle, walkie-talkie, beach towel.

The constant booming makes it nearly impossible to think, but I pull out Lenora's knife and start ripping the towel into long shreds. I twist them into a clumsy braid and then tie the ends together so that it forms a circle. If this works, there's going to be an enormous amount of pressure building over me, and I'm not sure the towel will hold, but it's better than nothing.

Still the heart thunders, and I desperately wish it would stop for just a minute so I could clear my head. I drop underwater again, this time searching with my fingers for a crack in the rocks near the opening. It takes a long time—precious minutes where Jonah must be wondering what's happening and Billy must think I'm dead—but I need to get this exactly right. Finally, I find the perfect spot, and I gather up my towel sling and Lenora's knife, sinking down and driving the knife through the thickest part of the rope knot.

On my first try, I miss the crack I'm aiming for, and the blade glances off the stone and slips out of my hand. Swearing, I fumble around until I find it. I'm sure I've cut my fingers but I can't feel anything and I can't worry about a little blood. On the second stab, the knife finds the crack, but the angle is wrong. If I'm not careful, I'm going to snap the blade.

And if I die down here, they might never find my body.

I can't do this to my mother. This will absolutely break her.

Come on, Addie. Breathe. Do this with your fear, and do not screw it up.

The next stab goes in straight and true, and the towel rope holds fast, floating just inside the opening. I start sipping in breaths, stretching my lungs and stilling my mind. It would be so much easier to do this without the constant booming, but maybe there's a way to harness the negative. With each beat, I'm going to relax a little bit more. I'm going take Jonah's advice and stop resisting the island.

Boom.

I roll out my neck.

Boom.

I pull in another slow breath.

Boom.

I loosen my jaw.

Boom.

Fear still flutters like a trapped bird in my chest, but I give it the space to be there.

Boom.

I suck in my last, deepest breath, and sink.

There's a steady current now, pulling the water into the hole, and I'm careful to hold my body upright as I maneuver toward the makeshift sling. I ease into it backward, tucking it around my hips and under my knees, and then I fold my body around the backpack. The bag and the positioning give me just enough volume that I can't quite fit into the hole. My body's buoyancy keeps trying to pull me toward the surface, but I wiggle backward until I'm wedged into the opening. This would hurt if I could feel any pain.

Now I wait.

Now I sit at the bottom of a cave, deep underground, while gallons and gallons of water pour down on top of me, and I hope that my oxygen holds out longer than the island's heartbeat. I try to push away all the panicky thoughts, all the images of myself dead and bloated and stuck in this tunnel until my flesh comes off my bones. Of my body falling out of that waterfall, covered in bruises with my eyes turned a different color. Of my mother sobbing in her wide-brimmed hat . . .

Let it go, Addie. Let it all go.

The pressure builds as the water deepens over me, and I let it crush away my fear. I've got two lungs full of air, no pain in my body, and I've been training half my life for something not unlike this. If anyone on this earth has a shot at beating this island, it's me.

Still, the heartbeat pounds, and as the seconds tick past, my legs start to tremble, and I wonder if I'm actually stronger than an entire island. I wonder how I'm going to get out of here, even if I succeed. I wonder what will happen if my body gives out in the middle of the process, whether the island will still take me, knowing what I tried to do, or whether it will kill me. All of these options lead to terrible ends.

Let it go, Addie.

My arms are shaking now, and my shoulders, and I'm trying to push through it along with my fear, like I'd do when I was diving, but there's nowhere to push through to. If this were a dive, I'd have a target in mind, either the plate at the bottom of my dive or the surface at the top. Now my target is death, either the island's or mine.

Boom, boom, boom.

It might be slowing, or I might be losing consciousness. I've been under for least three minutes, and I can feel my lungs collapsing. Every instinct in my body is screaming, and the urge to kick out of this hole and swim to the surface is unbearable. I reach for the knife to make sure it's still wedged in the crack, and something makes me change my mind and tug. I barely catch myself before I rip it out of the crack.

Get, out, get, out, screams my brain in time with the heartbeat, and I squeeze my eyes shut and shove those words away. I trust my body. I trust myself. My abdomen starts to convulse.

Something reptilian deep in the back of my brain keeps telling me it's fine if I want to breathe now. If I just let go, it will all be okay.

Boom.

Silence. My eyes flick open, but there's nothing to see.

Boom.

It's slowing, weakening. I'd be elated if I weren't about to die.

Now the heartbeat is a slow, stuttering thud. The water's crushing pressure isn't lessening, but it's no longer increasing. I just want to breathe. Shapes are swimming in my vision, things I know aren't actually in this black cave. Swirls of color, random objects from around the island. A thatched roof, a palm tree, a braided bracelet, a harp.

My mother's face, slowly filling my vision. She smiles, her face a radiant beam of light, and love pours from her to me, filling my chest and spilling into my stuttering heart. My body hums with indescribable lightness. I am not a failure. I am loved. I don't know what comes next, but whatever happens is okay.

Everything goes silent.

The heartbeat is gone.

The pressure is gone.

The cave is gone.

I'm gone.

Chapter

48

I WAKE UP vomiting huge, burning stomachfuls of water. I'm curled on my side in some place that's slick stone on the bottom and dry everywhere else, but I can't stop retching long enough to look up. Everything smells of stone and plants and sick, but I can smell again. I can see again. I can breathe again, when I'm not throwing up.

Holy sheep, I'm alive.

And I'm fairly sure my ankle is broken.

I choke out another mouthful of water that feels like fire in my throat and nostrils, and then I start to cough, spraying bloody pink all over the place. I've never, ever been so happy to cough. It's like daggers stabbing my chest, but it means I'm alive. I hope my eyes are still the same color, but I haven't ended up in the pool by the waterfall, and the island's heart still isn't beating.

Spent, I roll onto my back, and everything smears and swirls before my eyes manage to focus. I'm in a huge cave with daylight streaming through several holes in the ceiling. A shallow stream runs from one side to the other, and bones lie scattered on either side of it. Legs, ribs, fingers, skulls, others I can't identify. I'm both sickened and relieved that my own bones are still safely inside my skin. Spongy, bush-like trees fill the space. These must be the island's lungs. They don't appear to be breathing. The air is clean and light, and my ears ring with the silence.

"Hello?" I call, my voice ragged from all the water and acid. "Can anybody hear me?"

A tremor goes through the ground, and the lung trees shiver. I sit up to inspect my ankle. It's swollen, but I can flex and point my foot. Maybe not broken after all.

"Hello!" I yell again. "Is anyone there?"

The hole on the other side of the room is just as tiny as the one I came out of, and the last thing I want to do is crawl into it. It might be my only way out of here, but my body starts to tremble every time I look at it. The stream of water appears to be getting deeper, the current speeding up.

"Addie-dee?" A tiny voice filters down from far overhead.

"Violet, is that you?" My own voice is almost gone.

"I think it is me." Her tone wobbles. "But I'm very strange now and I don't have my body anymore."

My heart leaps. "Violet, that's really good!" This means something changed. Hopefully it means the island's connection to her is broken.

"Do you still have your body?" calls Violet.

"Yes!"

A pause.

"That's not fair."

I start to laugh, but another shaking rumble cuts me off. The spongy trees begin to contract, revealing white bones intermingled with the branches.

"Violet, have you seen Billy anywhere?" I rasp, as loud as I can.

"Yes, he came out of a different hole and he's all wet and very dirty."

Relief floods through me. "Can you get him and tell him to find some rope and come back here?" I call.

There's no answer.

"Violet?"

Another shudder races through the lung trees as they contract. Bones and skulls clatter to the floor as the leaves blacken and crumble and fall like ashes.

"Violet?"

Still no answer, and I desperately hope it's because she's gone to find Billy. I can't bear to look at the lung trees, but whenever I shut my eyes, it feels like I'm underwater with the heartbeat pulsing around me. I'm starting to shiver, even though it must be ninety degrees in here.

A soft thud startles me out of my shivery daze.

"Addie!"

I could sob at the sound of Billy's voice. A length of rope stretches from the bottom of the cave all the way up through the hole in the center of the ceiling.

"I'm here!" I struggle to my feet, trying to ignore the black stars swimming in my vision and the agony in my ankle.

"I can't believe we found you!" he yells, and my throat closes up when I try to respond, because I can't quite believe it either. "Put your foot in the loop at the bottom of the rope and hold on tight," he says. "I'm going to use the golf cart to pull you out."

As I step my good foot through the rope, the ground shakes again, and one of the lung trees tips sideways. It crashes to the floor, exposing long, bloody roots. I gag as another tremor, this one even stronger, sends chunks of stone and dirt raining down from the ceiling.

"I'm ready!" I yell. "Hurry!"

The rope flies up, burning my palms and throwing me off balance. The loop jerks from my foot to the back of my knee, and I bend my leg and grab hold as it sweeps me into the air. The cave shakes and rumbles as I rocket toward the crumbling ceiling. Another lung tree makes a hideous wheezing sound as it tips.

"Slow down!" I scream, barely dodging a rock the size of my head.

The line goes slack, and the sudden jerk almost sends me tumbling to my death, but then I begin to ascend again, this time at a slower pace, and finally I reach up and dig my fingernails into the edge of the hole, though I've got no strength left to pull myself out.

"She's here!" yells Violet, and the golf cart's engine cuts out.

"I've got you." Billy tugs on my wrist, then my forearm. It feels like my shoulder might pop out of its socket, but then we're both tumbling and landing in a heap in the dirt. We're beside the path, somewhere between the cenote and the Wells house. Billy's elbow is in my ear and my knee is in his bony armpit, and we try to untangle ourselves, and we both start to laugh, harder and harder until we're gasping. And then

I'm coughing. But as the flecks of blood land on the ground, nothing happens.

"I did it," I say. "I stopped the heart."

"Yeah, you did," says Billy. "Right when all the booming stopped, Jonah collapsed. Like, flat-out on the floor. I thought he was dead and I was going to be stuck in that cave forever if I couldn't figure out how to freedive back through all those caves and that scary tunnel. But then he sat up and yelled, 'What color are my eyes?' I was like, 'Bro, I can't really tell down here. Everything looks kind of blue,' and I swear to God, I thought he was going to cry."

I wipe my own tears of laughter off my cheeks. "I can't even imagine it."

"That guy is so weird," says Billy. "He pulled me back through the tunnel and hoisted me out a different hole, and then he ran off to the east side of the island—he said something about a waterfall and making sure it really happened—I don't even know."

I jolt at the mention of the waterfall. "Billy, are my eyes the same color as before?"

He squints at me. "Still brown. Still . . . really pretty." He flushes for a second, then continues. "I went back to the lighthouse, and Sean said he'd call the cops, even though he didn't believe me about why you were missing. He also said my dad called from the hospital and they're keeping David overnight, but he's going to be okay."

"Oh, thank God," I say.

"You can stay with us at the lighthouse until they get

back," he says. "Unless you need to go to the hospital too? Are you okay?"

Wincing, I roll out my ankle, then flex and point my foot again. "It's probably just a bad sprain."

"I think I sprain-ded my hands too." Violet drifts out of the trees. She doesn't look like an animated corpse anymore—her skin is no longer gray or bloated, and she's almost transparent. She holds her palms to her eyes, peering straight through at us. "What's wrong with my hands, Addie-dee?"

"You're not bound to this island anymore," I say. "You're not trapped in that dead body anymore." Billy gives me a horrified look, and I shrug. "It's true."

Violet juts out her nearly invisible lower lip. "What does that mean?"

"It means you can move on," says Billy. "To heaven or the afterlife or wherever."

Violet gawks at him. "How do I do that?"

"I think you might need your sister," I say.

"I always need my sister!" wails Violet. "But she is never here."

A tremor goes through the ground. Leaves and petals and dead bugs rain down from the trees.

"Let's try your house," I say. "I have an idea, but I don't think I can walk all the way there. Billy, can you drive?"

Billy breaks into an enormous grin as he holds up the golf cart key.

Chapter
49

AS WE CAREEN through the forest, the flowers are all blackening and shriveling and falling. Branches keep crashing down around us, and the air smells of sulfur. The small earthquakes have become almost constant. I'm carsick from Billy's chaotic driving, my ankle is throbbing, and I feel like I've been run through a washing machine. As we roar into the valley, I'm tempted to ask him to slow down, but something tells me we don't have much time. I don't know what will happen if and when the island's heart starts up again.

Billy pulls up next to the Wellses' crumbling house and helps me hobble closer, Violet drifting along beside us. A putrid odor fills the air.

"Are you sure we need to go inside?" he asks, pulling the neck of his T-shirt over his nose.

"You can wait out here if you want." I try to sound nonchalant for Violet's sake, but my eyes are watering from the stench and I don't want to go inside any more than Billy does.

The ground shakes again, and a branch the length of a car smashes onto the ground behind the house.

"I'll come in," says Billy.

The stench grows sweet and rotten, the unmistakable smell of a corpse, and I wonder if we're about to find Violet's actual body. That can't be a good thing for a tiny girl to see, even if she's been a ghost for hundreds of years.

"Violet, maybe you should wait out here while I check something first?" I say, but she darts around me and flits inside.

"Nooo!" she wails, and Billy and I struggle after her.

On the ruined hearth in the kitchen, an iguana lies dead.

"Edwin!" sobs Violet, pressing her transparent cheek to its mottled flesh.

"Was . . . Edwin a ghost iguana, or did he just die the regular way?" I ask Billy, who shrugs.

"This is your fault!" Violet's head snaps up, tears running down her face. "You said you were going to fix everything, but I'm still here and Nora is still gone, and now Edwin is dead too. And you losted my bracelet!"

"I didn't—" I start to say, but Violet flies away with a ferocious scream. The ground shakes again, and the cracking snap of trees echoes through the woods. Gritting my teeth, I limp to the bedroom and heft Lenora's harp onto my shoulder.

"What the heck are you doing?" asks Billy as I drag my hand across the space where the strings should be.

"Shh." I rake my fingers through the gap again, and the ancient wooden frame begins to vibrate. "Lenora, are you out there? You can come back now. The island can't stop you."

From deep underground comes a terrible rumbling. A heavy stone tumbles from the wall, and bricks fall off the broken top of the chimney. Ominous clouds billow overhead. The woods are black with dead flowers, and their sulfurous odor is making me dizzy.

"I think we'd better find Sean and get off this island," says Billy.

"Just give me one minute." I drag my hand across the harp's center once more, and this time it lets out an eerie, warbling note. Billy's mouth drops open.

"That is creepy as f——"

Somewhere deep in the woods, Violet screams.

Not bothering to wait for Billy's help, I hobble outside, shoving through branches full of rotting blossoms. The stench of death is everywhere, and the constant shifting underground sounds like thunder.

"Violet!" I yell. "Where are you?"

"I'm . . . I'm h-here," she sobs, and Billy overtakes me, crashing through the undergrowth. He swerves around the bloody roots of a newly fallen tree, then stops on the other side, both hands over his mouth.

"What?" I trip and nearly scream as I land on my bad ankle. "What happened?"

"Look." Billy grabs me and points.

Violet stands on a boulder in the center of a small clearing, bathed in a strange golden light that isn't coming from the sky. All around her, black petals float down. She's crying and trailing her tiny hands through the shimmering light, and she keeps repeating the same word, over and over.

Nora.

"She's here," says Violet. "Can you hear her?"

I shake my head. "What's she saying?"

"She says thank you."

The golden light contracts, darkening until I can just barely make out the shape of Lenora. Her lovely face no longer looks like a skull, and her black hair gleams. Her arms are wrapped tightly around Violet, her chin resting on top of her sister's head. She meets my gaze and mouths the words again. *Thank you.*

"You're welcome." I choke on the second word as the enormity hits me. These sisters haven't seen each other in almost two hundred years. I'm sobbing for them and for the time they lost. For everything they lost.

"Nora says we can go now," says Violet, and I can only nod, tears dripping off my chin. "She says she knows the way."

There's a sickeningly loud crunch, and Lenora fades out as a tree sways and crashes down. In the space where its roots once burrowed into the soil, there's a gaping hole. Stumbling, I run to Violet and reach for her hand, but my fingers pass right through.

"Go with Lenora," I say. "You're safe now. I'll miss you both."

"Goodbye, Addie-dee. Goodbye, Billy." Violet blows us both a kiss and flashes a triumphant smile. "I'm going to win hide-and-seek for ever and ever now."

"You're the grand champion." Billy looks like he's fighting back tears. I thread my arm through the crook of his elbow and squeeze.

The golden light expands, pulling us into its glow, and warmth floods through me. Then it's gone, and Violet is gone. The woods look emptier than they ever did before. I spent so much time hoping for this moment, and I never expected to feel this gutted when it happened.

"Bye, Violet," I whisper.

Another shattering crack echoes through the woods, and there's no more time to cry.

Chapter
50

THE GROUND OF the clearing begins to sink, and Billy and I throw ourselves backward as a sinkhole opens up and the boulder tumbles inside.

Boom.

It's not the sound of the boulder landing. It's the sound of the island's heart starting back up.

A plume of smoke pours out of the gaping mouth that was once a clearing, and we watch, horrified, as the air fills with humming. Bees. Or wasps. Or hornets. We don't stick around to find out. The insects engulf us as we race for the golf cart, and shots of pain hit my body, one after the other. I want to drop to the ground and howl, but I force myself to run through the agony. We throw ourselves into the cart, and Billy guns the engine. As we skid down the path and through a low-hanging curtain of moss, the swarm thins.

"You're not allergic, are you?" Billy slaps the back of his neck.

Gingerly, I touch my cheek, where three welts are rising. "No, are you?"

"Nope. Is Jonah doing this?" Billy waves his arm in the general direction of the bees, the woods, the sinkholes.

"I think this is the island," I say. "It lost Jonah and Violet, it has nobody now, and it's angry."

Furious is a better word for it. *Seething.* Shriveled vines are crawling all over the path, and our wheels skid and jolt over them. Black shadows keep darting overhead, and the booming underground is getting faster, more regular. Stronger.

"Hurry up," I say.

"The pedal's all the way down," Billy mutters, gripping the wheel with both hands.

Our rear wheel slams over something, and the entire cart tips. Too startled to scream, I grab the overhead handle as Billy cuts the wheel and hits the brakes, somehow managing to get us back onto four wheels. He steps on the gas again, and I peer over my shoulder as we roar off: a root the size of my leg is curling out of the dirt.

Another dark shape drops out of the trees and slaps our windshield, leathery wings splayed. The bat fixes its feral, shining eyes on me and bares its teeth.

Addie, it rasps.

Yelling a string of swears, Billy throws on the windshield wipers. One of the bat's wings catches in the blade, and as it gets dragged backward across the glass, it lets out a hideous hiss. The golf cart swerves and we're skidding sideways, then backward, then sliding down an embankment hidden by bushes. With a sickening crunch, the back of the vehicle hits a tree, and the fumy scent of gasoline fills the air.

"Come on!" I climb out, but Billy just sits there staring at the cracked windshield. A rotten vine is snaking around his elbow, crawling up his arm, and he doesn't seem to notice. Eyes watering from the pain in both my lungs and my ankle,

I hobble around to his side of the cart. Lenora's knife is gone, lost somewhere down in the island's underbelly, so I rip the decaying, squelching plants off him with my hands.

"I think I hit my head," Billy groans, and I suck in my breath as I spot the bloody gash on his temple.

"It's not too bad," I lie, grabbing a towel from the back seat. Billy yelps as I press it to the wound. "We'll bandage it up at the lighthouse. Do you think you can make it there?"

He scoffs. "What, you're the only one who can walk with an injury?"

"Well, no." I eye the plants that are slowly engulfing the cart. "But I'm thinking we're going to need to run."

Holding tight to each other's hands, we abandon the golf cart and thrash through the woods, heading toward the beach. Clouds of insects billow and swirl, trees groan and lurch and fall, and the tiny patches of visible sky are twilight dark.

"Watch out!" I yank Billy sideways as the ground where he was about to step gives way, tumbling into a sinkhole.

"It's like the island is trying to eat us," he says, and a chill races over my skin. That's exactly what it's trying to do.

We cut away from the sinkhole, moving slower now. The rotten-corpse stench of the plants is unbearable, and I can't believe I ever thought the regular flower scent was unpleasant. This is a million times worse. I'm coughing every few steps and need to stop, but we're almost to the beach, and that's got to be safer than these hungry woods.

As we near the edge of the trees, I step in a deep puddle, and my first, panicky thought is that it's quicksand again, but then I realize it's the ocean crawling in. The island is flooding. We pick our way through the last of the forest, and there's no beach left. The gray sea is sloshing into the palms, the water littered with leaves and branches and black flowers.

I did this. I broke the island. But if the only other choice was to let the island keep me, I have to be okay with what I've done. An engine roars and sputters down by the lighthouse, and Billy and I stumble through the water where the beach used to be. The catamaran lies half on top of the jetty, its hulls smashed and its mast leaning at a drunken angle. As we clamber around the ruined watercraft, I spot two figures struggling on the other side.

Jonah crouches in the Zodiac boat, tugging on the engine's start cord, and Sean is trying to shove him out. There's a tiny strip of sand left beside the jetty, and I stop to spit out several mouthfuls of blood while Billy charges into the water to help his brother. There's a lot of yelling and thrashing, but I'm coughing so hard I can't look. Blood spatters the white sand, instantly soaking down, and I shuffle backward, gasping for air as the red stains become widening tunnels. Then one big, yawning hole.

"Who the hell is this guy?" yells Sean.

"Don't even ask," says Billy. "Just start the engine."

The boat sputters to life, and I force my legs to carry me through the water. Someone pulls me into the boat and I press my forehead to its rubbery side and suck in oxygen. Beside me is a plastic cat carrier with Kylo yowling inside. The engine roars and strains, but when I finally manage to look up, we haven't moved.

"The current is too strong," yells Billy.

Sean steers us left, then right, but no matter which way he tries to angle us away from the island, waves shove us back.

"Let me." Jonah tries to push him away from the tiller, but Sean grabs a yellow waterproof bag and slams it into his shoulder.

"Stop it," I yell. "If you capsize us or flood the engine, none of us are getting off this island."

Jonah whips around to face me. He's different now, and it's not just that his eyes are blue. His features are still handsome, but he's no longer glowing with whatever energy the island gave him. Something about him seems older, more ragged. More human.

"The island is never going to let both of us leave," he says.

"Then maybe you should go back," I say.

He glances over my shoulder, and his mouth curls into a wry smile. A wave gushes over the boat, sweeping everyone into its foamy chaos. I tumble overboard, cartwheeling in the roaring water, and for several long seconds, it's impossible to tell which direction is up. Then something grabs my arm. Someone. The waves are still rolling and smashing everywhere, I can't see the boat or Billy or Sean, and I can't find my footing as Jonah drags me toward the shore. I suck in a mouthful of ocean and the water goes red as I cough it back out.

"You can't force me to do it." I twist away as we reach the narrow strip of sand, the gaping hole. "I have to go willingly."

With a black look, Jonah grabs me again. "I'm willing to try it and see what happens."

I spin back toward the water, but he hooks his foot around my injured ankle, and I fall with an agonized scream. He grabs my other ankle and hauls me toward the hole, and there's nothing to hold on to, no way to stop myself from sliding closer, closer along the sand. I kick and thrash, but his grip is unbearably strong.

"You should have believed me," he says. "I would have come back for you. But instead, you ruined everything."

Tears stream down my cheeks, and blood bubbles on my lips. The edge of the hole is inches from my face; grains of sand stream over the lip and tumble into the chasm. Jonah pauses, and something like pity flits across his face.

"I'm sorry it has to be you," he says.

There's a piercing shriek, and a creature as red as my blood soars out of the trees. The bird bombs down, claws reaching for Jonah's face. As he throws his hands up to protect himself, I rock backward, tuck my legs in, and kick out as hard as I can, catching him in the back of his knees. Pain explodes in my ankle, and for the flicker of an instant, Jonah looks back at me, his beautiful, terrible face twisted in shock. Then he pitches forward and tumbles into the hole. A tremor goes through the island, and the heartbeat booms.

"Guess it didn't have to be me after all," I mutter as I get to my feet.

"Addie!" Billy thrashes through the waves, which have slowed, although there's another big set rolling in. "Are you okay? Oh my God, when you kicked him in? Most incredible thing I've ever seen. But seriously, are you okay?"

"Yeah." I ease away from the hole. The boat's engine groans and then roars.

"Come on!" yells Sean, and we flounder through the water, which is now sloshing in all directions like the island isn't sure it wants what it's been given. Wind roars through the palms, scattering black flowers everywhere.

Aa-dee-dee-dee, cry the birds.

Sean hauls me into the boat, and I'm relieved to see Kylo's carrier still there, with a very wet and angry black cat inside. Before Billy is even fully on board, Sean guns the engine, and we shoot over a wave, crashing down the other side and splashing water everywhere, but moving forward.

"Go, go, go," I whisper as we drift back with the curling tide, then zoom forward again. Beneath the waves, I can hear the ground shaking, and Billy and I cling tight to Kylo's carrier as we careen through the sea, engine straining. Still, the birds keep screaming my name, but the sound is getting fainter and fainter.

Then we're rolling instead of crashing over the waves, and the sun breaks through the bruise-colored clouds. Kylo lets out a long, plaintive meow, Billy laughs, and even though Sean's jaw is tight as he maneuvers us through the water, the corner of his mouth twitches.

"Get the satellite phone," he says, nudging the water-proof bag with his foot. Billy finds the phone and it blinks to life. The ocean is glass-flat ahead of us, and the island grows smaller and smaller behind us, but I won't breathe easy until it's completely gone. Billy's talking into the phone now, telling our rescuers where to find us, and they're promising it won't be long, it will all be okay, and for the first time in a long while, I start to believe it.

Salty wind streams through my soaking hair, and the sun beams down, warm as love. The island is a green slash, then a sliver, and the only heartbeat now is my own, bounding in my ears. It feels like waking up from a nightmare—cloudy shreds of terror still linger, but daylight is rapidly chasing them away.

Eulalie Island disappears over the horizon, and I count to one hundred, two hundred, three hundred, and still, we are safe. We escaped. Leaning over the side of the boat, I trail my fingers through the dazzling blue water and breathe, just breathe.

Chapter
51

SIX MONTHS LATER, I'm lying on a different beach, this one firmly attached to the continental United States—Florida, to be exact. Billy sprawls on a towel beside me, eating Skittles and watching a girl play with a dog in the waves.

"Where do you think Violet and Lenora are now?" he says.

"I guess they're wherever we didn't get to," I say. "Because we were supposed to come back."

Billy nods. "I kind of wish they'd come back and tell us about it, though."

"It's probably better if they don't." I draw in a deep, painless breath, still marveling at the feeling. The recovery was brutal, but I'm diving again. I'm still massively out of shape compared to Evie and Mia, but I'm not pushing it. I probably won't break any records this year, or even the next, and maybe it doesn't matter. Maybe I am not a world record. Maybe I'm just me. I'm still working on liking myself through my failures, but it turns out I can't be perfect at that either.

We never went back to the island, not even to collect our things. The authorities declared it a disaster zone—the official report was that an earthquake caused a tsunami that flooded the island. According to Ken, about a month after we left, the plants started turning green again and the beach reemerged from the ocean, but he had already quit his job as caretaker. David made him the manager of one of his hotels about thirty minutes away from our town, and Billy's been going to the local high school there.

"How did everything go with Taylor?" I ask.

"Pretty good." The sunburn on Billy's cheeks turns pinker. "We're hanging out again tomorrow, probably going to a movie."

"That's fantastic!" I say. "What are you going to see?"

Billy tosses a yellow Skittle up and catches it in his mouth. "She wants to see *Trembler 2*, you know, that earthquake movie?"

"Oh no." I burst out laughing. "Are you sure you can handle that?"

"I may have to hide in the bathroom if it gets too intense," he says with a chomping grin. "Hopefully there won't be sinkholes."

"God, I hope not." I drag my fingers through the soft sand, grateful that the only thing I have to worry about here is a sunburn. Or maybe a jellyfish sting.

"What are you doing this weekend?" asks Billy.

"I'm meeting up with Evie and Mia on Saturday," I say. "If you can believe it, we're not training. We're going to hang out in Miami for the day. Go shopping, have lunch, stuff like that."

"The shopping part sounds boring, but okay." Billy throws an orange Skittle, missing his mouth entirely.

"It definitely won't be as fun as hiding in the movie theater bathroom," I say, and he clutches his chest in mock outrage.

"How dare you!"

Laughing, I get to my feet and dust the sand off. "Race you to the water. One, two . . ."

"Hey, wait!" yells Billy, dropping his bag of candy. "I'm not ready."

"Three!"

Arms pumping, feet churning through the sand, I race for the glittering sea that will always feel like home. I smash through the shallow waves and keep on running, slower and slower, until the water is so deep it takes me off my feet. And then, I dive.

EPILOGUE

IT'D BEEN HUNDREDS of years since Eulalie set foot on that tiny crescent of land in the middle of the blue-green sea, but she never lost the connection. She felt it all, every single moment.

The island's wildly beating heart as it fell in love with a tiny girl with the name of a flower. Its fury when the wrong sister jumped into its heart and the girl it wanted died. Its aching boredom and frustration as the deceitful boy's days stretched on and on, the occasional nameless victims he offered but the island rejected.

When more than two hundred and fifty years had passed, Eulalie began to wonder if the boy had learned his lesson. She decided to open the island up to visitors, give the island a chance to fall in love. See how he reacted. For a while, she felt nothing. And then came the island's deep annoyance when a nosy man with scuba tanks went poking and prodding all through its insides. Its relief when that ended.

And then the girl came.

Eulalie felt the stirring in her chest early one morning. The flowers in the garden of her remote Italian cottage began to turn pink. As the days went on, they deepened to fuchsia and violet, then scarlet and bloody crimson, and her own heart began to beat with passionate, obsessive love. She was drunk on it.

Eulalie was cutting lemons in her kitchen when her heart stopped. One minute she bent gasping over the counter; then she woke on the floor. According to the clock on her wall, two hours had passed. Thick hanks of her white hair had fallen out, her fingernails were broken and blue, and all of her flowers were dead. Her heart still beat, but it was unsteady and weak.

She left as soon as she was strong enough, taking an airplane across the Atlantic, then another short flight to a bustling island where she bought a boat. Eulalie didn't need technology to find her own island; she closed her eyes and let it call her home.

The island knew her before she set foot on its shore. The water turned from gray to aquamarine as her boat sped closer. The palm leaves began to rustle and shift, brightening from black to brown to green. From deep in the forest, the birds called her name. Not the name those men had given her all those centuries ago, and not the false names she'd assumed over the centuries, but her real one.

She walked every inch of the island, putting it back together. The plants greened at her touch, and white blossoms sprouted. The trees that had fallen couldn't be helped, but moss grew soft on their sides, and animals would make their homes underneath and inside. She took her time, and as the island healed, her own stuttering heartbeat steadied.

She grew a thick blanket of white violets to cover the

ruins of the sisters' house. Then she walked to the stone pool at the center of her island and dove. As the glowing blue water streamed around her, she wondered how she'd ever managed to stay away so long. The world was stunning, with its never-ending surprises, its splendors and its horrors, but this was where she belonged.

She found him curled up on the floor of a cave.

Jonah.

The beauty of his face still stirred something deep inside her, but she no longer felt the same wild infatuation, the same greedy need to keep him all to herself. The island hadn't wanted him back either, and he was broken. Fading. She wasn't certain how that made her feel. She asked him if he'd learned his lesson after all these years. He told her he'd learned it centuries ago, and then gradually unlearned it as the years spiraled away.

She realized she was responsible for creating this monster, but she also recognized pieces of the monster in herself. For the first time in hundreds of years, compassion flooded her beating heart. She offered him her boat. She told him the name of a man on the larger island who would take him anywhere he wanted. But if he chose to leave, he'd have only a few days left to live. Ashen-faced, he accepted this fate. She asked him what he wanted to do with that time, and he told her.

A week later, the man came to the island and told her he'd taken Jonah to England. Jonah had pretended not to marvel at the airplane, the crowds, the cars, the buildings. He'd grown more and more somber as they left the city behind and wound through rolling, grassy hills. Finally, they came to an ancient stone church with a graveyard behind it. Jonah found the grave he was searching for. He asked for privacy, and the man left him there. Hours later, the man returned to find only bones lying on the grave. He left Jonah there with Annabel.

Eulalie Island is a green, quiet place now. Vines have grown over the bungalows at the top of the cliffs. The lighthouse still stands, but its foundations are crumbling. Birds sing in the forest, and waves whisper over the sand. Eulalie is content; she braids white flowers into her long white hair and sings along with the birds. She sits on a branch high in her tree, watching the horizon. Waiting.

Deep down underneath it all, the island's heart beats.

ACKNOWLEDGMENTS

I started writing this book back in 2016, then abandoned it for several years and picked it back up again in the middle of the pandemic. It has gone on a long and strange journey, and many people have shaped it along the way.

Kathleen Rushall, your enthusiasm for this project (when it was still a tiny piece of a half-revised draft) made all the difference, and I'm so glad you encouraged me to keep going with it and turn it into a whole new book.

Gretchen Durning, it's been a joy working with you on both *The Wide Starlight* and this book. You've got such a great eye for how to put a story together, and your guidance has made this so much better than I ever could have dreamed of on my own.

Krista Ahlberg, Cassie Gutman, Camilla Kaplan, and Abigail Powers, thank you for your impeccable attention to detail, and for catching all of my random errors and inconsistencies. Thank you to the entire team at Razorbill and Penguin Teen for making this book, promoting it, and sending it out into the world.

Tara Phillips, your cover art still blows me away every single time I look at it, and Kristin Boyle, your vision for the design and aesthetic has been impeccable since day one.

Brianna Bourne, Lindsay Currie, Margot Harrison, Anne-Sophie Jouhanneau, Shanna Miles, Nina Rossing, Grace Shim, Jesse Sutanto, and Marley Teter, my wonderful writing friends, I cannot thank you enough. Whether you read a draft and gave me feedback, listened to me vent or ramble about plot, helped me figure out a sticky situation, or were there for general bookish chats, it means more than I can say.

Sufjan Stevens and Lord Huron, I doubt you will ever read this, but thank you anyway for your music. I listened to *The Ascension* and *Vide Noir* on repeat while writing this book, and both albums undoubtedly contributed to the atmosphere and gave me so many ideas.

Mom, I don't know where to even start with all the things I should thank you for, but the main one is your unwavering belief that I was going to do this author thing. So much love to you. Alissa, thank you for being such a strong and inspiring sister.

Isla and Neil, I love you both to pieces. I'm sorry I spent so much time hiding away in my office on various deadlines this past year. Hope you enjoyed the screen time!

Ciaran, thank you for being there for me, and for helping make all this writing possible. You might be the original brooding love interest, but I promise you weren't the inspiration for this book!